EPICENTER

JASON FLYNN SERIES : BOOK TWO

LUKE SWANSON

Black Rose Writing | Texas

ISBN: 978-1-68433-882-5
PUBLISHED BY BLACK ROSE WRITING
www.blackrosewriting.com

Printed in the United States of America
Suggested Retail Price (SRP) $19.95

Epicenter is printed in Book Antiqua

*As a planet-friendly publisher, Black Rose Writing does its best to eliminate unnecessary waste to reduce paper usage and energy costs, while never compromising the reading experience. As a result, the final word count vs. page count may not meet common expectations.

Praise for

EPICENTER

"Swanson's characters are perfectly flawed and authentic. *Epicenter* is a fast-paced thriller that promises to keep you turning the pages."
— **Christy Cooper-Burnett, award-winning author of** *No Way Home*

"*Epicenter* has bite and knows how to use it. Swanson continues to keep us on the edge of our seats with this well-crafted follow up. Is it too early to ask for a third book?"
— **Nicholas J. Evans, author of** *The Ones Who Could Do Anything*

"Readers will find *Epicenter* littered with off-beat characters, morally ambiguous heroes, and surprising twists."
— **Timothy Gene Sojka, bestselling author of** *Politikill* **and** *Payback Jack*

"Gritty and suspenseful, *Epicenter* takes you on a terrifying thrill-ride with a cast of flawed yet realistic characters. You won't want to put it down."
— **Mary Ellen Bramwell, award-winning author of** *The Apple of My Eye*

"A strong sequel that takes us on another enthralling journey."
— **R.J. King, author of** *A Shepherd of Wolves*

EPICENTER

PART 1: SACRIFICE

DECEMBER

1

Ah, Christmastime. A season of the year dedicated to peace, joy, and family. Roger loved every bit of it. The lights, the music, the bad TV movies. Something about the season always made the rest of the year worth it. No matter the heartache he had gone through from New Years to Thanksgiving, the month-long celebration of human kindness never failed to warm his heart.

Roger sat in his favorite recliner, taking the weight off his rusty knees. Not to mention his back and his bad ankle. He fumbled with a remote control for a minute, but he eventually persuaded his new stereo to play an Andy Williams Christmas album, and all the worry melted from his body.

He swapped out his thick bifocals for thinner, more precise glasses, then reached under the chair for his old grindstone and his 12-inch KA-BAR. He began sharpening.

Yes, Andy, it really is the most wonderful time of the year. Even in Los Angeles. Roger had lived in Colorado for the vast majority of his life: born and raised, from primary school to university, followed by a few years as a brick-layer, then a small stint in Vietnam with most of his boyhood friends, then back to Estes Park as a history teacher for nearly forty years.

He'd only moved to L.A. at the behest of his daughter, who lived in Huntington Park. So, at 76-years-young, Roger had left the mountains and hit the beach in order to retire close to his grandchildren.

It was God's hand, he supposed. He didn't necessarily want to live in L.A. He loved Colorado, especially around Christmas. The snow had a way of reflecting the red and green lights at night, just like a

Norman Rockwell photo. It was truly magical, and he hated to leave it.

L.A. didn't have snow. Or mountains. Not good mountains, anyway. It had crowds and earthquakes and traffic and heat waves.

But now things were coming together. It might all be a blessing in disguise.

He slid his thumb against the knife's blade. Yep. Good and sharp. Could cleave an iceberg in two.

Things were coming together.

Andy crooned, *"Hasn't snowed a single flurry, but Santa dear, we're in a hurry!"*

That's for sure. Roger rolled his eyes. It was about 50 degrees that day, and the morning weatherman had recommended a heavier coat for native Angelinos. Ridiculous. Roger would kill for some snow.

He hid his grindstone and knife under the recliner again.

That knife and he went way back. All the way to Vietnam. Yep, he'd slept every single night with that KA-BAR clutched in his fist. No Commie would get the best of him, no siree Bob. In fact, Roger had dubbed the knife Bad Bob.

Roger set his wrinkled hands on his knees and pushed himself to his feet, making far too much noise as he did so.

His wife hadn't liked Bad Bob.

She had eventually come around. After some persuasion.

Perhaps he should bring a contingency. Just in case Bad Bob didn't work that day. Maybe one of his switchblades. Or a hammer. Or even his Smith & Wesson Model 642.

Nah. Bad Bob had always performed. He'll do just fine.

"Tidings of comfort and joy," he sang with Andy. "Comfort and joy…"

2

He needed air.

Jason Flynn's brisk footfalls clapped across the linoleum floor of Los Angeles's Superior Court. He adjusted his suit jacket and yanked at the garish noose most people call a necktie, weaving through huddled groups of worried families, self-important legal teams, and "others" who seemed to only be there to clog traffic.

He strode with blinders on, not looking anyone in the eye. He only wanted to reach the front doors and get outside. The air may be of the L.A. variety, complete with exhaust fumes and wafted garbage, but anything was better than the recycled vapor the courthouse called air conditioning.

Jason had probably swallowed the same air O.J. Simpson had when he'd done his charade in this court decades ago.

That made his stomach clench even more. He picked up the pace.

He outstretched his palms and slapped open the door, stepping into the afternoon sun. The bright day was deceptively chilly — rather brisk by L.A. standards, in the lower-50s. He turned up his jacket's collar.

In his rush to escape, he'd forgotten the swarm of reporters lying in wait. One red-haired woman recognized him and stepped up, recorder at the ready.

"Detective Flynn!"

He set his jaw and kept walking. "Hello, Jessalyn."

Jessalyn Hooker of NewsNine scampered after him as quickly as her skin-tight skirt allowed. "Detective, are you pleased with the sentencing?"

Jason kept walking without a destination. He replied, "The L.A.P.D. and the district attorney will each have a press conference later today. They will give their official statements at that time. I, on the other hand, am going to get some pho."

"Did you speak with Northwood? Did he show any remorse?"

"A bad man is going away for a long time. That's the gist."

Her camera-ready veneer broke for a moment. Just a moment. "Detective Flynn," she sighed, "I know we've had our ups and downs—"

"Remind me of the ups again?"

"—but the public deserves answers. Citizens are still on edge after the horrific crime spree perpetrated by Abel last summer."

"Is this one of the ups?"

"Abel's legacy still hovers over this city like a thundercloud, Detective! How—"

Jason screeched to a stop, and Jessalyn nearly ran into him. "I don't talk about Abel." The words dropped out of his mouth like stones. "Now, the press conferences about Jordan Northwood will begin at 3 p.m. outside the Superior Court." He started to walk away. "Happy holidays, Jess."

Jessalyn nodded once, letting him go, and allowed a small smile to tug at her lips. "And to you, Jason."

The sun was a cool ball in a pale sky, a welcome change from the blazing spotlight it tended to be. The sidewalks were sparse, but they usually were at this early afternoon hour just outside the courthouse. This was a rideshare driver's prime location as lawyers in power suits and flocks of families came and left the halls of justice.

Jason looked down and realized his hands were balled into fists. Inch by inch, he forced his fingers to unfurl, hoping his anger would do the same.

Over the last year, he'd found that emotions were habits, just like actions. If he smoked twenty cigarettes a day, he'd likely continue to do that for the rest of his life. It was the same with happiness and anger. If he forced himself to smile and laugh and engage in positive interactions with others, he would eventually do those same things naturally.

In theory.

So as he walked from the courthouse, he carved a smile on his face and tried to shake the thoughts of Jordan Northwood out of his mind.

Jordan Northwood, the man who'd stalked and killed three of his own ex-girlfriends.

The man Jason had caught just before he'd cornered victim number four.

The man who'd pled *not guilty* and forced an extensive trial. Forced the families of all three victims to listen to every grisly detail of their loved ones' deaths.

The man who, on the final day of the trial—not ten minutes ago—had stood up and stated he had only claimed to be innocent to force those families to hear all the evidence of his exes' murders.

A woman on the sidewalk walking toward him grimaced and gave him a wide berth.

Jason's forced smile apparently looked more psychopathic than genuine. He ditched the effort and stuffed his hands in his pockets.

All's well that ends well, he thought. Another killer behind bars, without parole or visitation rights. So there's that.

His phone buzzed. Probably one of the lawyers or officers wondering where he had stormed off to. He dug it out of his suit jacket's inner pocket and answered. "Flynn."

"Jason, are you near your car?"

It was Garth Jameson, one of Jason's closest friends and colleagues. His voice was serious, all business. Not a good sign.

Jason didn't respond immediately. "Maybe."

"Take down this location and get there quickly."

"Don't do this to me, Garth."

The fellow detective didn't humor him. "The bluffs overlooking Marina Del Rey, west side of the Westchester neighborhood. Follow the black-and-whites already there to the body. It's on top of a little hill."

Jason rubbed a palm across his eyes. "C'mon, Garth. I've been in Northwood's trial all morning, I haven't even had lunch, and you're already sending me after another psycho. Can you catch some Christmas spirit and give this to someone else?"

Garth's voice, digitally distorted through the phone, shuddered a bit. "The victim is a boy."

The breeze made Jason's hairs stand up. He stopped in his tracks.

Garth continued, "Six years old."

Jason turned and strode back to the courthouse parking lot. "I'll be there in twenty."

3

The birds in the trees were silent. At first, Jason wondered if maybe they had flown south for the winter or something, but as he walked through the bluffs, he saw a few white-crowned sparrows watching from their nests. Just watching.

His shoes crunched against the dry grass and dusty rocks, creating the only ambient sounds in the area. From his vantage point, he could look down upon busy streets filled with cars and bikes, but they were the size of Hot Wheels. They motored back and forth without a sound. The cityscape of Los Angeles was merely a hazy portraiture up here on the bluffs.

No talking. No revving. And even the birds were speechless.

The cop in the bluffs' parking lot had told him a couple more officers were with the body on top of a crag the locals called the Point. A gravel path led to the top, a handful of benches and trashcans decorating the way.

Jason was almost there. Now he could hear the low chitchat of the two warm bodies at the top of the hill. He pulled his brass badge from within his suit jacket and clipped it to his belt, on the hip opposite from his Glock. He'd woken up this morning hoping he wouldn't have to don either. Guess Santa hadn't received his wish list.

He reached the top of the Point and stopped.

There.

The body. Small. Sprawled out on the rocky ground. In the dead center of the hilltop.

God, he was so *small*...

He cleared his throat and stepped forward. "Afternoon, everyone."

A man in white looked at him and nodded. "Detective," he greeted and stretched out his hand, which Jason shook. "Reggie Lau, forensics."

Jason turned to the other person on the Point, a female officer in a crisp uniform and a windbreaker. She had eyes round as eggs and wildly curly hair that was barely tamed within a big bun on the back of her head. "I take it you're the responding officer?"

"Yes sir," she answered in two clipped syllables, just like a cadet.

"Jason Flynn."

She cracked a wry grin. "Really? Detective Flynn?"

His eyebrows narrowed. "Yes...?"

The officer saw his displeasure and shuffled her feet. "I'm sorry, sir. Danielle Zahn." She offered her hand, which Jason shook and she retracted a bit too early. "Honestly, sir, I'm a big fan. You taking out Abel last year..." She let out a breath and smiled. "It was amazing. Real high-level stuff. You actually saved the city."

Not everyone, Jason swallowed. He noticed his fists balling again and clasped them behind his back.

"I did what I could. Thank you." He gave Danielle a polite smile and turned to what he dreaded most. "Do we have his name?"

Reggie nodded and stood beside Jason. "Trevor Riley. Written on the inside of one of his shoes. Confirmed by yearbook photos from his elementary school. Six years old."

"What school?" Jason opened a mental map of L.A.'s geography.

"Brooklyn Ave."

Interesting. Brooklyn Avenue Elementary was in East Los Angeles. These bluffs were within walking distance of the Pacific Ocean, on the far West side of the city. Not a short trip.

Jason started a new line of questions. "Has anyone notified his parents?"

"A few officers are doing that right now."

Jason took a deep breath and steeled his nerves. He hadn't yet taken a close look at the corpse, but that was his job here.

Custodian.

He pushed the thought aside and stepped toward Trevor before his brain could convince his legs otherwise.

The body rested on its back, arms and legs splayed out—definitely positioned that way after the murder. A pool of dried blood surrounded the boy's neck and shoulders, making him look like the center of a bullseye. His eyes were closed, but his mouth was agape.

The cause of death was evident. His neck was sliced wide open, along his jawline from ear to ear. Flecks of crusty blood dotted his pasty skin. It had spurted, meaning it wasn't done postmortem. The kid had been killed here.

Jason exhaled and turned away. Part of him wanted to get used to crime scenes so that he could do away with this nauseous vertigo feeling. But most of him hoped he never got used to it. Especially not with kids involved.

His brown hair. Just like Ted's—

Jason started talking to interrupt his own train of thought. "Loss of blood is the cause of death?"

"That's right," Reggie said. "Severe laceration of the throat. A very large, very sharp knife, done in one swipe. Trevor didn't stand a chance. Also…" He gestured to the boy's limbs. "He was bound."

Jason jerked slightly, but caught himself. He didn't want either colleague to see him rattled. He leaned over the body. Sure enough. Thin red marks were etched into Trevor's wrists and ankles.

"Looks like it was twine," he said.

"I think so too," Reggie agreed.

"He was probably tied up when his throat was cut." Jason stepped away. "The ligature marks are deep. Agony, I would think. Adrenaline at the moment of the killing would make him try with all his might to break free."

"But," Danielle murmured, "he wasn't strong enough." She clinched the bridge of her nose.

A cloud passed over the sun for a moment. Jason pulled out his phone to check the time. "It's a school day, isn't it?" He glanced around for Danielle and found her hovering by the edge of the hilltop, muscles tight, eyes on the young corpse.

"Mhmm, Friday." She put her hands in her windbreaker's pockets. "For most schools, it's the last day of class before Christmas break."

"Oh yeah, that's right." Jason pocketed his phone. "It's 2:30. And how long has he been dead, Reggie?"

"I'd say, based on what I see right now, he's been dead for three or four hours at most. Definitely today, not last night. The guys at the lab will be able to able more precise in a few hours."

"No, that's good, Reg, thanks. So whoever picked him up at school is who we want to talk to next. Who found him?"

Danielle answered, still keeping a healthy distance from the body, "A couple from the Catholic college a mile up the bluffs. They came up here for the view, to say their good-byes before the break. Found something much less romantic."

Reggie snorted. "One way to put it."

Danielle shifted, lost in thought. "Why would you kill someone like that? A little *kid*? Slaughtered like a ram."

"Yes," Reggie sighed, "it's brutal."

"Well, yeah, that," Danielle said, "but it doesn't make much sense either. If you wanna kill someone, you can shoot 'em, stab 'em, hit 'em with something heavy. But such a precise wound like that, on top of a mountain? And a kid? A gun would be way easier. There's something else going on here." She rubbed her forehead, brushing back some stray curls.

Jason moved away from the body and began to pace the perimeter of the Point's peak. He looked out at the city—the clouds floating among the steel jungle were like smudges of paint, some gray, some purple, all thick and suffocating.

What had the killer seen as he brought Trevor up here?

"It took me about eight minutes to walk up from the parking lot," he said.

Danielle nodded, bouncing her huge volleyball of hair. "Same. A gravelly path leading up a hill on the bluffs overlooking Marina Del Rey? On the other side of the city as Trevor's school? That's a long car ride and a pretty extensive walk up here."

"That's assuming he and the killer came here right from the school. But I agree with how you're thinking, this place is definitely outside a six-year-old's sphere of familiarity."

"So you think...?" Danielle prompted Jason with her big brown eyes, hesitant to throw a theory into the ring.

Jason placed his hands on his hips, nodding at Danielle. "He and the killer came up here this morning. Trevor wasn't carried or forced — someone would've noticed. They both walked. Together. It's still a theory, but..." He prompted Danielle to finish.

She said, "It looks like Trevor knew his killer. It wasn't a random snatch."

Reggie hung his head. "Christ."

My thoughts exactly.

"Plus," Jason resumed his pacing, fingers unconsciously grazing his badge and gun, "look at the position of the body. Spread eagle. His bounds were cut and he was placed that way after the act. Intentionally."

Danielle furrowed her brow. "Why?"

"I'll ask as soon as we find who did this." He averted his eyes from Trevor's frail body, suddenly very lightheaded. He needed to get off this crag as quickly as possible. He knew it was stupid, but he felt as if Trevor was watching him. "Can you hold down the fort, Reggie?"

"Sure thing, Detective."

Jason looked at Danielle. "I'm headed to Trevor's school, see who picked him up today. Care to come?"

"Me?" Danielle took a few steps back, shooting a quick glance at her uniform. She clearly wasn't accustomed to tagging along with detectives.

"Yeah. I don't see anyone else clamoring to be my partner on this one."

A wide smile broke across her face. "Absolutely, sir. I'll do what I can to help."

Jason patted the pocket holding his car keys. "Alright. Let's move."

The L.A.P.D. detective and officer began descending the Point: the man who had caught Abel and the woman who hoped to follow in his footsteps.

Their crunchy footsteps pounded rhythmically like a metronome, and Jason focused on each one, trying to distract himself from the truth.

Yes, he liked Danielle enough for having just met her. She was sharp and eager and kind. Enthusiasm was a big bonus going into a new investigation.

But that wasn't why he had asked her to come.

He needed someone to keep him accountable.

This case made him sweat.

A young boy.

Just like his son.

Dead.

Just like his son.

Once Jason found whoever did this to Trevor, he would need a good cop—a good soul—to keep him from beating the bastard to a bloody pulp.

4

The elementary school came into view. A squat building shaped like a submarine sandwich with a red roof. A handful of cars were in the parking lot, but trash blew all over the asphalt as if a mass of people had cleared out mere seconds before. In fact, Jason's car passed a full yellow bus as he parked.

Jason left his gun in a lockbox hidden in the car, and he and Danielle entered the building.

They passed a bulletin board covered in multicolored notices and cartoon characters telling the kids not to smoke and to respect their parents. And then a glass trophy case. Then a map with an enormous font pointing the ways to the library, cafeteria, and main office. As much as Jason liked Clifford the Big Red Dog and tater tots, he only needed to visit the latter.

A Christmas tree stood in the hallway, covered in plastic orbs and glittering tinsel, as well as figurines of Captain America and Garfield the cat and others. Hand-cut paper snowflakes dangled from the ceiling.

Jason hoped no students or parents would be around when they made their inquiries. Blood pressure would spike and an avalanche of panicked moms would bury them.

He and Danielle entered the school's office, in which a middle-aged secretary sat behind her desk. The lady wore a blindingly bad holiday sweater—complete with actual jingle bells—and was staring at a bulky computer from Dubya's first term.

"Excuse us?" Jason painted his voice with saccharine politeness, doing his best to hide the tension and urgency that gripped his heart. "Ma'am?"

The secretary turned her bespectacled gaze to the cops. The beaded chain attached to her frames dangled by her chin. "Yes? Can I help you?"

"This is Officer Danielle Zahn," he gestured to his partner, whose smile actually extended to her wide eyes, "and I'm Detective Jason Flynn. Los Angeles Police Department, ma'am."

"Oh my." The secretary quickly minimized whatever window she was looking at on the computer.

Jason sighed.

Danielle quickly spoke up. "We have a situation, Miss. One of your students, Trevor Riley, is missing, and we've been assigned to finding him."

Good. Low-pressure. Keep things easy but efficient.

"Trevor?" Another voice spoke from the back of the office. A tall woman in a blue dress, black tights, and polka-dot flats entered the scene. Her nails were painted black, and her make-up was minimal, if she was even wearing any.

"Yes, ma'am," Danielle addressed this new woman.

"I'm Principal Okubo. That's..." Worry creased her face. "Gosh, Trevor, that's horrible."

"Obviously, ma'am, we want to locate him as soon as humanly possible," Jason said, "and we're wondering if he left school early today."

The secretary perked up, looking like an ostrich that had just yanked its head out of the dirt. "I remember the Rileys being checked out today. But I've already filed the sheet in the back. Let me see if I can find it for you." She stood on quaking legs and staggered to the steel cabinet in the corner.

Principal Okubo rolled her eyes at the other woman. She composed herself and turned to the cops with resolve in her voice. "I can access the security feeds for you, Officer, Detective. We love the Rileys, and we'll do anything to help." She beckoned to her own office and took off, Jason and Danielle rushing to keep up with her lengthy gait.

As they moved, Jason cocked an eyebrow at Danielle, who shrugged in equal confusion.

"Ma'am," he said, "the Rileys?"

"Yes," she looked back at them, "Trevor and JT. Twins. Good kids. I just…" She shook her head and opened her office door. "We have to find Trevor. Come in, come in."

Jason's heartrate doubled. Every second stretched into an hour. He locked eyes with Danielle for a moment, and he could tell she was thinking the same thing.

There's another one out there. He might still be alive, but the killer has him.

We have to find him.

Principal Okubo sat at her desk, poked her sleeping computer, and began typing like her life depended on it. The office was cluttered to capacity, filled with more books than Jason had ever seen. Every shelf, corner, and inch of floor space held a stack, and the L.A.P.D. officers had to high-step over a drawbridge of encyclopedias to get to the desk.

"Okay, got it. Trevor and JT were checked out at…" she leaned toward the screen, "…10:35 today. Here they are, clear as day."

All three of them leaned toward the computer. Grainy footage of the main office filled the screen. Sure enough, at the front desk, chatting with the avian secretary, was Trevor Riley, alive and well.

The way he moves his hands when he talks –

Jason dug his fingernails into his palms.

Standing next to Trevor was another boy of similar height and stature, but this boy's nose was pointier, and he had shaggier hair. JT Riley. They were obviously fraternal twins, not identical. Still, though, Jason was shocked, righteously irked, and somewhat embarrassed they didn't know about Trevor's twin brother in the first place.

The brothers stood and talked in the office, completely unaware of their fate. It chilled Jason's bones.

A man stood beside them, signing the check-out sheet the secretary was now searching for in her filing cabinet. He was an elderly man, his spindly fingers uncertain with the pen. Thick glasses encircled his eyes. Powder-white hair sprouted in patches on the rim of his head, but he had a beard like Methuselah.

"Got him," Danielle breathed.

"Well, he's on the approved list to take the Rileys out of school," Okubo said. "That's their grandfather, Roger Shore."

"He's taken them home before?" Jason asked.

"Many times," the principal nodded. "Why?"

Someone Trevor trusts absolutely.

Jason and Danielle were already out the door.

We're coming, JT.

5

The air was chillier than Roger had anticipated. He stood by his earlier sentiment that L.A. locals needed to grow some thicker skin, but he was older than most. Yes, his beard kept the lower half of his face warm, but his bones were brittle, his body ached, and his bald head went numb after a few minutes outside.

He rubbed his hands together to generate some friction. He was almost done, anyway. He'd make some hot chocolate when he went inside.

The trees of the park stood over him like steadfast sentinels, guarding him from prying eyes. He loved his house, and he was glad his daughter had found it for him when he moved out here. It was quaint but efficient, and its backyard opened into a local park. He sometimes took walks when his rusty ankle and knees were up to it. The aroma of fresh leaves and rich soil always cleared his head and settled his soul.

Well, time to wrap things up.

He tossed Bad Bob onto the grass beside the wooden pyre. Sticky blood gleamed on the blade in the low sunlight. He'd pick it up for a good wash later.

Or not. He doubted he'd sleep in this house tonight.

Blood dripped from his hands too. And his old topcoat was stained all down the front. It arced diagonally across him, as if he'd been hit with a ketchup sprinkler.

Bad Bob had served him well.

Maybe now he'll be at peace—

A rustle in the brush caught his attention. He peered over his thick bifocals, heartrate tittering slightly. He considered going for Bad Bob, but he instead faced the visitor head-on.

A small brown rabbit hopped out of a bush. Its black gaze flickered from him, to the bloody knife, to the pyre, and back to him.

Roger deflated. He stared at the rabbit, the woodland creature that could have changed everything.

"You're five minutes late, my little friend." Sorrow wracked his body, nearly bringing him to his knees.

He nearly cried to the sky, *"Was this the plan?"*

But then it struck him. Yes, this was the plan. If this rabbit had been destined to come along earlier, it would have done exactly that.

In that moment, his resolve hardened.

What's done is done, it is what it is, and all that.

Let them come. Let them all come.

Roger went in to wash the blood off his hands, change into clean clothes, and make some cocoa. He hoped his wife had bought marshmallows.

6

They burst into the school parking lot, and Danielle began fuming.

"The grandpa!" Her lip curled as she hissed, revealing teeth like a caged Rottweiler. "That cretin, that…that…" She stomped, at a loss for insults.

Jason felt similar fire in his veins, but he forced himself to say what a senior detective should. "We don't know Shore is the killer. He could be abducted just the same as the boys. Now, call the Chateau and get his address."

"On it." She was already dialing.

Jason leapt into the driver's seat of his car, Danielle in the front passenger's. After returning his Glock to his hip, he squealed onto the bustling streets of L.A. He'd told Danielle to call their precinct's station—the Chateau, they mockingly called it, since it was the most boring-looking building you could imagine—for Roger Shore's home address, and already being on the road would hopefully shave precious seconds off their trip.

Danielle hung up her phone with relish. "689 Figueroa Street. Right on the edge of Sycamore Park."

Jason flipped the steering wheel and drove north, knuckles white.

He shot a look at his partner. She sat on the edge of her seat, knees bouncing like a child waiting by the chimney on Christmas Eve. A line of sweat had formed under her eyes, and strands of her wild curls had escaped her bun.

"How're you doing, Danielle?"

She noticed her posture and relaxed. Slightly. "Um, good, sir, good." She dabbed at the perspiration. "To tell the truth, Trevor's is the first body I've seen. In the real world, I mean. They have cadavers for us at the academy, but it's…it's different."

"I know what you mean." He found himself leaning back in his seat as well. "The first…" He scratched the day's growth of stubble and dug through the journal in his head. "The first body I saw. Lemme think."

He tapped his thumb against the wheel. He'd seen more corpses than he cared to remember. But where had it all started?

He remembered. "I was an officer at the time. A month and half into it. I worked with a guy named Jacky Talbit. About two-hundred pounds of solid muscle, four feet tall, half of it hair. We served in the Beverly Glen and Bel Air neighborhoods."

"Too bad beat cops don't work for tips," Danielle smiled.

Jason laughed. "No kidding. A lot of the people were nice as can be. But, y'know, people are people, which means there were some grade-A a-holes too. For every compliment, there was a threat to tattle on us to our superiors. For every Christmas card, there was a flicked cigarette butt."

"I know that story." The officer crossed her arms, lost in thought, inadvertently emphasizing the L.A.P.D. crest on her windbreaker.

"Anyway," Jason continued, "one morning, something's going on at the Stone Canyon Reservoir. Me and Jacky are called in for crowd control, since we're familiar with the population, or so they said. So we show up and, I dunno if you've seen it, but the reservoir is absolutely gigantic. It's like King Solomon's pool, cupped in the mountains, trees all around it. And they called in me and Jacky the Goombah to keep the whole thing civil."

"Baptism of fire."

"Baptism of stupid. So, as we're talking to the people, trying to shush them like rich people do with their horses, a crane was reaching into the reservoir. Eventually, it pulled out an old refrigerator, one of those doomsday deathtraps. Looked like it'd been in the water for years, and it had holes drilled into the sides."

"Of course." Danielle knew where this was going. She had inched closer, hanging on each word.

Jason turned west. He checked his watch. They were making great time. Almost to Roger Shore's home. He inched closer too.

"As the crane was moving over to set the fridge on the grass, the old hinges gave out. The lid flopped open and out came dozens of lifeless fish, a bunch of stringy weeds, and a bloated sack that used to be a human being."

Danielle scrunched up her face. "Geez."

"That's what I said. The whole thing hit the ground…and *splat*. We didn't even have to ask the people to leave — 'There's nothing to see here, folks.' The noise and the stench made them scatter in ten seconds flat."

"Did you find out who it was?"

"Eventually. Dental records pointed to it being a guy called Aaron Moya, some poor accountant who had ticked off boss Peter Milano sometime in the mid-90s."

"Boss Milano? You found a body put underwater by the big bad Mafioso?"

"Well, I didn't find it. I was just crowd control. But yeah. About fourteen years ago, I saw my first cold body in 'the real world,' as you said."

"So…" She seemed to build up the courage to speak again. "Have you ever killed someone?"

Pause. The car hummed across the road, among a sea of other drivers.

He'd been in tight situations before. Almost every week, he put himself between the people of Los Angeles and a deadly fate. Naturally, he'd drawn and fired his gun more times than he could count. Fistfights were an expected occurrence when he left his home every morning. He'd certainly put several men in the hospital. Intensive care, even.

But there was one man he'd nearly killed. One man he'd *intended* to kill.

Abel. The monster who had held the city hostage. Devious. Merciless. Brilliant. He would never stop his murderous rampage, no matter what a judge and jury would say. Many had suffered under Abel's hand, and many more were in his plan. He'd needed to be put down like a rabid dog.

So Jason had attacked. Heel to the jugular. Blows to the sternum. Abel had been his to execute.

And then he'd stopped.

"No, I...Almost. Once. He had a gun on me, but I knocked it away and took him down. Broke a few of his ribs. My hands were around his throat. Squeezing. Almost."

"That's terrifying. Thank God you didn't do it."

Jason didn't respond.

He had nearly killed Abel, but his conscience had stopped him. He'd stepped away and prepared a transport to L.A.P.D. lockup.

And a moment later—a *moment* after sparing him—Abel had picked up a gun and fired two rounds into Ted's chest.

Ted. His son. His friend and confidant and soul and integrity.

His hands were cramping from clutching the wheel. He didn't loosen his grip.

In the distance, between the glass and concrete structures, Jason started to see trees and hills. Sycamore Park. The leaves were still green and vibrant, with a strand of white lights every now and then.

"Almost there." Danielle vibrated in her seat, her nerves showing themselves again.

"Keep a level head," Jason said. "We don't know anything. Remember that."

"Yes, sir." A fierce smile pulled at her mouth.

Danielle clearly thought Roger Shore was the Riley boys' abductor and killer, but Jason had a hunch he was a victim as well. The feeble old man they had seen in the security video made for a target similar to two small boys.

There. A modest home built right on the edge of the park. Trees shot up behind the roof and chimney. A bench sat in the front lawn, a foldout table holding a chess set next to it. The breeze tickled an American flag hanging by the front door.

Jason parked and took a breath. "Ready?"

"Absolutely." Danielle popped open the car door and moved out.

Thanks to the lack of daylight saving time, the sun was already preparing to exit stage left. Shadows stretched more and more each second, and Jason pulled his suit jacket closer to his body. He shivered a bit.

Danielle unconsciously stepped aside to let him knock on Roger Shore's front door.

He balled his fist and slammed it on the wooden door five times. "Mr. Shore!" he yelled into the house. "This is the L.A.P.D. Are you home?"

Nothing. Jason wondered if his hunch was right—Shore was a victim too.

"Alright," he said, bracing himself for action. He gave Danielle a quick glance and placed his hand on the butt of his gun. "In we go." He backed up and positioned himself to kick in the door.

Then, it creaked open. Jason jerked to a halt, his heart hammering in his chest like a piston. He quickly pulled his jacket over his gun.

A wrinkled face peered at them from within the dark home. "Yes, officers? You're looking for me?"

Jason was still pulling in big breaths. He instantly calmed his body and sent his adrenaline back into reserve. "Roger Shore?"

The door opened more. The white half-donut of hair. The shiny dome. The huge glasses and beard. "Yes, officer, that's me." He spoke with patience and power, like a soldier who had spent most of his life in a foxhole.

"Detective Jason Flynn and Officer Danielle Zahn. Los Angeles Police. Sir, we have a few questions regarding your grandsons."

Roger arched an eyebrow. "Of course. Trevor and JT." He hobbled back into his house. "Took you long enough."

Ice slid through Jason's veins. He saw Danielle's face twitch too.

Their feet brought them into Roger's home. His living room.

The old man settled into a musty recliner and took off his Coke-bottle glasses, looking at them with clouded eyes. His thin hands were folded, rested upon his lap. He wore a wool sweater, old slacks, scuffed black shoes, and a countenance of laser focus. And, Jason noted, a wedding band on his left hand.

The living room fit his attire. Well-worn recliner, outdated sofa with a floral pattern, brown carpeting, pinstriped wallpaper, popcorn ceiling, decorative china plates in racks on the walls. A Carpenters

Christmas song leaked out of a stereo system: "Logs on the fire fill me with desire, to see you and to say…"

Jason and Danielle exchanged wary glances, thrown by Roger's blasé answer and hardboiled demeanor. They both sat on the sofa, lowering themselves slowly and staying perched like hawks.

Roger watched every movement with his gray gaze.

"Mr. Shore," Jason put iron in his voice, "you seem to know where your grandsons are."

Roger nodded and let out a breath. He'd been expecting this. "Yes, Detective Flynn. Trevor is dead on the bluffs by Marina Del Rey."

"You killed him." Not a question.

A clock ticked somewhere. Roger set his jaw and thought for a moment before responding. "Conviction is a tricky thing. It's not flexible or convenient."

Jason saw the man's eyes ticking back and forth, as if he was reading a script. He'd planned this confrontation for some time.

"When you believe something," Roger gestured with his spotted hands, "you must follow it through. Scripture is full of examples of great men doing strange things because of faith."

No. Jason balled his fists. He didn't like where this was going.

"In the book of Genesis, chapter 22 —"

"You lunatic…" Jason hissed.

Danielle looked between the detective and the old man. Her eyes were wide, breath unsteady. "What? Why? What is that?"

"You have quite the knowledge of Scripture, Detective." Roger looked impressed.

"Enough to know…" Jason bit back the fury coursing through his body. "Enough to know that you led your grandson up a mountain, sliced open his throat, and drained his blood on an altar to — what? — sacrifice him?"

"I don't claim to know God's will." Roger spoke calmly but pleadingly, truly trying to make his case. "Abraham was tested. It was my turn."

"What is it, Jason?" Danielle's voice cracked.

"Genesis 22," Jason said, never taking his eyes off Roger. "Abraham hears God's voice. He tells him to take his son Isaac, 'whom he loves,' up a mountain and give him as an offering."

Danielle turned her wide eyes to Roger.

"I know how it sounds." Roger stared right back at them. "It sounds like I'm insane. And you will say I am. The papers and news reporters will line up for interviews with me like they did with Manson. They'll dig into my history. 'Oh, he was in 'Nam, that must be why he snapped.' 'No, it's schizophrenia. Poor old man.' 'He's a freak, give him the chair.' But I will say until my dying breath what I believe. I heard God's voice."

"And He told you to murder two children?" Danielle bristled.

"He told me what He told Abraham. He said to take Trevor and JT and offer them to Him." Anguish crossed his face, and his eyes clouded further with tears. "That's where the similarities end. God didn't give me an exact location, as He did in Genesis. Also..." He wiped the moisture from his cheek and stared at Jason, steely once more. "Also, He didn't stop me."

Jason recalled Trevor's frail body, spread on the Point, a pool of blood around his open neck. His small hands, his dark hair.

He ground his teeth until the images disappeared.

"And since we've no place to go," Karen Carpenter serenaded, "let it snow, let it snow, let it snow..."

"I fully expected," Roger pressed, "that the Lord would intervene, just as He did with Abraham. So I took Trevor to the bluffs, bound his arms and legs, drew my KA-BAR. And nothing. Not a sound. I knelt beside Trevor, who was writhing on the ground..."

This man is dead.

"...but still, nothing." Roger rested, sizing up the cops' reactions. "He was dead very quickly, I promise."

"You're a monster," Danielle scoffed.

"I'm not hiding, Ms. Zahn. I'm not running from you or my actions. I have given a full confession and I accept the consequences of what I've done. I know the world will label me a monster, a psychopath, a pervert, anything and everything. But I'm looking into your eyes and saying right now, I am merely a man of faith. You cannot separate a person from his convictions any more than you can cut off his shadow."

"Where's JT?" Jason said, eyes sharp as daggers.

Roger nodded to himself, set his hands on the armrests of his recliner, and pushed himself to his feet.

In a flash, Danielle was on her feet, gun drawn and leveled at Roger's nose. "Sit down, old man." Her jaw was clenched, gun trembling in her wrathful hands.

"Danielle," Jason thundered as he also stood. "Put your gun away *now*." He spoke like a coiled snake.

Slowly, painfully, Danielle slipped her Glock back into the holster on her hip.

Roger watched all this with a resolute stare. Once no firearms were pointed at his face, he said, "When God allowed Trevor to die, I thought it was because I hadn't followed His instructions closely enough."

Jason's mind began to race. *Instructions? What do the Scriptures say?* He scoured his exhaustive memory of Bible verses left over from his time in university.

Genesis 22.

Now it came to pass after these things that God tested Abraham, and said to him, "Abraham!"

And he said, "Here I am."

"When we finally kiss good night, how I hate going out in the storm..."

Then He said, "Take now your son, your only son Isaac, whom you love, and go to the land of Moriah, and offer him there as a burnt offering on —

No.

Burnt offering.

It felt like Jason was falling.

"...but if you really hold me tight, all the way home I'll be warm!"

Still standing by his chair, Roger went on explaining, "I had left JT here while I dealt with Trevor, tied and gagged in my broom closet, so I returned, took him out back into the park —"

Jason took off like a shot. He shoved the old man out of the way and bounded through the house, aiming for the back door. It should open right up to Sycamore Park.

The music faded as he dashed.

He passed a decrepit kitchen filled with grout, stained dishes, and rotted food. Mounted on the walls of an office were several rifles and classical works of art. A closet with almost no clothing, a pristine bathroom scrubbed to a shine. In all the rooms, Jason never saw a bed.

But the back door was all that mattered.

Jason slammed his body through the door and stumbled into Roger's backyard. Weeds and dry leaves covered the ground, grabbing at Jason's ankles as he sprinted. The trees of the park loomed before him, creatures in the ever-darkening L.A. evening.

He squinted as he ran, looking for JT among the trees. The darkness blended together like a fog, so he just kept running, cold air burning the insides of his lungs.

There. Among the trees. A block of some sort. Something that didn't belong there. Dots of orange light glowed at the base.

Embers.

As he ran closer, the scene became clearer.

A pile of burnt branches. Smoldering ashes. Dried blood covered the grass, looking like black paint at this point. A charred, grotesque mass rested on top of the altar.

JT Riley.

Jason fell on his knees before he reached the corpse, skidding to a halt. He gaped at what he saw, almost not believing his sight.

Was this a nightmare? A horror story brought to life?

But then, he did believe it.

He had spoken with monsters. He'd met them the same way he had met any other person. They were real. They walked among humans, went to the supermarket, paid parking tickets, watched *Wheel of Fortune*, and, at the end of the day, slaughtered their grandchildren.

What is happening to this city?

Last year, Abel had unleashed his fury upon Los Angeles, hoping to create his own holy police and wipe out the sinners of the world.

In that moment, hands shuddering, on his scuffed knees before the burnt body of a six-year-old boy, Jason wished Abel had succeeded.

Maybe Roger Shore wouldn't be alive to hear voices and kill the Riley boys.

Jason's mind flashed back several months earlier.

His hands were around Abel's neck. Squeezing down on his Adam's apple. The fear of death in his weasel eyes.

Then a flicker of compassion. Regret. An act of mercy, for the sake of his son. Ted. Ted, the one who had prompted Jason to let Abel live.

Jason let go of Abel. He knelt before his son. A tear fell to the hardwood floor. He embraced his son.

Abel shot the boy. Twice.

Ted flew through the air and crumpled on the floor like a sack of laundry. His heart still beat at that moment, but he would never open his eyes again.

Jason knelt beside his son for the second time in less than a minute. This time, blood spurted from the boy's chest, and his mouth gaped like a fish on dry land.

Footsteps. Shadows. Crunch of leaves. Cold.

Opening his eyes, he returned to the present and exhaled. JT was still there, unrecognizable, a black and red heap atop the branches. The KA-BAR knife Roger had mentioned sat in the grass, dried blood on its silver blade.

He glanced over his shoulder. Danielle and Roger had followed, the old man in handcuffs.

Danielle clapped her hands over her mouth. Her legs shook, her eyes trembled in their sockets.

Roger simply watched, forlorn and seemingly remorseful. But unrepentant.

A few seconds passed—maybe an hour, for all Jason knew. Time had warped in that backyard.

He released a shuddering sigh, lurched to his feet, and began to move back toward his friend and the old man.

As he walked, he saw realization trickle over Danielle's face.

They had failed. Both boys were dead. They had the killer, yes. But they'd failed.

Roger opened his mouth to speak. "Detective…"

Jason glared at the lowlife. "The world would be better without you." His hand flew to the gun on his hip.

But Danielle was quicker. "No!" She leapt in front of Roger and planted her feet.

"Danielle!" He growled as he jerked to a halt, fingers curled around his holstered firearm. "*Move*, or you will *be moved*."

"No," she repeated. "I can't." Her eyes were round. Fearful. Terrified…not of Roger the crazed killer, but of *him*.

Jason's world started to blur, and not from tears. His fury had begun to stain his vision.

He wanted nothing more than to draw his gun and fire two shots into Roger's cozy sweater. Two shots—just like Ted.

But Danielle was blocking his shot.

"He deserves it. Everyone would be better off." He took another step forward.

Danielle's hand flew to her hip as well, and she drew her own weapon: a mobile radio. She pressed the *speak* button and started talking frantically. "Dispatch, this is Officer Danielle Zahn. I'm at 689 Figueroa Street, by Sycamore Park." The tenor of her words slowly increased, as if she were at gunpoint. "I have a man who confessed to murdering the boy on the bluffs this morning. His name is Roger Shore—he's detained, but he's alive. He is alive." She held out the radio between herself and Jason with a trembling hand. Her shoulders heaved as she took shallow, panicky breaths.

It was an unthinkable image: a young, fresh-faced officer, standing between a hero detective and an elderly murderer, preventing the slaughter of the latter.

"Why did you do that?" Jason seethed like a rabid animal. He stamped his foot. "Why did you *do that*?!"

The radio bleeped in response: "*Understood. Back-up is en route.*"

Jason wanted to scream at the sky. Now, other L.A.P.D. officers were on their way, and they knew Roger was still breathing. If Jason managed to kill Roger between now and when they showed up, there would be hard questions.

Roger spoke from behind Danielle. "I know you two don't believe what I—"

She snapped at him over her shoulder. "Shut up, Mr. Shore, right now." She returned her focus to Jason. "You didn't kill Abel, and you will not kill this man."

"WHY NOT?!" He hadn't meant to yell those words, but he did. They echoed against the trees. "We can say he attacked us! Charged at us. Something! We're officers of the Los Angeles Police Department. He heard voices and killed his grandsons today. They'll believe us."

"*Us*?" Danielle sputtered. "Sir, what are you doing? This is wrong."

"What's wrong is letting these things exist!" he shouted and pointed a damning finger at the old man. "We accept this by letting them live. This isn't just crime, Danielle. Robbing, speeding, manslaughter, those are crimes. This," he jabbed his finger again, staring right into Roger's cold eyes, "is an *atrocity* against humanity. Locking him up won't help. I didn't finish Abel when I had the chance, and he—"

A *buzz* cut him off. His cell phone. For a moment, the only sounds in the world were the buzzing, his weary breaths, and the rippling tree branches.

He took his hand off the butt of his gun, pulled the phone from a pocket, and glanced at the screen. Garth was calling. He turned it off.

Danielle lowered the hand holding her radio. She looked at him with...What was it? Compassion? Terror? Both?

Jason inhaled deeply, catching the smells of embers and burned hair. His fury was reignited anew.

"You know what Abel did," he rumbled.

Danielle slowly shook her head. "If you kill him, you'll lose yourself, Jason."

Jason looked away. In his head, he responded, *What if that's exactly what I want?* But he didn't dare say that.

All was quiet.

The wind rustled the brittle leaves. Danielle shivered.

In the distance, Jason could hear approaching cars. The cavalry was almost here.

He clenched his eyes shut.

In that moment, even though he hadn't fired a single shot, Jason became a killer. In his heart and his mind, he craved violence. He yearned for bloodshed. The only reason Roger Shore was still breathing was because...

His eyes snapped open. "That monster is still alive because of you. I hope you can live with that." He shoved his hands in his pockets and left the park, giving Danielle and the old man a very wide berth.

PART 2:
SHATTERED

JUNE

7

The L.A. sun blazed down like a flashlight, illuminating the entire city. The entire world, it seemed.

The neighborhood was quiet. Tranquil. Sprinklers watered a few lawns, mostly in vain—the sun evaporated the water before it could nourish the dead grass. There was an abandoned bike on a sidewalk. An ajar mailbox. An American flag, limp in the breezeless day.

A car roared onto the scene and screeched to a stop. Tony Reynaldo leapt out of the driver's side and took off, leaving the engine running and the door open.

Dozens of cops were right behind him. At least, Tony assumed there would be dozens of cops, and not just one or two. He'd gotten wind that the L.A.P.D. had connected him to the four women who had gone missing over the past month.

Earlier that afternoon, he'd heard a knock on his front door. Before the officer could even knock a second time, Tony had slid out a window, hopped into his car, and bolted. Sure enough, as he drove away, he'd seen a flock of black-and-whites parked outside his house.

They'd found him. About time, to be honest. All criminals like to think they're masterminds, but honestly, they know the police will show up sooner or later. In Tony's case, it had been later. Four dead women later.

A memory blinked in the back of his mind. His second target. A nice lady named Pam. Pam*ela*, rather.

He had a charming smile. No one had ever told him that directly, but he must have a certain charisma. How else could he get complete strangers to follow him into his house and down the stairs?

Later. He could reminisce later. Right then, he was running. Fleeing on foot.

It was kind of fun. Like he was in a movie. He could almost hear the thrumming bass of the background music.

Within a minute, he was dripping. The summer heat was merciless. His shoes pounded against the pavement as he ran and ran and ran. Heat emitted from the ground like an oven, but he didn't slow down.

He moved through the neighborhood. The trees offered little shade. It was about noon, so not many people were out and about. School had just let out for summer vacation, but he was lucky—the kids were either inside where it was cool, or at a community pool or something. Regardless, the residential streets were mainly empty.

A smile flashed across his face. He might actually give the police the slip.

In the distance, sirens. Authoritative voices. Pounding footsteps.

Tony exhaled and kept running. He wasn't in the clear yet.

Just up ahead—a narrow road between two houses. Tony turned and ran down it.

No one in sight. Empty road. Garbage cans on the curb. He slowed to a jog to catch his breath.

Cute houses. Quaint. Waist-high fences surrounded the dry yards. One was painted red several years ago, and its natural color was showing at the roots. Laundry hung to dry. Tony didn't know people still did that.

The next house was a bit nicer, a bit newer. White windowsills, a swing set in the lawn, satellite dish on the roof—

CRASH. THUNK.

Something hard slammed against Tony's head. He fell to the concrete and scraped his palms. "What the...?" He could feel a welt growing on the back of his skull.

A toolbox landed next to him. A full, heavy toolbox.

Who'd thrown that?

Instinct yelled at Tony to get to his feet, and he obeyed, ready to face whoever had screwed with him.

A man stood in the lawn of the house with the swing set. He was tall and lean, and he wore a loosened necktie, slacks, and a white shirt soaked through with sweat. He'd been out in the heat for a while.

The stranger in the tie — the prick who'd thrown the toolbox, most likely — hopped over the waist-high fence and took a few slow steps toward Tony. He seemed casual, leisurely, in no rush at all. But his face was hardened, his jaw set. He was on a mission.

"Anthony Reynaldo." The man said the words as if they tasted rotten. "Kidnapping and homicide. Four counts."

"Ugh..." Tony spat. Who was this nutcase?

He was a little off-balance, thanks to the toolbox to the head, but he tried desperately not to show it. He growled back, "Yeah, and who're you?" He held out his fists, prepared to tear the guy into ribbons. Then something shiny caught his eye. The sun reflected off of something on the man's belt.

A detective badge? Tony blinked. Why wasn't this cop chasing him with the others? Or calling in his position or something?

No gun either. Odd, seeing a detective with no weapon.

The cop nodded. "L.A.'s finest. The pleasure's yours."

Tony'd had enough. He threw a fist at the cop's chin...but the guy easily sidestepped it. As he stepped, the cop pulled something out from behind his back. Something long and heavy — Tony didn't get a good look at what it was.

Suddenly, all the air rushed out of Tony's body. The cop had punched him in the gut. He stumbled back until he bumped into the fence of a house across the street. The cop swept his legs out from under him, and Tony plopped to the ground.

Heat radiated from both the sky above and the concrete below as Tony tried to regroup. What was going on?

The cop knelt in front of him and raised an arm. He held up an old hammer...and he brought it down hard.

Tony felt the big toe of his right foot crunch into a thousand shards. "*Gahhh!*" he shrieked. His body clenched and convulsed, then shuddered and wilted.

"Sorry about that," the cop said. He lifted the hammer again and smashed Tony's other big toe.

Tony wanted to scream until his throat was raw, wanted to snivel and cry, wanted to beat this cop into a pulp. Instead, he ground his teeth. "You're gonna pay for this, deck. You're finished. As soon as those other cops hear about this, you'll be in jail right next to me."

The cop wiped a bead of sweat from his temple. Then, in a flash, he slapped Tony's head, right where the toolbox had hit. It would've hurt less if he'd punched him.

"The world would be better without you," the cop rumbled.

Those words hung in the air. Despite the shimmering sun, Tony felt a chill.

It must have been a surreal scene: a pleasant-looking residential street; a criminal sprawled on the ground, leaning against a fence; a detective knelt in front of him, holding a rusty hammer.

"Listen," the cop said. "You're a killer—there's no point playing dumb. You have a dozen cops on your tail. You'll be arrested in a couple minutes. The press will have a field day. You'll be branded a murderer for the rest of your life. That's done. But I have evidence no one else has. Evidence of what you do with those bodies after you've killed them."

Tony's heart almost stopped, then went into overdrive. This cop knows? He knows about what he does in the cellar? There's no way this cop has evidence of that. No way. Tony was way too careful.

He's bluffing. He's a lying scumbag cop.

Unless…

Tony's mind galloped at a million miles an hour. It all came down to whether he believed this mysterious detective had evidence or not.

He looked into the cop's eyes, and the devil looked back.

Tony gulped.

"If you say a word about me," the cop continued in a low tone, like a tidal wave that hadn't crashed yet, "if you say one little syllable, I'll leak what I have. Once the world sees that, you won't just be a killer anymore. Your wife, kids, nephews and nieces…When they look at you, they'll see a twisted, perverted freak." He cocked an eyebrow— he may as well have cocked a gun. "Choice is yours."

Footsteps on concrete. Yelling. The police were getting close. Tony had completely forgotten about them somehow.

The cop smiled wickedly and stood. "Better start running." He grabbed the toolbox sitting on the road and hopped back over the fence. A moment later, he was gone.

Tony took a few shallow breaths, but he couldn't quite fill his lungs. He pushed himself to his feet, then took a step. His toes screamed all the way up his legs, as if his nerves were on fire. He couldn't cry out, though. He didn't want the police to hear.

Another step. More agony. And another. Tears dribbled down his face.

He staggered halfway down the street. Just as he was about to collapse, he heard a shout.

"There!" The police had found him.

He was almost relieved. The pain was blinding. He fell to the hot concrete and held his hands in the air. "I'm not resisting!" he yelled. "I'm cooperating!"

A dozen uniformed officers swarmed around him, red-faced and sweaty, guns drawn, yelling like soldiers in a war zone.

If they asked, he'd say he stubbed his toes. He had no intention of telling them about the cop with the hammer. Not even one little syllable.

8

The bus smelled, but at least it was air-conditioned.

Jason sat toward the back, where the bumps in the road were more pronounced. The toolbox he'd used against Anthony Reynaldo was on the seat next to him. A nice buffer between his sweaty body and the rest of the sweaty world.

A few passengers chitchatted, but on the whole, the only sounds were the wailing brakes and dragon-like engine. The dull roar almost lulled him to sleep. Almost. He didn't sleep much anymore.

His tie dangled loosely from his neck, and he slackened it even more. He hated ties enough already—on a scorching day, it felt like a scarf.

He stared out the window as he passed through the city. The skyscrapers, cars, hazy air, gaudy billboards...It all seemed surreal, like something a science-fiction writer from the 1920s would create.

Are we living in a dystopia right now? Jason mused. *We always read about cruddy societies in lit class, but have we actually arrived?*

Garbage everywhere. Dirty skies. Monolith corporations. Evil monsters disguised as humans. Other humans completely apathetic toward the evil monsters.

Jason rubbed his eyes. He needed more sleep.

Los Angeles had become haunted for him over the past year. The ghosts were always there, but only recently had he been able to see them.

Abel. It had started with Abel last summer. A year ago. A religious lunatic whose goal had been to execute ten people, each of them having broken one of the Ten Commandments.

In the year since, a dozen books about the killer had hit the tops of bestseller lists, and TV psychologists constantly spouted off new insights into his mind: His mother was mean, capitalism was stacked against him, the world was cruel, religion, God, blah, blah, blah.

Abel was still alive, locked away somewhere, but he didn't talk. He didn't share his inner thoughts and motives, which was just how the pop-psychology people liked it—that way, they could fill in the blanks themselves and sell more books.

As Jason had drifted through the year following Abel's spree, he had learned the general population didn't overly care about the nitty-gritty details of Abel's motivations. At the end of the day, the man had wanted to kill, so he did. Period.

But, Jason knew, merely killing people hadn't been Abel's goal—that had been the means to an end. His true ambition was to spark a holy war and garner a following. He'd wanted to create disciples who would continue his work and enforce his crazed vision of biblical justice all over the world. If Abel had succeeded, that's very likely what would have happened.

Jason hadn't been the one to stop him. He'd failed.

Abel had killed all ten of his intended victims, the last being Jason's son, Ted.

Ted, who had just been ten years old at the time. He'd be eleven now, if Abel hadn't shot him twice in the chest.

Abel had been arrested and carted away, then attacked in public. He barely survived. That's why his doctrine hadn't spread, not because Jason and the L.A.P.D. had stopped it.

Ted had hung on, lying in a hospital bed for a while. Unconscious, only breathing with the use of a machine. He was small for his age, and the big mattress made him look like he was shrinking every second.

Eventually, the wounds ran their course, and Ted Flynn lost the fight.

Jason had lost against the most heinous killer he'd ever encountered, and he'd lost his son too. That's when sleep became a stranger.

And then Roger Shore had come into his life.

He didn't have an evil lair. He gave a full confession to his horrid crimes, and he'd even led Jason to one of the bodies.

And he was a monster.

Jason had spared Abel earlier that year, and he was determined to never make that mistake again.

But Danielle Zahn had stopped him.

Thanks to her, he has never killed another human.

He still had nightmares about that day. Not because he had come close to killing someone—because he hadn't succeeded. He desperately wanted Roger Shore dead, and he wasn't sure what kind of person that made him.

"The world is a better place without you."

Those words thrummed through his brain like a semi-truck.

It was his responsibility. His burden and sacrifice. Jason was a garbage man, taking out the filth and trash. Making sure no monsters would walk free.

"My army of warriors, punishing the sinners of the world…" A voice whispered in his head. A voice that sounded like…Abel's?

The bus hit a pothole and whipped Jason's head around. He jolted and gasped, his entire body tingling as if a bucket of water had been dumped on him.

He'd dozed off.

A middle-aged lady across the aisle looked at him fleetingly, then back down at her phone.

At the next stop, Jason hopped off, deciding to walk the last few blocks to the precinct. As the bus rumbled away, he realized he'd left the toolbox in his neighboring seat. Oh well.

Against the cityscape, a proud white skyscraper peeked out amongst the clutter. L.A.'s City Hall. Historic, classical architecture. It was a welcome break from the glass and glam that the rest of the city wore.

That's where Jason was headed. Not there exactly, but his precinct was just a few blocks away. City Hall provided a convenient landmark, in case Jason ever got turned around.

"If you're ever lost," he'd once said to Ted, *"just make your way to that skyscraper, or to the precinct right next to it. You'll find friends there."*

He stuffed his hands in his pockets and paced down the sidewalks of Los Angeles. A few pedestrians brushed past, but most were in air-conditioned cars on the road.

He spied a Chinese take-out place ahead. Some food might energize him.

He should have killed Anthony Reynaldo today. Just as he should've killed Roger Shore.

What pleasant thoughts to be having while ordering take-out, Flynn. It's a real mystery why the dating scene hasn't tilted in your favor.

Jason left with his box of noodles, pretending he didn't know the answer to that question.

His perpetual bloodlust felt like a noose around his neck, one he would wear for the rest of his days. And maybe beyond—despite his early spiritual prospects, he didn't know what happened to the soul once the body stopped breathing. He hoped monsters went to hell, so that logically meant he must believe in a heaven. But then again, based on his own experience, no one was remotely good enough to make it into heaven. So hell must be really crowded, like DisneyWorld but with fewer churros and even longer lines.

But.

As he walked, Jason started to imagine. What if Reynaldo got out of custody? He was a smarmy guy—he might worm his way out of serious jail time. How many other people would he hurt? Those dead, desecrated victims would be Jason's responsibility.

He stopped walking and almost vomited on the sidewalk.

How could he have let Reynaldo live? He had let him limp away—why? Because killing was too *hard*? If he had been stronger last year, if he'd made the tough choice, Ted would still be alive.

He was lightheaded. The sun cackled at the fool with the badge, the so-called hero who couldn't even keep his own wife and son alive.

"No." He said the word out loud. He needed to hear his own voice. He began walking again—he needed to get inside, around people he trusted.

At last, the Chateau came into sight. Jason's precinct, full of friends and allies. The nondescript pile of beige concrete was a sight for sore eyes. He burst in and inhaled as much AC as he could.

"Ah, thank you, Willis Carrier," he muttered to no one in particular.

Willis Carrier was the inventor of air conditioning. Ted had told him that last year. He'd been full of fun facts.

He hopped up the stairs to the third floor, entered the precinct's bullpen, and, even though he saw this every day, he was a little amazed. Officers and detectives bustled through the enormous room, as if part of a perfectly choreographed dance. They handed off files, traded info, and worked together in a manner that would be impossible without a pitch-perfect leader. The L.A.P.D. was in full swing.

Jason shook off the wonder and dove in, weaving his way between the dozens of desks. A wall-sized window let in the sun's light but kept out the Venus-level heat. The city stretched out before him, the skyline more than a little intimidating.

Back at his desk, he shuffled through the piles of paperwork until he found something to keep his mind occupied: a form requesting security clearance for a gala next week—the President was visiting L.A., and the interim captain thought they could use a few more cops patrolling the perimeter.

Jason started filling out the blanks and boxes, but soon enough, his mind wandered back.

Maybe I can find out where Reynaldo is being kept. Roger Shore too. I can sneak into their cells, finish the job...

He massaged his temples.

No, Reynaldo and Shore were in the past. There was nothing Jason could do about them now. They were both in police custody, where they would stay. Ideally.

If either of them set foot *outside* a jail cell, though...

"Hey, man."

Mercifully, someone came along to capsize his train of thought. Garth Jameson approached then sat down at his desk, next to Jason's. Hair perfectly trimmed and coifed, wearing a navy suit and slim tie. Jason couldn't see his shoes, but he bet they were shiny.

One of his best friends. A steadfast ally, especially during Abel's reign of terror.

Jason smiled and nodded. "Afternoon."

Garth checked his watch. "Where've you been?"

He gestured to the soggy box of noodles. "Lunch."

A beat of quiet. Officers and detectives moved around the bullpen, their shoes sputtering and scatting on the linoleum floor.

Garth knew Jason wasn't telling the entire truth, and Jason knew Garth knew. For all Jason's strengths, he'd never been a compelling liar.

Eventually, Garth took a sip from his mug. "What're you filling out?"

Jason tapped the form with his pen. "The Cap wanted more officers at the President's pep rally next week. She recommended thirty officers, and Secret Service needs all their info so they can run their own background checks."

"Frustrating," Garth shrugged, "but I get it."

"Mhmm." The conversation stalled. Usually, Jason and Garth would trade banter or ask how each other's mornings were.

Not today.

Jason's pen screeched as he went back to writing.

The door to the captain's private office popped open, and Cheyenne Childers hobbled out, struggling to carry two cardboard boxes at once. Every few steps, she stopped to balance the boxes on her knee and get a better grip.

Jason rose halfway from his chair. "Need help?"

"I got it, I got it," she huffed then laughed. "I figured getting both boxes in one trip would be easier. Looks like I was wrong." Her destination — the desk she'd used when she was a detective — was on the other side of the bullpen. A perilous journey, but she was determined.

After Captain Slate Jones had been killed by Abel, the precinct went through a revolving door of acting-captains. Most stayed for less than a few weeks for one reason or another. Mainly, they weren't up to snuff. They simply didn't have the experience, savvy, or skillset to lead the precinct.

Elevating Detective Childers to interim captain had been a hail-Mary attempt to establish some order. All the cops and decks knew and respected her, so it was a good idea, in theory. In practice, it was a *great* idea. Cheyenne had been acting as captain for the past four months.

Finally, she was moving out of the office and back to her detective's desk. The new captain was coming in a couple days—middle-aged, bullish, probably a veteran who'd been in the thick of it.

Jason watched as Cheyenne bustled through the bullpen. "She was good. Really good."

"We've never been so organized," Garth agreed with a chuckle. "This place is running like clockwork. The new recruits who came onboard while she was in charge will be sad to see her go."

"*I'll* be sad to see her go."

"Well, for us, she's not going anywhere. She's coming back."

Across the room, Cheyenne dropped the boxes on her empty desk, sending flecks of dust into the air. She wiped her hands on the legs of her pants and made her way back to the office.

"Gonna rent that space out?" Jason asked. "Rooms with AC and a view could make you a fortune in L.A."

"I'm your captain for two more days, Flynn," Cheyenne leered. "Watch the quips!"

Jason saluted, she saluted back, and she closed the door.

Just like that door, the levity Jason had felt for a moment shut down too.

Garth sipped again. "She has a lot to be proud of, no doubt." His computer dinged, and he checked the screen. "We got surveillance footage of the store on Massey Street."

In one motion, Jason swept the box of noodles into a trash bin and pushed himself away from his desk. "Any passersby?"

"Haven't watched it yet. Care to join?"

"I'll get the popcorn."

A storeowner named Dillon had disappeared three nights ago, only to show up forty-eight hours later in a gutter on the east side of Royal Heights. Knife-wound between the ribs. Garth and Jason were looking into it, but they had very few leads so far.

Dillon's store peddled odds and ends that grandmas love—card games, shoe polish, travel-sized mouthwash, old books, and so on. It was the sort of place that CVS and Walgreens had put out of business decades ago. Why would anyone kill a guy like that?

They'd finally gained access to the security camera footage of an ATM across the street from Dillon's store. The store itself didn't have a camera of its own. Hopefully, they could identify the last people to see Dillon alive before he disappeared.

Jason and Garth went into a dark back room where the only light came from a small monitor mounted to the wall.

Grainy black and white footage of Massey Street flickered on the monitor. Dillon's storefront was about twenty yards in the distance.

"Alright," Garth muttered, maneuvering the screen's controls. "This is the day before Dillon vanished. Let's find when he left the store." He began to fast-forward the footage.

People and cars zipped by like fleas hopped up on caffeine. Not many of them entered Dillon's old store. Eventually, the sky began to darken, and Garth played the footage at its normal speed.

"There." Jason tapped the screen as a figure exited the front door. The presently-deceased Dillon locked up and went home, where he lived by himself. And that was that. No one ever saw him alive again. "He left at eight p.m. Now back up and see who his last customer was."

Garth was already on it. He rewound the footage until he saw movement around five o'clock.

"Got him." Garth paused the screen. Stepping out of the glass door, holding a stack of used books, was a kid in shorts and a t-shirt. No branding that Jason could see. Probably twelve or thirteen years old. He wasn't short for his age — in fact, he was tall and gangly — but he was frail, bony, and in desperate need of a haircut. His arms were so thin, he was struggling to hold the stack of hardcovers with both hands.

But the footage was too grainy and distant to make out his face.

"I'll try to ID this kid." Garth flicked the monitor off and left. The door quickly swung shut, leaving Jason alone in the small room.

He moved toward the door. Only the faint afterglow of the screen allowed him to find the door handle. He held the knob for a moment, taking a deep breath, and letting it hiss out of his nose.

That moment turned into a minute. He realized he didn't know whether his eyes were open or not. The monitor's glow had faded entirely, and he stood in total blackness.

If I step outside this room, I'll try to learn where Anthony Reynaldo is being kept. Never mind the fact that he's in police custody. If I know where he is…I might go and find him.

He couldn't tell if this was a good thing or not.

His hand hurt. He was gripping the door handle so tightly, his fingers were throbbing.

He yanked open the door and went straight back to his desk, ruining the flow of the precinct's dance. He sat, picked up a pen, and leaned over the paperwork. Those security clearance forms weren't going to fill themselves out.

9

Tobin Vivek jogged into the apartment building, his breath quivering as if he'd just run a marathon. Everyone at school always made fun of him for his scrawny legs and low stamina. But he wasn't going to see them for a whole summer.

Except for the kids who lived in his building too. That was fine, though—Tobin had gotten good at ducking them. He could be invisible, if need be.

Dong.

The elevator used to *ding.* Now it *dongs.*

The door slid open and an old lady hobbled out. She was probably a gorgeous young supermodel when she'd first gotten on the elevator, it was so slow.

The building's lobby looked like the waiting room for the world's worst dentist office. Sofas and chairs and carpet, all stained, stolen from a thrift shop. Brown splotches decorated the ceiling, and it always smelled like a wet dog had wriggled its way under the floorboards and died.

But it was good. Nothing horrible to complain about. People didn't kill each other or anything.

He stood in the lobby for a second to catch his breath and wipe the sweat out of his eyes. In the heat of the day, his long hair was like a wet mop. His hair hadn't been cut in over a year—he didn't want to pay for one, nor did he have the confidence to do it himself.

Middle school gym hadn't been kind to him this year...but again, he wouldn't have to worry about that all summer.

Next year, though...His stomach churned. Eighth grade was gonna suck.

A low sound caught his attention. Someone was playing ear-piercingly loud music on the third floor. He could hear it, even in the lobby.

Looked like his mom was home.

The elevator was available, but only grandmas and people carrying groceries used that. He headed for the staircase.

Tobin had lived in this building for...He stopped to think. His mom and brothers and he had moved here when he was ten years old, and he was thirteen now. So three years, maybe a little more. That wasn't a huge amount of time, but even so, he'd never heard of someone getting robbed or beaten up here. Pretty good stats, the way he saw it.

Then again, no one really held open doors for each other or helped old ladies cross the street. And come to think of it—if they saw you getting robbed or beaten up, they'd probably avoid eye contact and walk right on by.

So to recap: Tobin's neighbors wouldn't kill him, but they wouldn't stop him from being killed.

On the ladder of the social contract, he was one rung above "passable." And that was all he needed.

The air conditioning in the stairwell was self-generated—the faster he went up the stairs, the stronger the breeze blowing on his face would be. He stopped on his floor and walked down the hall.

Though he'd only been in this building for a few years, he'd lived in Royal Heights his entire life. Just on the outskirts of the center of the city. If he wanted to, he could drive to Hollywood. He was tall enough to reach the pedals in most cars, and he had even hotwired one or two before...but getting inside would be the tricky part.

As he neared his family's apartment, the music got louder. His mom loved '80s metal, and she played it at such a high volume, it became all distorted and he couldn't tell what they were saying. She always had some sort of noise going: music, TV, or both. Tobin thought it was so she wouldn't have to talk to anyone.

He reached the door, opened it, and the music just about peeled off his eyebrows. He walked across the small sitting room to a coat closet. His four big brothers were all there—one was playing guitar, although Tobin had no idea how he could hear the notes; another was lifting barbells; the other two were rolling around on the floor, pseudo-wrestling. The door to his mom's bedroom was closed, the deafening music exploding out. The floor trembled with the bass.

He slipped into the closet and shut the door without anyone noticing him. Mission accomplished.

A chain dangled from above. Tobin pulled it, and dull yellow light filled the closet. He sat on the floor and leaned against the back wall. Pant legs and shirt arms tickled his face. This was where he worked. Where he thrived.

Hidden in the corner was a tall stack of books, all of them old and dusty. He'd bought most of them from second-hand shops, but many of them were found in alleys or on empty diner tables.

Tobin picked up the book on top of the stack. He held it with reverence, because he knew of its potential.

Its potential to make cold hard cash.

He reached into the pocket of one of the winter coats hanging above him, and he pulled out an old iPod Touch. He got online and searched the book's title.

The author was barely successful. And still alive.

He tossed the book aside. Next.

Aha. The next two books in the stack caught his eye. *Gone With the Wind*, by Margaret Mitchell—an old edition with a solid gray cover and brown pages, not very pretty. And Richard Nixon's memoirs. Both of them were massive, hundreds of pages, maybe even a thousand. He had to use both hands to hold each. Some people just wrote and wrote as if they had something to prove.

He set Nixon aside and thumbed through *Wind*. He'd never read it, but he'd seen the movie on cable. A racist old book that had inspired a racist old movie. Just the sort of thing rich people love.

The pages were in good condition. He smiled and jittered with excitement.

Behind his stack of books was a shoebox. He dragged it over and flipped open the lid, revealing a dozen pens. What color and style would old Margaret use?

He used the iPod to look up an image of Margaret Mitchell's signature. He studied it for almost ten minutes, paying close attention to every swish and swipe. Then he grabbed a thin black pen and got to work.

Tobin had steady hands. It sounded insignificant when said out loud. Not many kids rush home from school to brag to their parents about their hands. But you could accomplish a lot in the world with steady hands—you could perform brain surgery, conduct a symphony, or paint the next *Last Supper*. Or, if you had a certain inclination, you could pick locks, snatch wallets, or forge signatures.

And Tobin Vivek had the latter inclination. He could reproduce any signature just by sight. It wasn't easy, of course—it took a lot of practice and patience, but he was good at it.

Bad forgers simply copied a person's signature, as if tracing it onto another sheet of paper.

Tobin knew better than that. He knew humans never signed their name the exact same way twice. Letters and sizes and slants were always just a little bit different. For example, Margaret Mitchell made the lowercase A's in her first name lopsided, not identical. So it stood to reason that the L's in her last name should be a little lopsided too.

Details like that made him a great forger, and he'd found great success online.

If he found an interesting book with a famous/infamous author, he would sign their autograph on the title page and sell it on the internet. He used a different account every time so no one could track him down if they found out it was a forgery, as unlikely as that was.

He finished Margaret's first name and set it aside to let his hand rest. He looked at his pen collection the way some other kid might admire a pile of baseball cards.

A surprising amount of thought went into choosing which pen he would sign any given autograph with.

For example, if he were to sign Nixon's name in the memoir, he would choose a maroon-colored fountain pen. Was it more accurate? Tobin didn't know. But it *seemed* more accurate.

In fact, if he was pressed for a specific number, Tobin would estimate that a blue-ballpoint Nixon signature would sell for thirty percent less than a red-fountain one, despite both signatures being one hundred percent fake.

Facts were circumstantial. It came down to how things felt.

All that being said, Tobin wouldn't do Nixon. A signed presidential memoir would draw way too much attention…and a lot of anger, if it was found to be fake.

Over the years, Tobin had learned the tricks of the trade, mainly because he invented both the tricks and the trade. Big signatures sold poorly. But so did tiny ones. Female signatures should be a little more flowery and slanted…unless it was a feminist author. In that case, he wrote bold letters, and pressure on the pen made for a good effect. Tobin was a master at feeling these things out.

He wasn't raking in the dough with these books—not by a long shot. If he swindled people out of too much money, he would have been tracked down and beaten up a hundred times by now. No, he sold the books at prices just high enough to have a solid payday, and just low enough so that his customers would shrug when they found out the signature was false. Most of his buyers were filthy rich with disposable cash—a drop in the bucket for them was a swimming pool for him.

For a kid in Royal Heights, this was life-changing. He hadn't been caught, and the results spoke for themselves.

He'd made thousands of dollars. But he hadn't spent a nickel. He saved every dollar so that one day, when he was old and confident enough, he could leave. Get his own apartment. Forge his own future away from indifferent brothers, stupid classmates, and blaring '80s music behind closed doors.

These books were his future.

It was getting hot in the closet. A bead of sweat formed on his forehead. He scooted away from the open book so the drop wouldn't soil a page.

10

A voice broke through Jason's mental haze.

"Got him." Garth slapped the side of Jason's desk as he buzzed past.

"Him?" Jason murmured, still emerging from his fog. *Reynaldo? Shore? Abel?*

"The kid in the footage. The last person to see Dillon alive, that we know of."

Jason shook away the last cobwebs. "Yeah, yeah. Good." *Get it together. Now. Not later, not when it's less difficult. Now.*

He dug a key from his pocket and unlocked the desk's bottom drawer. He reached in and felt the metal of his gun.

He affixed his Glock in a holster on his belt, mirroring his badge on the other hip. He stood and followed Garth, who was almost at the exit. "Who is it?"

Garth answered over his shoulder, "Tobin Vivek, thirteen years old. Lives in Royal Heights. Let's pay him a visit." He cinched his necktie and adjusted his suit jacket, preparing to step out into the world.

Jason, on the other hand, tugged at his tie and dreaded venturing out into the wasteland without AC. "Let's."

They passed the massive window, and Jason stared out it for a moment. Despite living in L.A. for many years, he'd never felt like he truly knew it. There was so much potential, so much mystery, and so much danger out there.

He spied a blue water cooler in the corner of the bullpen. A dry patch in the back of his throat felt like the Gobi Desert—he wanted a drink, but Garth was energized, his gait speedy, a man on a mission.

I can get water later. He ignored the cooler and kept up with his friend.

The two detectives descended the stairs and passed through the reception area. A kind, older woman named Lois waved at them from her desk, then went back to replacing the lemon-scented air-freshener with a new cartridge.

"Ms. Cabrera," Garth nodded politely to her.

She smiled at them, and Jason did his best to return the favor.

They burst out the precinct's doors, and the heat sucked Jason's breath from his lungs. They moved across the parking lot. The sea of metal cars simultaneously absorbed and reflected the sun's rays, and Jason shielded his eyes from the glare.

A beep came from the middle of the lot. Garth jingled his keys, and they followed the chirp to his department-issued car.

Garth slid into the driver's seat, and Jason got in next to him. The engine rumbled to life, and the air conditioner blasted them in the face, feeling more like a hairdryer.

Off they went, turning east, away from the heart of the city. The white spire of City Hall loomed in the rearview mirror.

The AC wasn't doing its job. Jason squirmed and tensed up, feeling like his skin was a size too small for his body. He glanced over at Garth—he was barely sweating. There were no fat drops on his forehead, just a faint sheen. *He's practically in a tuxedo and wingtip shoes. How does he do that?*

They drove in silence for a minute. Traffic wasn't bad, surprisingly. They flew past the Chinese take-out place Jason had visited earlier that afternoon—he pretended not to recognize it.

Royal Heights sat east of downtown L.A. Just a few miles from the Hollywood sign, the Walk of Fame, and the ivory obelisk of City Hall...But those few miles might as well have been filled with valleys and deserts. They were worlds apart in all the ways that mattered.

Garth flexed his fingers on the steering wheel—ten and two, all the time. He cleared his throat and ventured a question. "How're you doing?"

Jason shrugged and obfuscated. "I'm a little hungry, honestly. Didn't get to eat my noodles."

"No, Jason, about today —"

The question landed in Jason's gut. He barely contained his sigh. "Garth, I know you mean well, but I…Not now. I'm not in the mood. It's just…" He gestured out the window. "It's so friggin' hot."

Of course Jason knew what Garth was hinting at. It was what had made Jason pursue Anthony Reynaldo earlier that day. It was why there was a fire in his chest at that moment…and every moment.

It had been exactly one year since Abel had shot Ted.

One year ago, Captain Slate Jones and Detective Sam Washington had died at Abel's twisted hand. Jason had found the killer in his own home. He'd beaten Abel to a pulp, and it had felt good. Then he'd spared Abel, because he'd wanted to show Ted that his father wasn't a violent man. And then Abel had shot Ted twice.

How time flies.

"I'm just checking in," Garth said. His eyes were fixed ahead, his neck muscles taut. He was hurting too. "It's not your fault."

Jason felt for his friend, but he had very little sympathy for him. Not today.

His head pounded like a war drum. The fire in his chest rose to the surface. "What's there to talk about?" He clenched his fists. "I didn't kill Abel when I had the chance. Then, a minute later, Abel killed my son. It's simple logic, Garth. There are monsters who need to be put down. It might not be my fault, but it's my responsibility, and I don't take that lightly."

Bit by bit, Jason opened his fists. His fingernails had punctured his skin. Red drops blossomed from his palms. He grabbed a tissue from the glove box and wiped away the blood, but tiny pink half-moons remained etched in his skin.

They didn't speak for the rest of the drive.

The car zoomed past an old, weathered church. Jason didn't catch its name. The walls were gray and crumbly, but a colorful stained glass window shone with all the power of the sun. A few people were carrying tables onto the brown lawn—there must be a picnic scheduled for the evening.

A minute later, Garth pulled over to the side of the road and put the car in park, but he continued to stare straight forward.

Jason took in his surroundings: Royal Heights. A lower-middle class neighborhood mainly comprised of apartment buildings and small businesses. A few low-rent homes here and there. Bike racks on the sidewalk. Unpainted doors and dusty windows. Litter and bottles tangled in the grass. Weeds clawing their way through the cracks in the pavement.

A lot of cars drove past—very few stopped. Not many pedestrians, and Jason got the feeling the heat wasn't the only factor.

The brick apartment building up ahead was where Tobin Vivek lived. Jason only knew that from the address—Garth didn't tell him.

They sat in the faux breeze, waiting to see the thirteen-year-old kid, and they didn't speak.

11

Ajax stood on the street corner and checked the time on his cracked phone screen. The BMW should be coming any minute now.

Good thing it was hot today. Very few people on the sidewalks. It's always helpful to have fewer wandering eyes around.

The cartel he worked for was based in rural Mexico, and it got hot there. Hotter than L.A., he thought.

Cars whizzed by—none of them slowed, and none of them were BMWs. His hands jittered a little, and he wondered if he'd told the couriers the right address. If he got this wrong…

No, no, he'd told them right. He sighed and shook his head. He needed to have more faith in himself.

He went back to watching the cars drive by. He loved cars. Their shapes, their designs, even their names. Everything about them screamed *power*. A poor man with a dented car had more freedom than a millionaire who took the bus.

Ajax smiled to himself. Next year, when he got his license, he was going to get a silver Maserati with leather interiors—

He gulped and caught himself.

The driving age in Mexico was eighteen. He was only seventeen and didn't have his license yet…but when he'd joined the cartel, he'd lied and said he was nineteen.

He quietly chided himself. "Can't make mistakes like that, Heck…"

His real name was Hector. In high school literature class, though, when they'd read snippets from Homer's *The Iliad*, his peers had found out "Hector" was a great warrior, brave and respected. Apparently, he didn't meet any of those qualifications. "Ajax," on the other hand, was a crybaby who killed himself when he didn't get his way. For the rest of his time in high school, his classmates had called him Ajax. When he left home and joined the cartel, he'd realized he liked the name.

"Screw them," he'd said. "They don't get to name me. I name myself."

He'd been in the cartel for less than a year. He was mainly a holster for a gun, a body to add numbers to an army.

But that was merely his starting point, not his destination. Ajax had goals. Not exact goals — vague ones. The motivational tapes he listened to said to set specific, attainable goals, but what did they know, anyway?

He wanted to be on top. On top of what? He didn't know…yet. But step by step, he was going to taste the sweet waters of power, or die trying.

Today, the cartel was going to eliminate a couple of rats they'd found burrowing in their garden, and Ajax was in charge of finding a good place to take care of them. Rats had a tendency to scream and make a mess when they were moments away from being killed.

Royal Heights was an okay neighborhood, he supposed. Not the best he'd seen. Not the worst, either — not even close.

He'd chosen this location for today, and he was always very careful. He wanted the neighborhood to be at least a little nice, so they wouldn't run into any trouble. Hostile gangs and crappy neighbors could be major headaches.

At the same time, they couldn't exactly kill rats in Bel-Air. Snooty socialites liked to ask questions and butt into other people's business. Also, a lot of them were buddies with police captains and commissioners or whatever and had them on speed-dial. If they saw a group of Mexicans wandering around…well, the cops would be there faster than you could say "ICE."

Royal Heights was right in the sweet spot. Livable enough to not run into any thugs, but there were also quite a few abandoned buildings to choose from.

Ajax had picked a small empty warehouse. One door, grimy windows, plenty of space inside.

A few other guys were already inside the warehouse. They had laid out plastic tarps so they could bundle up the corpses like a burrito and scram.

The plan was simple: At the designated time, a black BMW would stop next to the warehouse. In the car's trunk would be the two rats, blindfolded and tied up. Ajax and the driver would bring the rats inside, one of the guys would pop them in the head, and that's it. Rats taken care of.

Most of his colleagues wore black suits. They wanted to blend in. Not Ajax—he wanted to stand out as much as possible. He wanted his boss to notice when he did good work, so when he had joined the cartel, he'd gone to the store and bought all the Hawaiian shirts he could. It was his unofficial uniform. A lot of the older guys groaned and tsk-tsk'd, but there was no rule against it, so he wore them every day.

Even as he stood on the street corner in Royal Heights, he looked like he was ready for a luau.

Of course, if someone looked closely, they'd see the bulge of a pistol under the floral design, tucked into his waistband.

Yes, if he was going to rise up the ranks, he needed to stand out to the big boss.

The man in charge of the cartel was a millionaire a hundred times over. Cash isn't what Ajax respected, though. The boss wasn't powerful because he was wealthy—it was the other way around. He commanded men's lives every single day, and incidentally, he'd become rich along the way. That's the sort of power Ajax sought and admired.

Gore Rodriguez. Seventy years old. The big boss. He was a little paunchy, a little slow. But as soon as someone saw his cobalt eyes, they knew the truth. He wasn't merely a lethargic old man—he was a vampire who had grown fat after decades of slaughtering and consuming his rivals.

The day Ajax had joined, he had witnessed Rodriguez's full might.

His very first assignment had been to cover a rear exit of *casa de Rodriguez*. They called the estate "Xanadu." The mansion had two guest houses, a garden, a hedge maze, and three separate garages.

Lush. Opulent. Bursting with wealth and luxury. It had mesmerized Ajax the moment he stepped onto the grounds. Someday, he would live somewhere just as magnificent. Perhaps next door, if he and Rodriguez ever got as chummy as Ajax wanted them to.

Ajax had been loitering around the mansion's back door, decked out in his Hawaiian shirt, fiddling with the shoulder holster that held his pistol. Ironically, given the lush plant life and multitude of weapons, he blended right in.

It was a quiet day. Until it wasn't.

A bodyguard named Salva had burst out of one of the greenhouses, fuming, screaming, cursing to the sky. Ajax knew he should report this to his superior...but then the boss himself, Gore Rodriguez, followed Salva out of the glass building, smoking a massive cigar.

It was just Salva and Rodriguez, by themselves, in the middle of Xanadu. This was going to be good. Ajax had ducked behind a shrub to watch.

The bodyguard yelled, "I'm sick of you, old man!" He stabbed a finger at the boss, practically foaming at the mouth. His face was red, his veins throbbing. "Who do you think you are? All the money in the world, and you think you're better than me, huh?" He continued ranting and raving, waving his arms around.

Rodriguez just watched, chewing on his cigar.

Finally, Salva's rant reached its crescendo. "You know what?" He reached for the gun on his belt and approached the boss.

He never got the chance to draw his weapon.

Rodriguez sent a fist into Salva's gut with enough force to crack a few ribs. The bodyguard doubled over and opened his mouth to cry out...and Rodriguez shoved his lit cigar far down into his throat.

As the boss had lumbered away from Salva's convulsing body, he'd locked eyes with the rookie hiding behind the shrub. Rodriguez didn't say a word, didn't change the look on his face. He'd simply walked away.

Other men appeared out of nowhere to take Salva away, and in less than ten seconds, Xanadu was quiet again.

From that moment forward, Ajax had devoted himself to earning Rodriguez's respect. He would bathe in hot coals if it got him a nod from the boss. And today was his chance to prove that he was more than just a teenaged gunman.

An engine purred, and Ajax stilled his thoughts.

A black BMW pulled up, then parked on the side of the road, right in front of him. A brawny man named Marco got out of the driver's seat, leaving the car running. He wore a dark suit that strained against his pecs and biceps.

"You're late," Ajax said.

Marco held up a hand to calm him. "Less than five minutes."

"Well," Ajax checked the time again, "you're less than five minutes late."

Marco's sigh turned into a snarl. "Get over yourself."

The guy had never liked Ajax. Most of the men in the cartel didn't like Ajax. A few of the wives thought he was cute, but Ajax wasn't crazy about that. "Cute" wasn't the reputation he was going for.

No matter. Ajax had never been liked—he was used to it. He wasn't trying to win any popularity contests.

"C'mon." Marco gestured to the BMW's trunk.

The rats.

Ajax looked up and down the street. No pedestrians, but plenty of cars on the road. The engine rumbled as it idled. "Turn off the car."

"No," Marco said. "Air conditioning."

"You're wasting gas."

"There's no way in hell I'm turning it off. It took an hour to cool the car down, and I'm not starting over." He tapped the trunk. "Help me get the first one inside."

"What about all the people watching?" Ajax gestured to the moving cars on the road.

Marco chuckled once. "They aren't watching. No one will notice."

He popped open the trunk, and Ajax couldn't help but lean in for a closer look.

Two unconscious men were shoved into the small space, their arms handcuffed behind their backs, rags tied around their eyes. One of them had a bloody nose.

"Who are they?" Ajax said quietly, not wanting to wake them up.

"Yakuza," Marco answered loudly, as if to spite Ajax. He then added condescendingly, "That's like the Japanese mafia."

Ajax sneered, "I know that," even though he didn't.

"The Yakuza has been getting meth and heroin into L.A. for years. Rodriguez doesn't like it, but lets them be, for the most part. Three days ago, though, we caught these two morons on our turf. Rodriguez *really* didn't like that, and now he wants to set an example." Marco cocked a thumb toward the warehouse. "He doesn't take kindly to trespassing."

Ajax's eyes almost popped out of his skull. "Rodriguez is *here*? I mean, in *there*?"

"Shut up and lift."

Marco grabbed the legs of the mobster with the bloody nose, and Ajax took the top half. As they shuffled toward the abandoned warehouse, Marco slammed the trunk shut, leaving the other unconscious man alone in the dark.

12

The sun passed overhead, moving into the perfect position to reflect off a window, against the rearview mirror, and into Jason's eye. He squinted from the blinding assault and propped his hand against his face.

He and Garth had been sitting in the car for an hour, watching Tobin Vivek's apartment building. Somehow, against all odds, the day had gotten even hotter. Plenty of people had come in and out of the building—men and women, old and young—but no sign of Tobin.

Jason glanced in the rearview mirror. The old church they had passed was a few blocks behind them—he could still see the brightly colored window, but just barely. The colored glass reflected the sun into his face, either mocking him or trying to get his attention.

The window's design featured a man standing in a field of green. If Jason were a gambler, he'd bet it was Jesus. Ninety-nine percent of church stained glass windows feature a haloed Jesus.

Jason decided it was mocking him.

He sighed and scanned the road in front of him for the hundredth time. In the late afternoon, Royal Heights had come to life a bit. A few people were on the sidewalks, holding grocery bags or pushing strollers. The small stores seemed to be attracting a good amount of business. Cars moved to and fro, back and forth, ebbing and flowing.

The traffic showed no signed of ending, and he doubted it ever would. Probably since the second day of cars' existence, the world has been in a constant state of gridlock. Or was it the other way around? Humans are gridlocked creatures, always creating conflict and wrecking things. It makes sense that they invented machines that lent themselves to discord. People's default setting is "road rage."

Jason was going crazy.

Is there a car version of cabin fever?

Despite the heat, a chill came from the driver's side. Garth hadn't said a word since they parked. He just kept staring at the apartment building, his eyes flicking around, scrutinizing every pedestrian's face.

Long stretches of waiting were nothing new to Jason. It came with the job. He'd sat in a car and stared at nothing for entire nights before. Why had the past hour been so tedious?

Because I usually have someone to talk to.

His friend had suddenly closed himself off, and Jason didn't know why.

Had he offended Garth somehow?

If so, grow up, Garth.

The thought was jarring, but Jason realized he meant it.

Garth wasn't the one who had lost a wife and a son. Jason was.

Garth didn't bear the responsibility for every murder Abel, Roger Shore, and Anthony Reynaldo had committed. Jason did.

Garth wasn't haunted by nightmares. He didn't jerk awake in a cold sweat every night and instinctively reach for his gun. Jason did.

So yeah. Jason was a little snippy. If that was the reason Garth had clammed up, so be it.

The front door of the apartment building opened, and a kid shambled out. Long, mangy hair.

Finally. Tobin Vivek.

For the first time in over an hour, Garth glanced at Jason. This time, though, Jason didn't return the glance. Jason got out of the car, and Garth turned off the engine and followed suit.

Immediately, a coast of sweat formed on Jason's hairline, but he ignored it. He only had eyes for Tobin.

The kid was on the sidewalk, moving away from the detectives. His pace and posture suggested that he didn't know he was being followed. He had his hands in his pockets and his head tilted down, so his hair formed a shroud around his face.

Jason and Garth walked smoothly but briskly to catch up with the kid. In a matter of seconds, their adult legs had placed them about twenty feet behind Tobin.

Garth cleared his throat, and Jason shot him a glare. But it was too late.

"Mr. Vivek!" Garth bellowed.

Tobin spun around to look at the two men behind him.

Garth held out his hands and used a firm, patronizing tone, as if he were talking to a toddler, not a teenager. "L.A.P.D. We'd like a word with you."

While the words were still coming out of Garth's mouth, Tobin sprinted down an alley and out of sight.

Jason took off running. He looked over his shoulder and yelled, "Go to the next major street and try to cut him off!"

Garth darted back to his car, and Jason turned down the alley Tobin had disappeared into.

The kid was already at the far end of the alley, turning onto another street.

Geez, he's fast. Jason sighed and pumped his legs faster. *Should've stretched this morning.*

Jason exited the alley and caught sight of Tobin's thick mane bouncing down the street. The kid peeked over his shoulder and saw the detective giving chase. He leapt into traffic, weaving between cars like a video game frog. The drivers blasted their horns at him, but in a matter of seconds, Tobin was successfully across the street, not a scratch on him.

The road was full of cars, and crossing it seemed like a suicide mission, even though Jason had just watched Tobin do so.

The kid smirked and began to jog away.

It was the smirk that really got under Jason's skin. He wiped an arm across his forehead. With his gun on one hip and his badge on the other, he dove into traffic.

"Outta the way!" someone screeched at him.

"Are you serious?" yelled another.

Jason was too focused on not getting steamrolled to respond. While Tobin's crossing had been smooth and effortless, Jason's was jerky and more than a little precarious. He was nearly killed by at least five Ubers, but he made it.

He stood on the sidewalk, huffing and puffing, glaring at Tobin's back. The kid was still jogging away, thinking his troubles were trapped on the other side of the street.

Why is Tobin Vivek running from us in the first place?

There weren't many people around, but the traffic hopefully covered up any noise he might make. Jason scampered quickly, keeping his footsteps as light and quiet as possible.

But not quiet enough. Tobin's head tilted to the side, as if receiving a radio signal, and then he took off in a dead-sprint.

How Tobin had heard Jason through all the hair surrounding his ears, Jason didn't know. "C'mon!" he thundered in frustration and picked up his pace.

The last time Jason had chased someone through the streets of L.A., it had been nighttime. And raining sheets. Visibility had been nonexistent, but at least he hadn't keeled over and died of heat stroke.

As he ran, the perimeter of his vision got a little swimmy, and his chest felt tighter with every breath. The summer day was taking its toll.

He couldn't see Tobin up ahead, but there was another alleyway. The kid must've gone that way. Jason followed his gut and found himself blocked by a chain-link gate. It was only about seven-feet tall, though, and it swayed back and forth as if someone had just climbed over it.

Jason stuck his fingers into the grimy chain-links and quickly hoisted himself over the gate. He landed hard and nearly collapsed — his knees and ankles were getting weak. He should catch his breath soon. And he needed a gallon of ice-cold lemonade.

The old metal fence had left brown smudges on his white shirt. He shook his head as he jogged out of the alley and back onto the Royal Heights streets.

There. Tobin ran down the sidewalk. Jason tailed him.

Suddenly, Tobin's run turned into a sprint. He must've seen something.

Shoot. Up ahead, idling by the sidewalk, was a black BMW.

"Don't even think about it, kid!" he yelled.

But Tobin was already thinking about it. The thirteen-year-old reached the BMW, yanked open the driver's door, and hopped in. The tires squealed against the pavement as if they were in pain, and the car surged into traffic. It veered and knocked into other cars, and then it turned onto another busy street. And it was gone. A few seconds later, its rumbling engine faded into the L.A. ambiance.

Jason slowed from a sprint to a trot, then a jog, then a defeated crawl. He hissed one word—"Kids..."—and grabbed the agonizing stitch in his side. He walked in the general direction the BMW had gone, hoping Tobin would crash soon.

13

The interior of the warehouse felt artificial, as if the place had been created for a haunted house attraction. It was big and echoey, containing nothing but random litter and an ominous feeling. The floors were concrete and the walls metal, giving every sound an odd twang. The only light came from the grimy windows, casting everything in a brown haze.

Except for Ajax's gaudy Hawaiian shirt. His goal was to stand out, and in that dusty deathtrap of a warehouse, he definitely succeeded.

Five burly cartel men, including Marco, stood in a semicircle around a tarp that was stretched out on the floor. And stretched out on the tarp was a recently dead body—the bound and blindfolded Yakuza gangster whom Ajax and Marco had lugged inside a few minutes before. His bloody nose didn't seem like that big of a deal compared to the bullet hole in his skull.

The Yakuza man had woken up from his unconsciousness just as Ajax had closed the warehouse door. The burly cartel men had dragged him the rest of the way to the tarp and set him on his knees. That's when he'd started to cry and beg and plead…but it was all in Japanese, so Ajax didn't know exactly what he was saying. Tears had leaked out from under his blindfold, though, so it likely had to do with his wife and children or something.

Ajax had watched the whole thing from the doorway. He hadn't been invited into the semicircle, but he hadn't been told to scram either, so he'd hung around the exit, halfway between leaving and staying.

The five cartel men had stood around the Yakuza man as he pleaded. They had their arms crossed, scowling at the rival gangster.

Ajax wanted to tell them to take off the guy's blindfold—looking intimidating didn't mean anything if the victim couldn't see them. But he held his tongue.

Because Gore was there.

In a distant corner of the warehouse, cloaked in darkness, stood Gore Rodriguez. The boss of the cartel. Because he wore a dark suit, it looked like his head was floating in midair. He was just as terrifying as Ajax remembered: stocky, dominant, dripping with power. And he never moved. Didn't wipe his sweaty brow, didn't sniffle or scratch an itch. Nothing. He stood in the corner like a stone gargoyle and watched.

The Yakuza guy kept blubbering and crying, and the cartel men seemed content to let him wear himself out. If Ajax were running this show, he would kill both rival gangsters at once, *BOOM*, roll them up, and get out of there. It would take less than thirty seconds.

Eventually, Marco had drawn a big, shiny pistol from his suit jacket and pulled back the slide. The sound ricocheted in the empty warehouse, and the Japanese gangster shut up.

Then, Marco had shot him in the head. The pistol coughed through its silencer, a red mist erupted from the gangster's skull, and he flopped to the ground.

Ajax watched the execution and felt...nothing. The lack of emotion affected him more than the actual murder.

That was the first time he'd seen someone get shot in the head. It was brutal, violent, and shocking, to be sure. But it barely raised his heartrate. It was as if he'd seen dozens of mob-style executions in his seventeen years of life, even though he hadn't.

Well. He'd learned something about himself.

Marco popped the joints in his neck and bounced on his heels. The murder had gotten his adrenaline going...or maybe it was just an excess of testosterone. He looked at Ajax. "Go get the other one from the trunk. Take his blindfold off so he can see his buddy." He gestured to the pile of blood and meat on the tarp that had once been a man.

With a quick glance at the boss in the far corner, Ajax nodded. He didn't want to be seen merely as an errand boy, but he wanted to be a team player too. Someone who fit snugly in Rodriguez's network.

He opened the warehouse door, a strip of sunlight illuminating the dusty air. As he went to the sidewalk and listened to the sounds of the bustling city, he thought of his next step. His choice of location for these executions had been right on the money, so hopefully, his superiors would entrust him with more responsibilities. He might even be invited to join a crew that dropped off a load of product. That was Rodriguez's inner circle, the people he trusted most. If he trusted you with the goods, you know you've made it —

Wait. Ajax looked up and down the street. He shielded his eyes from the sun to make sure he was seeing things right.

Yep. His eyes weren't lying.

An icy knife eased itself into his spine. The execution hadn't affected him earlier, but now, his heart was pounding against his rib cage. He felt faint.

The car was gone. The black BMW. The one with the other gangster still in the trunk.

Ajax's hands started to tremble.

What will Rodriguez do? Best case scenario, Ajax will be kicked out of the cartel and sent to Canada. Worst case…he'll join the Yakuza guy on the tarp.

How had this happened? How the hell —

Suddenly, the icy panic in his veins disappeared, and hot anger replaced it.

Marco had left the car running. The keys were in the ignition, even with a captured gangster in the trunk.

Ajax set his jaw and patted the gun that was hidden under his colorful shirt. He went back inside.

The five burly cartel men were chatting, cackling, having a grand old time. Morons. Rodriguez still watched silently from his corner.

Marco looked Ajax up and down. "Well?"

The single syllable echoed against the metal walls.

Ajax let out a breath. "The car is gone."

All the air was sucked out of the room. Marco's smug face began to melt, and he turned the color of flour. He stared intently at Ajax, silently begging him to not say anymore.

Ajax didn't grant Marco's request. He spoke loudly so that Rodriguez could hear: "You left the car running on the side of the road, Marco. The Yakuza man escaped because you wanted the air conditioning to stay cool."

The other cartel men glared at Marco, and Ajax shot a glance at the boss to ascertain his reaction. Par for the course, Rodriguez's expression hadn't flickered. Instead, he started walking toward the warehouse's exit. Two bodyguards appeared out of the shadows and walked behind him, guns drawn.

Royal Heights was no longer safe for Gore Rodriguez. They were getting out of there.

"You little putz…" Marco snarled and lunged at Ajax.

Marco had a huge, muscular frame, and he'd likely never lost a fistfight in his life. But Ajax was ready. He drew his pistol from his waistband and whipped it across Marco's jaw. The big man toppled to the floor, dazed and moaning.

Rodriguez and his bodyguards were near the door, their footsteps clicking and clacking like bullets being loaded into a magazine.

Ajax began to tuck his pistol away and step out of his boss's path…but then he paused. Instead, he clutched the gun tighter and squared his shoulders. He felt something in his gut, some deep fire he couldn't quite identify. Was it fear? Nerves?

No. It was excitement. Adrenaline.

"We'll find the missing man, sir," he said, forcing his voice not to quiver. "We'll tear the city apart if we have to. We'll kill him. And whoever helped him escape."

Gore Rodriguez looked into Ajax's eyes for the second time in his life. He nodded, and left. The door swung shut with a *bang*, rattling the earth beneath them.

Ajax exhaled. Inhaled. Exhaled. Then he turned to the men still in the warehouse. Four stood around the bloody corpse, dumbfounded by the situation, looking to Ajax for direction. They were all at least a decade older than him.

Marco staggered to his feet. A dark red bruise was forming on the side of his face. He shot Ajax a glare that dripped with venom, but he said, "Now what?"

"Roll up that body and meet me outside in thirty seconds. Then…" he holstered the gun under his floral shirt and walked toward the exit, "…we go hunting."

14

Jason took deep breaths as he walked, trying to soothe the painful stitch in his side. His lungs felt like they were filled with sand, but he knew it would pass soon enough. He just needed to take it easy…and rehydrate very soon.

He turned onto the street where the BMW had disappeared a minute ago.

Hopefully, Garth had circled around in his own car, and he'd caught Tobin already. Finger crossed. Jason never relied on hopes, though. He was about as lucky as a black cat walking under a ladder. Coincidences rarely came out in his favor.

He did his best to walk with his shoulders back, confidently, like he wasn't about to die of heat stroke. But despite his best efforts, his steps were a bit sluggish, and the stitch in his side kept him from standing up straight.

He passed a storefront and peeked inside. There were a few shoppers—locals, judging from their clothes. It was an old mom-and-pop electronics store. TVs, stereos, even some CDs. Jason couldn't remember the last time he'd bought a CD.

Maybe they have a water cooler…

No. Find Tobin first. Don't let him get away. Or at least meet up with Garth and get a lead on where the BMW was headed. He squinted down the street, quickly skimmed the moving traffic and the cars parked on the sides, but he didn't see the black vehicle anywhere.

How did that kid hotwire the car so fast? One second he was hopping in, the next he was burning rubber down the street.

Over the years, Jason had tried to pick up skills like that. "Extracurriculars," he called them. Picking locks, dismantling security systems, hotwiring cars, telling a lie without blinking…He figured it would be useful for a detective to have the same skillset as those he hunted.

So far, he was failing in all categories.

His phone vibrated in his pocket. Probably Garth.

He twitched at a memory. His phone buzzing. Abel's grating voice on the other side. North Highland Boulevard exploding, turning into a war zone. It'd been a sunny day, like this one. And he'd been searching for a BMW — a silver one, that time, but still.

He ignored his phone until the buzzing stopped. His hands shook from the effort it took to not ball them into fists. He looked at his palms and was surprised to see tiny red half-moons imprinted there.

From my fingernails.

As Jason walked past an alley, a noise erupted behind a dumpster. Barking. A huge dog, it sounded like. Jason jumped back and held out his arms to shield himself, but the animal wasn't attacking him.

A grungy street dog came out from behind the dumpster, seemingly oblivious to Jason. It just thrashed around on the concrete, howling, scratching the metal container…whimpering too.

Jason didn't want to get within its biting range, so he kept walking. He looked over his shoulder and saw the dog crying at the sun. Like a whistle. A siren. A warning.

He heard screeching tires.

There. About a hundred yards ahead.

The black car! Swaying wildly as it moved down the street, driven either by a blindfolded drunk or a gangly kid.

He jogged after it as fast as his cramping muscles allowed.

"Gotcha, you little…"

Habit forced him to swallow the profane end of that sentence. Years ago, his wife Keri had been the one to soothe his anger and keep his darker instincts in check.

Then, the twisted hand of fate had taken her away, like a cosmic joke. Jason had thought he'd forgiven the young man responsible for Keri's death. He'd truly thought he'd moved past his anger.

And then Ted had died too.

His eyes zeroed in on the car and he picked up the pace, like a laser-targeting missile.

As he ran down the sidewalk, he suddenly stumbled to the right, almost falling to the ground. He shook his head and wiped away more sweat. *What in the world? This heat is really getting to me…*

But then he pitched again, this time to the left.

No. It wasn't just the heat.

The ground was moving.

A satellite dish snapped off a roof and crashed right in front of him. He swerved to avoid it, and his legs got tangled up as if they were made of rubber. He nearly face-planted on the concrete.

What's happening?!

It felt like he was running diagonally on a treadmill. He looked all around—the few pedestrians on the street looked just as confused as he was, and many of them were on the verge of panic. They held their arms out to keep themselves steady.

Several blocks behind Jason, the dog's barking turned urgent, almost frightened. It just kept going, even though its throat was hoarse.

The windows lining the street rippled like the surface of a pond after a rock had been dropped in. A car braked in the middle of the road, causing a chain-reaction of crashes behind it. Metal crunched, people yelled, horns blared. But Jason wasn't listening.

Underneath all the noise, there was a low sound. One he'd never heard before. He strained his ears to listen. It was a sort of earthy churning, like a rockslide or an avalanche. It was difficult to pinpoint exactly where the sound was coming from.

And every second, it got louder. The churning turned into a rumble, then a roar. Then a quake.

Jason realized why it was hard to figure out where the sound was coming from.

Because it was coming from everywhere. The earth itself was churning, rumbling, roaring. Quaking.

Oh God.

Being an L.A. resident for many years, Jason had felt plenty of earthquakes—little ones and strong ones. But never like this. The air trembled. His bones were jolted. Buildings shook like dead leaves clinging to a branch. The entire cityscape convulsed.

His brain shook too, dumbfounded, in shock, so his body switched to auto pilot, and he kept running on the trembling ground. He heard glass shattering above him, and he tensed up. He couldn't remember if it was better to be inside or outside in situations like this. His thought process wasn't just slow — it had vanished entirely.

Up ahead, a powerline fell into the road, sending sparks into the air. People screamed in horror as their world fell apart around them.

Shelter. Now.

Jason skidded to a stop, fell to his knees, and rolled under a parked car. The concrete tore his slacks and scuffed his knees, and the sun-heated ground just about burned him, but he barely noticed.

He huddled under the car and watched as Los Angeles shifted back and forth. Back and forth. Back and forth. It was unbelievable. The whole city wasn't just shaking — it was *being shaken*, like a snow globe filled with millions of people.

Is it just the city? An earthquake of this magnitude could affect entire counties, if not half the state…

Unsteady feet ran past the car. It seemed that people were coming out of the buildings, thinking it would be safer out in the open than confined indoors.

"Get under something!" he tried to yell, but his words were lost in the turmoil. "Take cover!" No one heard him.

Soon. This has to end soon. He waited for the screams to die down, but they only got louder. Most of the traffic on the road had stopped, except for a few fools who were trying to escape the chaos in their vehicles. Every driver that tried to navigate the rocking streets crashed.

He heard the shattering of glass, louder than a cymbal in an orchestra — windows everywhere were breaking. Deadly shrapnel rained onto the ground. Pedestrians screamed as the shards landed in their hair, eyes, and skin.

Cries of agony joined the screams of terror. Injuries. Casualties. Deaths.

How long has this been going? He tried to think. The noise and madness and scorching-hot concrete all clouded his mind. *Thirty seconds? A minute?*

People kept running past the car he was hiding under. They stumbled, fell, trampled each other.

One woman fell to the concrete sidewalk, but she didn't get back up. She didn't move. Blood leaked from her scalp. Jason saw a red-stained brick on the ground next to her. It must have dislodged from a building and fallen right onto her.

If this doesn't stop soon, more than a few bricks will come crumbling down.

The panicked stampede didn't slow. People stepped right on the fallen woman, crushing her hands, arms, and even her bleeding head. They either didn't notice her, or they didn't care.

Jason reached his hand out from under the car, grabbed her ankle, and pulled with all his might. It was difficult to get leverage, since he was lying on the ground, but he gritted his teeth and dragged her body to relative safety. A trail of red followed her, smeared on the concrete.

"Miss?" he said as he gasped for breath. He shook her shoulder and checked her wound. "Miss, are you—"

Her eyes were wide open, and her chest didn't move. Gone.

He nearly gagged, but he shoved his emotions into a small box somewhere far away. *Not now.* His eyes burned for a moment before he clenched them shut. When he opened them again, the unfallen tears were banished.

CRASH.

Dust and grime swarmed the air. Sure enough, buildings were collapsing. Or sections of them, at least. Jason couldn't see what was happening to the city, but he could hear and feel it, and that was bad enough. Part of him wanted to stay under the car for the rest of his life and never find out exactly how much damage had been done to the City of Angels. He could curl up and choke on the grimy air, then eventually stop breathing. They'd find him next to this poor, nameless woman whose only crime had been running for her life.

He wouldn't have to deal with the hardships to come. The mayhem. The inevitable lawlessness and violence that always bubbled just under the society's surface. All it took was a few good shakes to shatter the veneer of civility. Again, just like a snow globe…pretty as a postcard one minute, chaos the next.

If he stayed right here, that wouldn't be his problem. Someone else would shoulder that massive burden. Someone else would deal with the crazies that came out of the woodwork, the lowlifes that used disasters as an excuse to enrich themselves, or go on a violent rampage, or add to the anarchy just for kicks.

If I come face to face with criminals like that, there's no way they're coming out of it alive...

And right then, the earth stopped rumbling. The city itself, though, still shivered — the snowflakes in the globe still swirled. Jason could hear cracking, banging, shattering. Sounds he'd expect to hear in a demolition yard.

And screaming. Throughout the entire city, screaming.

Sweat dripped in his eyes. Jason grabbed his dangling necktie and wiped his entire face with it. Then he crawled out from under the car.

Royal Heights was in shambles. Entire walls of buildings had crumbled into gravel, and debris covered the streets. A fire hydrant had been ripped out of the ground, and water shot straight into the air. At the same time, though, no less than five buildings within Jason's sight were on fire. Black smoke rose into the sky, joining the destructive haze of thousands of fires from all over the city.

The concrete road was cracked all the way down, as if letting everyone get a peek of the center of the earth. The ground sparkled from all the broken glass.

The people of Royal Heights were shell-shocked. Some poked their heads out of windows, some were splayed on the ground. They looked at each other, confused, stunned, wanting someone to say that this was all one collective nightmare. This wasn't real. This hadn't actually happened.

No one said a word. This was real.

Somewhere unseen, a baby cried. No one comforted it.

Jason leaned against the car, his mind reeling. He'd always heard about "the Big One" — the earthquake of mythical magnitude that would someday, supposedly, send Los Angeles into a tailspin. Was this it? Had the Big One just reared its ugly head?

Jason couldn't know something like that. What he did know was that this one was Big enough...and aftershocks weren't out of the question.

He staggered forward, his legs still unsure of themselves. "Everyone," he called out with as much authority as he could muster. He unhooked his badge from his belt and held it up. "Everyone stay calm, and stay close to each other. Find shelter under a table, or...or..."

No one was listening. His words floated into the air, just like the smoke.

The shell-shock wore off all at once. People began running all over the place, like ants after their hill had been destroyed. Cars fired up and ran over chunks of broken concrete. Shoes crunched on shattered glass. Fires crackled and swallowed buildings whole.

Jason held a palm to his head, dizzy from the chaos. What could he do? Where should he go?

Up ahead, something caught his eye. There, in a long line of destruction and tangled rubble...The driver's door of a black BMW popped open. A boy popped his head out and looked around, eyes wide, trembling. Tobin Vivek.

Jason began to jog toward the car. He stepped over broken parking meters and fallen air conditioning units. He heard the faint sound of rotors and looked up—helicopters had taken to the sky, surveying the damage.

The whole city...Nothing will ever be the same.

A body was sprawled on the sidewalk. Unmoving. Elderly.

Across the street, a group of people worked to move a massive pile of rubble. They repeatedly yelled someone's name.

Jason kept focused on Vivek's car. He had to. If he let himself think about the scale of what had just happened, he'd...he'd...He didn't know what he'd do.

He approached the car with as light of footsteps as he could manage. "Tobin Vivek," Jason called as he held up his badge.

The kid looked up in response. He was lanky and shaky, a scarecrow in a windstorm. Undoubtedly terrified. He was barely a teenager, but he'd just lived through a horrific disaster. And on top of that, the cop who was chasing him had just caught up.

Jason clipped the badge to his belt and quickly identified himself: "Detective Jason Flynn. Are you okay?" His eyes scanned the BMW. It looked miraculously undamaged, other than a few dents from falling debris. No smoke, no flat tires.

Tobin nodded. "Yeah." He sat in the driver's seat with his shoulders pulled up near his ears, as if he were trying to disappear inside himself. "I stopped the car when the earthquake started. Didn't want to crash."

Jason nodded. *Smart.* "I'm gonna have to ask you to step out of the car."

Tobin slowly exited, setting his feet on the ground gingerly, one at a time, like a seaman stepping on land for the first time in a year. "I swear, officer," he said with a chuckle, "my license is at home, in my other pants."

Jason smiled too, in spite of himself. But it lasted only a moment. The sound of sirens in the distance and the smell of burning rubber made sure of that. "I've no doubt, kid."

Tobin leaned against the body of the car, pushing a mop of hair out of his eyes. "Is…Was that…Was that what I think…?"

Jason swallowed. "Yeah, I think so." He tried swallowing again, but there was no moisture in his mouth. His lips were sticky from dehydration.

"Hell…" Tobin exhaled and looked like he was about to faint. Then he stiffened and his eyes bugged out. "My apartment!"

He started to run again, but Jason set a firm hand on the kid's shoulder. "No, Tobin, no. It's too far and too dangerous right now. Stay here. We can wait for…"

For what? Who are we gonna wait for that will magically fix everything?

"My partner. He's nearby. The police and EMS will be on their way. If we wait right here, things will get sorted out."

Jason wasn't sure who he was trying to soothe.

But Tobin seemed to calm down. "Okay…" He took a breath and plopped down on the hood of the BMW.

As the kid took a moment to collect himself, Jason dug into his slacks pocket. He pulled out his phone and stabbed the screen with a sweaty finger.

No cell service.

He wanted to bark and throw the useless plastic brick into a ravine, but he repressed the anger. It'd be a bad look for an officer to act like an animal in the aftermath of a catastrophe like this.

With the phone back in his pocket, he had nothing to do except sit on the car's hood next to Tobin. The black paint radiated heat, and it felt like his buns were sizzling, but he was frankly exhausted, and it was a relief to sit down.

Tobin's hands twitched as they rested on his knees, as if searching for something to fiddle with.

Jason cleared his throat. "How'd you hotwire the BMW so fast?" He was almost impressed.

Tobin jolted as if he'd forgotten Jason was there, then looked up at him. "You think I know how to do something like that?"

"Well, yeah. How else would you make a stranger's car go?"

Tobin crossed his arms defensively. "I didn't hotwire it. The car was on. No one was in it, so I helped myself."

Jason paused in surprise. "Wait, hold on. The car's engine was running?"

Tobin nodded. "Door unlocked, AC running, radio on a country music station...I changed the music," he quickly added, as if defending his honor.

"And you didn't think that was weird? A hundred-thousand-dollar BMW idling by the curb?"

"Seventy-five-thousand," the kid corrected him. "And no. I didn't think it was weird. I didn't think *anything*. I was being chased by a cop. I heard the engine running, saw it was empty, jumped in, and went."

Jason sat quietly, absorbing the information. The Royal Heights street where they were had mostly cleared of people — only a few shell-shocked pedestrians wandered around, rustling through debris. At the far end of the street, a large-framed man in a black suit emerged from an alley, looked around at the damage, then dashed away. Likely frightened.

A blanket of black smoke hovered over Los Angeles. Jason couldn't imagine how many fires were tearing through the city. Streets were cracked and congested, keeping the police and fire departments tied up. Anyone trapped under rubble wouldn't be helped for a long, long time. The thought made him sick.

Every minute or so, a weakened wall collapsed somewhere in the neighborhood, sending up a puff of dust and a chorus of screams. The sounds of a city in turmoil were all around them...but they were in the distance, unseen, like the musical score of a horror movie making everything even tenser.

Eventually, Tobin couldn't hold in his pride any longer. A smirk bloomed on his face. "I mean, I *can* hotwire a car. I just didn't hotwire *this* car."

Jason didn't have the verve to smile back.

Tobin quickly followed up: "Hang on, why were you chasing me?"

It seemed like Jason and Garth had watched the surveillance footage in the police precinct days ago rather than mere hours. "There was a storeowner named Dillon. He was stabbed and dumped on the east side. We think you're the last person to see him."

Tobin's eyebrows bunched together. "Dillon's dead?"

Jason didn't have a response ready. Tobin clearly didn't know anything about the storeowner's murder. Yet, as crass as it sounded, Dillon's death was small news. Inconsequential. Easily forgotten, in light of the city-wide disaster.

"Yeah," was all he could think of to say. "Yeah, Dillon's gone."

Tobin didn't respond. He just stared forward, his shoulders slumping a bit as if he'd put on an invisible backpack.

This is all so much for a thirteen-year-old kid to absorb. His entire world has come crashing down.

Along with everyone else's.

15

The world was nothing but dust and darkness. And tons and tons of invisible weight. The feeling of unseen pressure bearing down, gravity doing everything in its power to crush him.

Ten minutes ago, as soon as the ground had started to shake, Ajax had stopped what he was doing and rushed under the closest cover, which had been a discolored old Puget parked on the side of the street. Debris had fallen all around the bulky car, and now he was trapped underneath. But he was alive and unhurt, which was more than he could say for Los Angeles.

"Hector!" That was Marco's voice. "Hector, are you under there?"

Ajax bristled. He hated being called Hector, but now wasn't the time. "Yes, I'm under the car!"

The chunks of concrete and metal that held him captive began moving. Rays of sun shot under the Puget, and shortly after, Marco's face appeared. He offered a meaty hand and pulled Ajax into the light of day.

Ajax was briefly awestruck by the disaster area he was now in. Roads were cracked in half. Walls of buildings had crumbled like wet cardboard. Oily fire and dirty water spewed all over the place. A handful of bodies littered the scene.

He, Marco, and the four other burly cartel men had been searching Royal Heights for the black car. Now, in the wake of the disaster, he didn't know where the others were…if they had even survived. For a moment, he was frightened. He was only a teenager, after all, and part of him craved adult leadership. Especially in the face of such a widespread, unprecedented disaster.

He snapped himself out of his stupor. He couldn't allow himself to act like a seventeen-year-old idiot. Not in front of Marco. Not in front of anyone.

Any and all feelings of doubt, fear, or weakness, he quashed. Destroyed. Banished to the far corners of his mind. He set his jaw and continued to survey the damage with a glare that he hoped made him look callous.

"Are you okay?" Marco looked at him with steely kindness, almost how a big brother would address a sibling.

Ajax hated it. He was no one's little sibling. He was in charge here.

He ignored the question and supplied one of his own. "Did Rodriguez make it to safety?"

Marco shrugged. "I don't know. Cell service is down. I'm sure he got somewhere secure." He looked Ajax over again. "Hector, are you sure you're not hurt?"

"If you say 'Hector' one more time, I'll pistol-whip you again." Ajax grabbed the butt of the gun tucked in his waistband to drive the point home.

Marco snarled. The tendons in his neck stood out as he restrained himself from striking—instead, he growled through his teeth, "Whatever you say, *Ajax*." He adjusted his suit jacket, which had turned from black to grimy gray. He noticed and slapped a layer of dust off his shoulders.

Heavy footsteps approached them from behind. Running. "Sir!" One of the cartel men appeared from an alley, sweaty, frantic. He began speaking to Marco. "The car—"

Ajax hijacked the conversation. "What is it?"

The cartel man's words screeched to a stop. He gave Marco a curious glance, as if asking for confirmation that Ajax was the person he should be talking to. Marco replied with a sharp eyebrow and a scoff.

"Sir," the man said to Ajax, "I found the car. The black BMW."

Ajax's heart clenched in excitement. "Where?"

"A few blocks over. A man and a boy are sitting on its hood."

"On the hood…?" Ajax hissed. Whoever these strangers were, they were mere feet away from the handcuffed Yakuza gangster in the trunk. *If* the gangster was even still in the trunk. "Why didn't you shoot them?"

"I..." The cartel man stammered. "I thought I should tell..." His eyes quickly shifted from Ajax to Marco then back to Ajax. "...you."

"What's your name?"

He cleared his throat. Despite him being at least two decades older than Ajax, his voice shook. "M-Manny."

"Well, Manny," Ajax snipped, "next time you have a clear shot at your targets, *take it.*" He followed Marco's lead and brushed dirt off the shoulders of his Hawaiian shirt. He snapped, "Find and gather the other three men. Manny here is gonna take us to our rats."

As the adults scrambled around, looking for the other men in Rodriguez's employ, Ajax took several calming breaths. He set his hand on the butt of his gun again, and he briefly wondered what it would feel like to shoot someone.

No, not just shoot someone. Kill someone. Better to aim for the head or chest. A bullet in the leg or gut would make a lot of noise, draw things out. Ajax nodded to himself. For his first kill, it was a good idea to be quick.

16

Sitting on the black car in the middle of the fractured street, Jason wondered what time it was. He never wore a watch—he usually counted on Garth for that—and he didn't want to waste the remaining battery on his phone. He craned his neck and checked the sun.

About three o'clock. Maybe four?

His stomach noisily complained that it was empty. He hadn't eaten the noodles he'd gotten for lunch, and dinner didn't seem likely anytime soon.

And *cripes* he was thirsty. He would crawl through a cactus garden for a bottle of water. Part of him wanted to run into one of the damaged buildings and stick his face under a running faucet. But logic told him that was idiotic—just down the street, a burst pipe was shooting water the color of Martian sand all over the sidewalk. It'd be a long, long time before L.A. tap water was safe again.

Tobin sat still next to him. He hadn't spoken since Jason had blurted out that the storeowner Dillon had been killed. That hadn't been Jason's finest moment. Of course, the kid was taking it hard. He likely hadn't encountered death yet.

How would Ted have taken it if you'd suddenly told him that someone he knew had been stabbed and dumped?

He clenched his fists. Thoughts of Ted were the last thing he needed.

Pinpricks of pain shot up his arms. He'd pierced the skin of his palms again. *Crap.* He wiped the blood away on his pant legs.

"Ew." Tobin had seen him do that.

Jason shrugged. "Judge me. These pants are goners anyway."

Tobin eyed the slacks. Torn, grimy, stained. "I guess you're right."

Jason held up a hand to shield his eyes. There wasn't a cloud in the sky. The sun cooked his bones, boiled his marrow. He wanted the day to go faster so the sun would set, but he knew the heat wouldn't leave, even at night.

Tobin kept shoving his thick hair out of his face. It was like a mane, hot and sopping with sweat.

Jason pulled his necktie over his head, undid the loose knot, and handed it to the kid. "For your hair."

Tobin looked at the tie, confused.

"Tie it back. I mean, if you want. Like a headband."

Slowly, Tobin took the necktie and wrapped it around his forehead. He secured the knot, and when his hair didn't immediately flop back into his eyes, he smiled in relief.

All was still. Calm. Quiet. Not a cloud, not a breeze.

Jason didn't trust such calm. It was always a prelude to tragedy.

Always.

Far down the street, a man appeared. He was large, and he wore a dark suit.

Is that the same guy who was wandering down there before...?

Another man joined him. They could be twins—tall and muscular, with heads shaped like trapezoids. They walked briskly toward Jason and Tobin.

A chilly inkling tapped Jason on the shoulder. Their gait was urgent, very purposeful. Something was wrong. He hopped off the car's hood and waved at the incoming men. "Hello, you two. Can I help—?"

Almost simultaneously, the two men reached their right hands into their suit jackets.

Jason sneered and spun around. He yelled to Tobin, "Get down!" He leapt over the BMW's hood, tackling Tobin to the ground, just as gunshots ripped through the air.

Tobin squirmed under Jason's body. "What's happening? Are those—?"

"Did you leave the keys in the ignition?" Jason dragged himself and Tobin behind one of the BMW's tires. That was the best cover they were going to get for the moment. He glanced around the car and saw the two men were still there, running toward them, guns outstretched.

"Yeah yeah yeah," Tobin frantically answered.

"Get in the back and stay down!" Jason ripped open the back door and then sprinted to the driver's seat. He slid in and heard the back door slam shut—Tobin was in. He strangled the key, brought the engine roaring to life, and smashed the gas pedal.

He zoomed straight at the incoming shooters. Their eyes widened and they jumped out of the street, narrowly avoiding becoming roadkill.

Jason didn't slow down. He kept the BMW flying down the road, but the cracked concrete prevented their getaway from being as speedy as he wanted. The car staggered and bounced along, the wheels trying and failing to navigate the uneven terrain.

BANG SMASH BANG SMASH.

Bullets shattered the rear windshield. The gunmen weren't giving up.

Tobin screamed. He was curled up in the floor space behind the driver's seat, hands over his ears. "I don't have any money!"

Jason ducked his head to make himself a harder target. His knuckles were white on the steering wheel as he scanned for an exit route. Collapsed walls, cracked streets, and abandoned cars limited his options. Even a few alleys were blocked off by debris.

Ding…Ding…Ding…

The BMW scolded him for not having his seatbelt on. He growled and drew his Glock from his belt, reached his hand out the window, fired once into the air. The attacking gunfire hesitated for a moment.

Yeah, that's right, fellas. I'm armed too. You messed with the wrong guy.

He glanced in the rearview mirror—he was leaving the two gunmen behind in a hurry. They were the size of action figures. He needed to get away before they wised up and shot out his tires.

"Who are they?" Tobin peeked out from his hidey-hole. "Terrorists? Robbers?"

"Assholes," Jason answered.

Just then, a flash of motion caught Jason's eye. By the time his brain reacted, it was too late.

Three more men in suits ran into the middle of the street, right in front of the speeding BMW. They too held handguns that were aimed at Jason's head. The man in the middle of the trio—the biggest and tallest, with muscles straining against his clothing—snarled and yelled, "*Hazlo!*"

Jason didn't wait to find out what was happening. He threw the wheel to one side, his instinct and peripheral vision telling him an open alley was there. The BMW squealed into the narrow opening, dodging the three shooters.

But another man was there, waiting for them. This one was smaller, slighter, wearing a gaudy Magnum PI shirt. Jason was taken aback for a second—this newest guy had soft features, almost no wrinkles, patchy facial hair, like a teenager. *Just* like a teenager.

The guy in the floral shirt—*Magnum*—stood twenty feet into the alley, his own gun raised. He smirked like he was about to pull the legs off a grasshopper.

Jason's foot came off the pedal. Could he really barrel through this kid? Flatten him against the concrete?

Magnum opened fire, punching jagged holes into the windshield.

Jason pushed the pedal all the way to the floor, and the BMW bolted forward. He returned fire, shattering what was left of the windshield.

Like a fearless matador, Magnum didn't move, didn't even flinch away from Jason's bullets. Driving and shooting at the same time hindered Jason's aim, and it looked like Magnum knew it.

The speeding car was only seconds away from splattering Magnum's innards all over the alley. At the last possible moment, he pushed himself against the wall, and the BMW flew past him.

Jason let out a quick sigh of relief. He navigated the car through the maze of alleys, back out onto the streets of Royal Heights. But he immediately realized he needed to get out of sight. There was no telling how many gunmen were on their tail.

At the far end of the street, there was a mechanic's garage with a collapsed roof. Plenty of cars, lots of crannies in which to hide. He aimed the BMW that way as he forced his heartrate to slow down.

Tobin sputtered in the back seat, never quite forming a full thought: "How the — Where did — Who could that — What's going — Why the hell — "

Jason guided the BMW into the damaged garage, positioned it in a dark corner behind many other cars, and turned it off.

Things were quiet again, except for the engine that ticked as it cooled, and his own rampaging thoughts.

Jason had been inches away from killing that guy in the floral shirt. Ultimately, he was glad none of the gunmen had forced him to take any of their lives.

Not because he didn't want to.

Because he did.

Because he couldn't escape the thought that running and hiding from them was so taxing, and it would be so much easier to just kill them and be done with it.

Tobin opened his door and stumbled out of the car. He wrapped his hands around his head, as if trying to squeeze the memory of this day out of his brain. He wandered deeper into the wrecked garage, muttering to himself. "Oh shoot oh man oh shoot oh man…"

It seemed even hotter inside the garage. The heat was contained, amplified.

Jason ground his teeth together and punched the steering wheel.

I just did it again.

He'd been in a position to kill a bad person. A gunman. Someone hell-bent on doing harm. Jason had been inches away from wiping that person off the face of the Earth. And he'd choked. Chickened out. He hadn't had the balls to follow through.

He'd spared Anthony Reynaldo. He'd spared the guy in the floral shirt. He'd spared Abel. And the world was worse off for it.

And now, this teenager Jason was calling "Magnum" would be after them again. Magnum wanted to kill them for some reason, and he seemed unlikely to quit. And he had a posse of shooters alongside him. He'll be back, guns blazing, and eventually, he'll win.

Given enough time, Jason will get tired or injured, and he and Tobin will die at the hands of these gunmen.

All because Jason hadn't made the hard choice and taken an evil man's life.

I'm a coward. I'm weak.

Jason stared straight ahead through the shattered windshield, panting, sweating, silently moaning.

"Detective?" Tobin stood next to the driver's side window. He spoke as if he'd been trying to get Jason's attention for a while. "You awake in there?"

Jason popped open the door and got out. His legs wobbled, but he leaned against the car body to hide that fact. He cleared his throat. "Tobin..." He leveled his gaze at the kid with a necktie around his forehead. "You have to be honest with me. Forget how we met—"

"You mean how you chased me through my neighborhood?"

"Yes, that. At this point, we're locked in this together, so be straight with me: Why were those men shooting at you?"

Tobin's eyebrows shot up. "*Me?* They were shooting at *you!*"

Jason paused. *Were they?* He rubbed his temples. "I have no idea who they are. Usually I know the people who are trying to put a bullet in me."

"First time for everything, I guess," Tobin shrugged.

Jason reached for a clue, an explanation, something to ground himself in this nightmare of a situation. "They were speaking Spanish to each other."

Tobin responded, "Yeah, they were. Good good good, that narrows it down to...all of Los Angeles, except for the actors and Instagram models. You've cracked the case, Einstein."

Jason glared at him. "Rule number one: Only I'm allowed to be a smart aleck."

Tobin opened his mouth to fire back.

But Jason continued. "Rule number two: People with badges and guns and driver's licenses make the rules. Now keep quiet and let me think."

He replayed the shootout in his mind. By his count, there were five muscular men in suits, plus the teenager in the bright shirt. But there could easily be many more throughout the neighborhood, or even throughout the city.

The gunshots echoed in his mind, and he pulled his Glock from his belt. He ejected the magazine and counted how many bullets remained. "Seven rounds left..." he whispered to himself.

Tobin responded with sarcasm, but more than a little fear bled into his words: "You didn't bring an extra clip thing with you?"

"I came here to talk to you. I didn't know I was walking into a war zone." He reinserted the magazine and holstered his gun.

The more he thought about the current situation, the smaller he felt. His heart trembled in his chest as panic took hold. He grasped for another thread of hope: "My friend should be somewhere nearby. Another detective. Maybe he'll hear the shots and come help."

Tobin looked about as confident as Jason felt. "Probably not. The way the city is right now, I bet no one'll notice a few extra gunfights."

Jason didn't want to admit it, but he agreed. Civil services wouldn't be rushing to their aid anytime soon. They were on their own.

Tobin could see the dread on Jason's face. "We gotta hide. Find a closet or a basement or something and wait all this out."

"No," Jason shook his head. "No, if they find us and we're cornered like that, we're done for. We need to keep moving."

"So you get to decide everything?" Tobin took a step back from Jason, letting the words hang in the air between them.

Then, a sound came from outside the garage. Tires rolling over the broken pavement, a rumbling engine. Someone was driving by.

Both Jason and Tobin froze. They barely breathed, in case the movement of their lungs alerted the passerby to their presence. Jason's pulse tapped a staccato rhythm in his ears.

The sounds of the car moved past them without slowing down. They had remained undetected.

"Yes," Jason firmly said, continuing the conversation, "I do."

It took Tobin a second to get back on track. "I don't even get a say?"

"I'm a detective, I'm an adult—"

"And? I live in this neighborhood. My apartment is a few blocks away. We could go there and hide. We'd be safe."

"You don't know that."

"And *you* don't know anything either! You're just as clueless here as me, so why are you in charge?"

Jason's temper began to simmer behind his eyes. He crossed his arms to conceal his clenched fists. "Who got us out of that gunfight? Was that you driving, or me?"

"Oh, excuse me, Mr. Mario Kart, I didn't mean to step on your ego. I'm just a little pissy because *the city was destroyed and people with guns are trying to kill us and I don't know what to do.*"

Jason wanted to respond, but he hesitated. Tobin was just a kid in a horrible situation. Yelling and arguing would help no one.

And then, a noise. *Thunk.*

Tobin's eyes, which had been locked on Jason's in anger, bugged out. He'd heard it too. It had come from inside the garage.

Thunk thunk.

Jason drew his Glock and put a finger to his lips.

Like a bat using echolocation, he strained his ears to find where the noise was coming from. It was tinny and hollow, irregular but increasingly frantic. With every passing second, the rapidity of the noise picked up its pace.

Thunkthunkthunk.

Jason gulped.

It was coming from the BMW.

The trunk.

The gunmen had shot out the back windshield, and a few bullet holes pierced the trunk. Someone...or something was inside, trying to get out.

Tobin tiptoed to the driver's side and retrieved the car keys. He held the fob up for Jason to see, and he set his thumb on the button that would pop open the trunk.

Jason nodded silently and leveled his gun at the trunk. He took a slow breath, telling himself to shoot only if he absolutely had to. He only had seven bullets left. Also, they were still in hiding—if he fired his gun, their nearby attackers would probably be able to find them.

He mouthed to Tobin: "*Three, two...one.*"

With a beep, the trunk opened like a yawning lion.

Two shoe-soles kicked out and caught Jason in the chest.

All the air burst out of Jason's lungs. He staggered back, too stunned to react immediately. Too stunned to breathe.

A figure rolled out of the trunk. An Asian man of medium height. He wore jeans, a dress shirt, and penny loafers. The shirt and his cropped hair were plastered to his body by a sheen of sweat. His mouth curled into a vengeful scowl.

The man staggered to his feet and rocked back and forth, like a fighter ready to go a few rounds. But his hands were bound behind his back. He also had a circle of loose cloth around his neck — a blindfold that had slipped off?

Jason put a hand on his chest to try to manually get his lungs pumping. He and the man sized one another up. *What in the world is going on?*

The man launched another forceful kick, and the next thing Jason knew, his gun clattered across the floor and under a car. He charged at Jason.

Tobin, crouching in a corner of the garage, grabbed something from a pile of clutter. It was a creeper trolley — a low frame with wheels that mechanics can lay on and use to roll under cars. He heaved it across the floor, right into the man's path.

The man's feet slipped on the wheeled frame, and he tumbled to the ground. And since his hands were bound, he fell hard. His shoulder landed on the concrete floor, and he let out a pained yelp.

All was quiet, except for the three sets of labored breaths. Tobin shuffled over to stand by Jason, who nodded his thanks for the assist, and they faced the mysterious stranger.

Jason held out a hand as if trying to calm a rampaging animal. He spoke in a steady voice: "My name is Jason Flynn. I'm a detective with the Los Angeles Police Department. Who are you, sir, and what were you doing in this trunk?"

The man spat some hateful words at him in Japanese. He twisted to his feet and moved to attack again.

But Jason was ready this time. He grabbed the man's collar and shoved him against the wall. He spoke again, not nearly as gently this time. "Who are you?!"

The man didn't respond — just stared at him with quivering hatred.

"Where did you come from? Why are those men trying to kill you?"

The Japanese man smirked. "*No hablo inglés.*"

Jason leaned in to respond. "*Muy gracioso, cabrón.*"

A beat of silence filled the garage. The man sized Jason up once again, an amused sneer pulling at his lips. But he didn't speak more.

Jason saw that the man's wrists were not merely tied together but were, in fact, handcuffed. Heavy-duty ones too. He let go of the man's shirt and stuck a finger in his face. "Don't move."

Tobin spoke up, "You think he speaks English?"

Jason stared in the man's sharp eyes. "He understands us." He cautiously stepped away from the hostage, ready to grab him if he started to run.

But the man didn't move. He simply flicked his gaze from Jason to Tobin, then back to Jason.

Biding his time. Like a caged tiger.

Jason retrieved his gun from under a car, then peeked out the front of the garage. The street was empty, but he could hear distant screams, screeching tires, crackling fires…The sounds of a city in chaos swirled all around.

Tobin stepped next to him and whispered, "So they were trying to kill *him*, you think?"

Jason kept scanning the outside world, but nodded. "I'd bet the BMW is theirs, and the *cabrón* from the trunk is their hostage. When you stole the car, you stole him too. And now…they're tying up loose ends."

"They're gonna take him hostage again?"

Jason debated whether or not to tell the truth. He decided honesty was the way to go. "They made that mistake once. I get the feeling those gunmen aren't in a taking-prisoners mood."

Tobin swallowed and adjusted the necktie around his head, as if preparing to charge into battle. "So who are they? Who's he?"

Jason shot a glance at the Japanese man. *Cabrón.* "I don't know."

Tobin lingered at Jason's side, waiting for the detective to say more. But Jason had nothing else. No insight or wisdom or solutions to offer. After a minute, Tobin slumped back into the corner of the garage, a healthy distance from both adults.

Cabrón stood where Jason had left him, handcuffed and sweating, but surprisingly calm. Alarmingly so.

Jason wiped his eyes and tried to think. *Where can we go? Who should we seek out for help?*

What really got under Jason's skin was that Tobin had been right. He had no idea what to do. He was just as clueless as the thirteen-year-old kid. He was used to spearheading investigations and being on the path to success.

Here, there was no investigation, no mystery, no clues. Just men with guns hunting them down.

There was only one objective: Run.

17

The ceiling of the mechanic's garage seemed to press down on Tobin, as if the weight of the universe was trying to crush them all.

Oh, wait. No, the earthquake had collapsed part of the roof. That made more sense.

He rubbed his eyes and nestled deeper into a dark corner of the garage. He kept moving until he was sure he was entirely hidden. No one could see him, he hoped.

So much had happened in the past hour. His brain could barely keep up with it all. Detective Flynn had chased him through the neighborhood. He'd stolen a car. The biggest earthquake in history — or so he thought — had torn the city to shreds. Men with guns had tried to kill him and the detective, they'd had a crazy car chase in the wreckage of the neighborhood, and now...

Now, the men with guns were coming after them, all because he had stolen the *one* car in L.A. with a kidnapped guy in the trunk. Of course.

He couldn't believe it all. He was barely able to absorb all the details of this insanity.

His neighbors — the people he'd lived next to for years — shrieking in horror as their lives came crumbling down.

The smells of gasoline and burning plastic and smoke and copper and dirt all mixing together.

The bodies, lying in the street, not moving. Some of them face-up, mouths open, bleeding from their heads.

Tobin had never seen a dead body before...Well, he'd seen his great-aunt Saira in a coffin at her funeral a couple years ago, but that didn't count. She'd been wearing a muumuu, and elevator music was playing in the background, and afterward, everyone ate potato salad and went home.

This was different. These bodies were in everyday clothes — bathrobes, t-shirts, sneakers, whatever they happened to be wearing when disaster struck.

And they were hurt, very clearly. Aunt Saira had died of something in her lungs, and she was really old. These people's lives were stolen from them, violently and suddenly. Their heads were cracked, legs mangled like Play-Doh, blood all over the place.

And they were scared. So, so scared. Terrified of what was happening, of the fact that they were having to face death much sooner than they'd expected. Their screams were frozen on their lips —

He put his head in his hands, trying to forget the images. But that was pointless. He'll remember this day for the rest of his life.

He slowly raised his head to face this new reality, one in which he'd seen such horrible things.

Detective Flynn was still looking out at the street, scanning for attackers, or making a game plan, or thinking deep thoughts in general.

The Japanese man — the guy Detective Flynn called *Cabrón* — stood against a wall, hands cuffed behind his back.

Tobin started examining *Cabrón*, really looking at the man. On the surface, he looked angry but calm, really held together. But Tobin knew what it was like to wear a mask, to pretend you weren't scared.

The signs were all there: the fidgeting feet, the constant swallowing, the crinkling at the corners of the eyelids. *Cabrón* was as terrified as they were.

Tobin laughed to himself a little — he didn't know what *cabrón* meant exactly, but he knew it wasn't very nice. His mom would smack him upside the head if he said it.

His gut lurched a little at that thought. His mom...His four brothers...

Were they alive? Are they somewhere safe? Did they even realize he wasn't around?

Those questions poked and prodded him, but another one rose to the top:

Did his stack of books make it through the quake?

Their apartment was on the third floor of a building that was barely up to code on a good day. It'd be a miracle if his second-hand books filled with counterfeit autographs were ever seen again.

All the money he'd made selling books online was tucked away in a digital account, which was a relief. But the signatures and books he'd accumulated over the past month were still hidden in his apartment's coat closet.

He remembered signing Margaret Mitchell's name in *Gone With the Wind* earlier that afternoon…even though it felt like a lifetime ago. That book alone would probably fetch him five hundred bucks, if he priced it very conservatively, as was his strategy.

One way or another, he needed those books.

He decided to try to convince Detective Flynn one more time to go to his apartment building to hide. Tobin knew that place inside and out—there were tons of nooks to curl up in and wait for the worst to pass.

And if he could grab his books while they were there, he wouldn't complain.

18

The crummy apartment building clearly hadn't been built to withstand such a quake. Wires dangled from the ceiling, and the walls were tilted in one direction, like a photo hanging crookedly on a hook.

Ajax walked down the hallway, gun in hand at his side. He strained to see—most of the electric lights had shattered, and those that were still intact weren't working. A few beams of sunlight shot through the cracked walls, but they waned minute by minute. Evening quickly approached, and dusk would take over in about an hour's time.

Then, it'd be even more difficult to find the man and the child who'd taken the Yakuza hostage from them.

L.A. in the dark, in the aftermath of an earthquake...The worst game of "hide and seek" imaginable.

Ajax felt the heft of his gun and smiled to himself. No, more like "tag."

Again, his mind drifted to thoughts of Gore Rodriguez. Had the boss made it somewhere safe before the quake hit? Where even was "safe" anymore? Perhaps in the air. Rodriguez seemed like the kind of strategist to have a helicopter loitering nearby, just in case.

A creaking noise came from somewhere deeper in the building. Ajax held his gun out and moved toward it.

Undoubtedly, cell towers and phone service were down, and would be for the foreseeable future. When Ajax caught and executed the fugitives, how would he let Rodriguez know? The boss needed to be told as soon as possible. Maybe Marco had a satellite phone or emergency radio Ajax could use to contact Rodriguez.

That is, if the boss was alive at all.

Ajax banished the thought and was determined to never let it back into his mind.

After all, he was hunting these fugitives to impress the boss. If there was no boss to impress, why would he risk his life hunting three people in the middle of a disaster-struck Los Angeles?

No matter how lightly he walked, his footsteps squeaked against the vinyl flooring. A mouse heard him coming and scurried for cover. The biggest mouse he'd ever seen — practically a possum.

When catastrophe hits, ugly creatures come out to play.

He had an impulse to follow the mouse and squish it under his heel, simply for having the gall to be so disgusting. But he kept moving forward, toward the creak he'd heard. Hopefully, it was the three fugitives, and he could shoot them and go home. He really didn't want to search every crumbling building in Royal Heights...but he absolutely would if he had to.

What will it feel like?

He tried to ignore the itchy question and focus on the hallway ahead, but it wouldn't leave him alone.

What'll it feel like to kill something?

The rush of knowing that a life is over...because of him, and no one else.

He'd had his fair share of highs in his seventeen years, but none of them suited him. The meth and heroin the cartel dealt in weren't his taste. Getting blind drunk was idiotic to him, and inhaling smoke was a one-way ticket to a funeral.

But stealing someone's life...That was something he'd been aching to try for a while.

Movement. A primal yell.

Ajax had been so wrapped up in his thoughts, he wasn't paying attention to his surroundings. Rookie mistake. A deadly one.

A person lurked around a corner. As Ajax stepped into view, the person hopped out and yelled.

"*AHHHHHH!*"

It was a piggish man in a dirty tank top. Fat arms. Bad teeth. He held a baseball bat high above his head, then brought it down hard on Ajax's arm.

His gun fell to the plastic floor as pain ricocheted through his body. He wanted to react, but his reflexes were too slow. All he could do was watch as the tub of lard swung the bat at him again. The thick wood connected with Ajax's shoulder, and he collapsed.

The man loomed over Ajax and brandished the bat like he was a knight. "Who are you? What're you doing here?" He spoke louder than he needed to in the tight indoor space, his eyes bugged out, tendons taut, sweat beading on his forehead.

Ajax could only gape up at his attacker. He knew he should be reacting and fighting back, scrambling for his gun or going at it with his bare fists, but...he was frozen on the ground. The ambush had shocked him into a living coma. His breath was short. He couldn't move. Could barely think.

In the warehouse, he had been so confident. He'd taken charge and made a snap decision. But now, in the dusty hallway, face to face with violence, he was impotent.

He hated that more than the fact that he might be beaten with a wooden bat.

"I won't ask again!" The fat man leaned in closer, getting more and more frantic. "Why are you here?"

Ajax briefly wondered why this man was panicking so much. But then he saw, huddled against the far wall, a woman and two children. Similarly obese, also in dirty clothes. The man's family.

And Ajax saw something else—a large figure in a dark suit, moving silently behind the man with the bat.

Marco appeared and kicked the back of the fat man's knee. The man let out half of a yelp. Only half, because Marco slammed a fist into the fleshy neck, cutting off the sound. The man gagged as he tumbled to the floor, clutching his throat, and the family screamed.

Marco held out a hand, which Ajax ignored and quickly stood up. He retrieved his gun and began to march down the hallway.

But with the weight of the weapon returned to his hand, and the fat man helpless on the ground, he paused.

This could be a perfect practice round. A low-stakes turkey shoot. He'd just been thinking about his first kill, and then an easy target had presented itself, prostrate before him. Couldn't be a coincidence.

A phrase from one of his motivational tapes whispered to him: "*Seize your opportunities.*" Maybe they actually did make some valid points.

His gun hand twitched, wanting to aim itself at the fat man. Should he go for the head, or center-mass? Which would be less messy? Or...which would be *more* messy? Part of him wanted there to be bloody evidence of his boldness. By the brutality of the act, everyone would know Ajax was here—

"What are you doing?" Marco's harsh whisper sliced through his thoughts.

Ajax tucked his gun away and continued walking. "Shut up," he said in a normal volume, which boomed in the crumbling hallway. "We're wasting time in here," he said over his shoulder to Marco. "We need to anticipate where they'll be headed, not dig through apartments until we happen to find them."

He felt Marco's hateful glare, and he worked hard to ignore it. He kept his eyes fixed ahead, trying desperately to break in his confident attitude like a new pair of shoes.

The echoing sobs of the family followed him as he walked. Those were easy for him to ignore.

PART 3:
BREATHLESS

19

Jason scanned the empty street one more time, then said, "We should get moving." He turned to face Tobin, but he didn't see the kid in the shadowy garage. Just *Cabrón*, standing silently against the wall.

A chill ran down Jason's skeleton when he realized he'd had his back to the handcuffed man for several minutes. He'd assumed Tobin had been keeping watch, but the kid was out of sight somewhere. *Cabrón* could have charged him, tackled him, slipped away…anything. But strangely, the Japanese man hadn't moved from his spot. That made Jason more nervous than anything.

A rustling sound came from a dark corner, and Tobin emerged. "Where are we going?"

"Well…" Jason rolled his neck, but his joints refused to pop. "Somewhere public. Lots of eyes, lots of witnesses. Those men won't try to kill us with lots of people around. They wouldn't risk the attention."

"You know that for sure?"

Jason thought back to the first attack. The gunmen had waited until the street was clear. No one was ballsy enough to kill someone in front of dozens of witnesses. That'd be ludicrous. Even nutcases like Roger Shore, Anthony Reynaldo, and Abel had done their dirty work in secret.

He bobbed his head, getting more confident with each nod. "Yeah. Yes. We'll be safe."

Tobin took a slow breath and said, "And you're sure—"

Jason didn't have time for this. "Yes, Tobin, I'm sure. Stick with me and you'll be okay."

The kid swallowed the rest of his words like they were sticky medicine.

"Now…" Jason turned his attention back to the handcuffed man. He spoke clearly and with force: "We're leaving now, and you're coming with us. If you run, yell, or do anything I don't like," he grabbed the butt of his Glock, "you won't like it either."

Cabrón just stared back at Jason, shifting faintly from foot to foot. His mouth was a straight line, completely neutral, but his eyes glittered as if he were telling a joke.

Oh, he knows what I'm saying. He might not be fluent in English and know every single word, but he knows what's going on.

Tobin's eyes, on the other hand, were wide and shaky, staring at Jason's hand resting on the gun handle. Jason quickly took his hand away—scaring the kid wouldn't help their situation.

He gulped as he remembered he only had seven rounds left in the Glock. Hopefully, they would be able to make it through the rest of the day without hearing another gunshot, and Tobin would reunite with his family, and they would get to the bottom of who *Cabrón* was, and the gunmen would turn themselves over to the police, and the people of Los Angeles would pull together to rebuild overnight, and everything would be okay.

Jason shook his head. *Yeah right.* The past year had made him more cynical than ever. And he'd been pretty cynical before.

"C'mon." He grabbed *Cabrón*'s forearm and dragged him out of the garage, into the beating sunlight. The man squinted against the day, having been in a car trunk for at least the past hour. His legs were weak too, from being cooped up in that small space. Jason almost felt a shred of sympathy for the man.

He focused and summoned his mental map of Royal Heights. Where was the place with the highest likelihood of a crowd?

"This way." He set off in the direction of the old electronics store he'd passed earlier in the afternoon. He kept a firm grip on *Cabrón*'s arm, and Tobin scampered behind them. He kept their small group close to the buildings, behind as much cover as they could get while still moving.

If Jason knew one thing for certain, he knew that looters would be on the prowl in the wake of disaster. The mom-and-pop electronics store would be the perfect target. Normally, Jason would either keep his distance from looters or try to subdue them, but today, he needed witnesses, and they would have to do.

The neighborhood was quiet, except for crackling fires and their own footsteps on the concrete. No one was around, which made Jason uneasy.

Cabrón wriggled in Jason's grip. He tried to reach his shoulder up to wipe the sweat from his eyes. Jason hesitated for a second, then wiped the handcuffed man's face with his own white shirt sleeve.

The sun descended inch by inch, but the air was still hot as a stovetop. Jason panted and felt the stitch in his side returning.

I'd do anything for a gallon of water right now. A glass. Hell, a drop.

Loud noises snapped him out of his thoughts. Voices yelling. Glass shattering. Crowds churning and broiling.

Tobin shot Jason a wary glance, but Jason avoided direct eye contact and looked straight ahead. The kid tightened the necktie around his forehead and followed suit.

A block ahead was the electronics store, and it was more chaotic than Jason ever could've imagined. Hundreds of people were gathered in front of it. Jason had no idea why—maybe they were looking for shelter, maybe everyone was going after some free merchandise, maybe they all ended up in the same place at the same time by sheer coincidence.

The "why" didn't matter. The reality was that half of Royal Heights had congregated on the street in front of the store, and they were scared, angry, and in a frenzy.

Fights had broken out. Punches flew through the air. People shouted in each other's bloody, sweaty faces.

A few fools tried to keep the peace, holding up their hands and yelling words of comfort, but all they did was add to the noise.

Jason stopped and stared. "God..." What had he led them into?

Suddenly, he heard small feet dashing away from him. Tobin took off running into the crowd, the tie trailing behind his head.

"*Tobin!*" Jason bellowed. "Tobin, what are you doing?!"

The kid didn't slow down or veer. He ran right into the throbbing mass of people.

"No!" Jason swore and tried to run after Tobin—but he jerked to a halt. *Cabrón* stood unmoving like a statue, fused to the ground.

Jason yelled at him, "Come on!"

The man looked down at Jason's hand clamped on his forearm. He seemed to be saying, "*You wanna run and catch the kid? Let go of me.*"

Jason sneered, "Not on your life." He kicked the back of *Cabrón*'s knee and dragged the handcuffed man toward the crowd. *Cabrón* fought against Jason's grip, but he couldn't get traction between his penny loafers and the pavement. Jason controlled where they went.

As if diving into a cold pond, Jason took a breath before entering the riotous swarm. He could see the electronics store through the mass of bodies, but just barely—the windows were reduced to shards on the ground, and the merchandise was long-gone.

So why are all these people still here?

One look around answered his question.

The brawling, the shouting, the punching and kicking...People were drawn to this riot because they didn't know what else to do. They had oceans of pent-up anxiety and fear, and this was the place to release it.

Bodies pressed against him on all sides, but he didn't dare loosen his grip on *Cabrón*. One slip, and the handcuffed man would surely bolt.

A teenager in a beanie jumped in front of Jason and roared, "Suck on this!" He pulled back an arm, revealing a heavy brick in his hand, preparing to hurl it at Jason's face.

Jason focused, blocking out the chaos of the riot. Despite his thirst and exhaustion, he could foresee the fight directly ahead. And fortunately for Jason, this teenager was an inexperienced moron. He could take the punk out in two moves.

Dodge.

Strike.

Done.

Jason could have tackled the teenager before he threw the brick, but he waited so the idiot would be off-balance.

A second later, the teen hurtled his arm like a catapult, and the brick was airborne.

Jason kept his eyes locked on the red brick and, at the right moment, ducked his head under the projectile. It sailed into the crowd, hitting some other unsuspecting rioter.

As Jason stood upright, he threw his fist into the teen's Adam's apple, then yanked the beanie down over his eyes. Jason didn't even look to see if the teen was beaten—the sounds of strained gasps told him he was down for the count.

Jason dragged *Cabrón* forward as he swept the area for Tobin's shaggy head. He called out, "Tobin!" But his voice barely registered among the storm of shouts.

Then, *Cabrón's* efforts to wriggle free intensified. He thrashed against Jason's grip like a desperate fish on a hook.

"Calm down," Jason hissed. "I'm not letting—"

Cabrón sputtered a word in heavily accented English: "No!" His face was pale, as if Death himself had just knocked on his door. The knowing glint was gone from his eye, replaced with pure terror. He looked at something over Jason's shoulder. "Cartel!"

The fear in *Cabrón's* voice made Jason spin around to see what he was looking at.

A man in a dark suit. One of the men who had shot at them before. He was making his way through the crowd, in Jason's direction. He reached into his jacket, murder in his gaze.

Cartel...

Crap.

Jason looked back at the handcuffed man he called "*Cabrón.*" In the midst of hundreds of rabid people thrashing and screaming, they silently stared at each other.

Then they both turned to face the cartel gunman.

With uneasiness resting in his gut, Jason peeled his fingers off *Cabrón's* forearm. They would both need mobility to get through this in one piece.

The cartel man's hand fumbled around inside his jacket. Maybe his fingers were too sweaty to grip his gun on the first try. Didn't matter— they had a few seconds' head-start, and that could make all the difference.

We can't let a gunshot go off in the middle of this crowd. Jason quickly took in the angry mob. *This place is a bonfire already, and if you throw bullets in the middle, everyone will get hit with the shrapnel. People'll stampede and tear each other to shreds.*

No matter what, he couldn't let the cartel men let off a shot.

He shrugged to *Cabrón.* "Sorry." He grabbed *Cabrón's* collar and hurled him at the cartel man. *Cabrón* shrieked as he stumbled forward, and the cartel man gasped in disbelief. They collided into each other, with Jason one step behind.

He grabbed the stunned cartel man's ears and brought his chin down onto his knee...hard. The gunman crumpled to the ground. Lights out.

Cabrón steadied himself upright, panting and completely disoriented. He looked like he'd just stepped off a roller coaster he didn't want to go on in the first place.

Jason slapped some grime off *Cabrón's* jeans. "Has anyone ever said you have a bright future ahead as a bowling ball?"

Cabrón scoffed and rolled his shoulders, preparing to reenter the fray.

"Oh yeah," Jason muttered to no one in particular. "*No hablo inglés.* Right."

Cabrón cackled and responded in rapid Japanese.

"You said it." Jason continued the search for Tobin Vivek's mane of hair amid the turbulent crowd. "Tobin! Tobin, come on!" No answer. Just more pandemonium and violence from the masses.

And then, like a flash, *Cabrón* ran off too. In a matter of seconds, he vanished in the sea of people.

Jason grimaced and balled his scuffed hands into fists. "Well, frick." That was the last thing he'd wanted.

Which do I look for: the man or the kid?

He began to wade through the crowd, shoving rioters out of his path. He wasn't in the mood for gentleness or diplomacy.

Or do I just leave? Get somewhere safe without two extra passengers?

The thought made him stop, like weights attached to his ankles.

Could he do that? Was that even an option?

A nearby shout interrupted his internal interrogation. He faced the voice and found...another cartel man in a suit. This one already had his gun drawn, pointed right at Jason's forehead.

Don't shoot, Jason silently implored. *If you shoot, we'll both be flattened like mushy pancakes.*

He locked eyes with the cartel man and slowly raised his hands in surrender. The gunman beckoned for Jason to approach him.

Gladly. Jason wanted to smile to himself, but resisted. *Idiot.*

As soon as he got close to the gun, this would be all over.

Grab his wrist, twist the weapon away.

Elbow in his kidneys.

A kick to the shin.

One last strike to the jaw.

Game, set, match.

Jason took a few clipped shuffles forward, leading the gunman to believe that he was compliant. A bead of sweat stung his eye, but he ardently ignored it.

When he was only a few feet away, the gunman held out a hand, signaling *stop.* But Jason kept shuffling just a bit more. When the gunman opened his mouth to yell, Jason struck.

He pounced at the man, grabbed the wrist of the hand holding the gun, and twisted his entire body. The weapon clattered to the ground, but Jason's feet slipped. His head swam as he fell through the air, taking the gunman down with him. They landed in a painful heap, with Jason on top. The cartel man shoved his knee into Jason's gut, but Jason punched the gunman's jaw, sending his skull backward into the concrete ground. He moaned and stopped moving.

Jason swayed as he stood. He felt lightheaded, unstable, almost as if he'd been drugged. But he knew he hadn't taken anything — and that was the issue. He was exhausted, overheated, and dehydrated. He'd only won that fight by sheer dumb luck.

He strained his eyes to find the abandoned gun on the ground...but it was gone. Kicked away by any number of panicking feet.

Not good. But he didn't have time to hunt down a lost handgun. He continued trudging through the throng of people.

The riot's unbearable volume was like a dagger that speared both of his eardrums. He wanted to run, but he couldn't. Every step was a monumental labor.

And it was still so hot. The sun had almost hidden itself behind the L.A. cityscape, coloring the sky various shades of orange, violet, and dusty black. But the heat of the day still wrapped itself around every inch of his body. He tried to imagine falling into a dunk-tank of ice water, to trick his mind into thinking he was cold, but he couldn't remember what it felt like to shiver.

Another figure blocked his path, and he didn't have the strength to shove this one aside. Plus, he couldn't if he tried—this man was a mountain packed into a suit two sizes too small.

Jason stood as tall as he could and planted his feet. He sized up his new opponent.

This cartel man was huge and muscular, seemingly able to bench-press an SUV. He had sharp eyes and a wedding ring on his left hand. A nasty purple bruise decorated the side of his jaw. He hadn't drawn his gun, and his posture suggested he didn't intend to.

I can't beat this guy. Not physically.

Jason took a breath, which he forced not to shake, and tapped the badge on his waist. "Sir, I'm with the L.A.P.D. You don't want to do this."

The man nodded once. "*Soy Marco. Encantado.*" He didn't step aside.

Jason gulped. Against a beefy guy like Marco, he had no choice. He reached for the Glock in his holster…

…and felt only air.

His gun was gone.

Sickly sweat raced down his back. Someone must have swiped it from his belt as he moved through the crowd. Hundreds of rioters had bumped into him—anyone could have taken it at any time.

That meant three things:

There are multiple guns floating around in the middle of this angry mob.

At least one rioter is armed.

And that person isn't me.

He stumbled back, away from Marco. The big man smirked and leisurely strolled toward him, flexing his fists.

Okay. Game plan. Quick.

Jason had to fight dirty, no doubt about it. That was the only way he'd survive the next sixty seconds.

The bruise on his face. Looks pretty fresh. And tender. Go for that. When he's stunned, kick his shins, knees, and balls. Then run.

He pulled back his arm and launched it at Marco's purple jaw.

But Marco's sharp eyes saw what was happening. With the speed and smoothness of a practiced fighter, he shifted his head ever so slightly. All it took was tilting his neck a few degrees.

Instead of a flexible, breakable jawbone, Jason's balled fist smashed against the side of Marco's skull. The punch made Marco wince and stagger a bit, to be sure…but it almost broke Jason's right hand.

Stars exploded in Jason's vision. He screamed and recoiled, his hand feeling like it'd just been run over by a truck.

Marco snorted and adjusted his suit jacket. He swung a punch into Jason's gut, then followed up with two quick strikes to both sides of Jason's face.

Not a single thought in Jason's head was in the right place after getting hit by the brawny cartel man. His legs gave out, and he fell to his back on the warm pavement.

He stared up at the charcoal sky. The day had quickly morphed into dusk. Time was behaving strangely, crawling in some moments, sprinting in others.

The air had an orange haze about it, filled with dirt and embers and dust and tears. It was like the atmosphere of another planet.

Suddenly, Jason's view was filled with a giant looking down at him. Marco stood above the man he had bested, thinking, pausing, weighing his options. That was unusual—cartel enforcers like him were typically shoot-first thugs.

Then, Marco lifted his elephantine leg high, and brought it down hard. His heel smashed into Jason's battered right hand.

Jason didn't know whether or not he screamed. He blacked out for a few seconds, and when he regained focus, Marco was looking into the crowd. A sneer was plastered on his face.

A voice. There was a voice yelling something: "Marco! *Eres un cabrón!*"

Through his mental fog, Jason recognized the voice and accent. He craned his neck and saw the handcuffed Japanese man yelling amid the crowd. He taunted Marco, antagonizing him.

Marco reached into his jacket and strode away, leaving Jason helpless on the ground, cradling his withered hand.

So Jason lay there, alone among hundreds of rioting strangers, simultaneously numb and in agony. He took long, deep breaths to try to mitigate the throbbing pain in his hand, but every passing second, it got worse.

Then: *BANG.*

A gunshot exploded in the middle of the crowd. Perhaps it was Jason's paranoia, but he thought it sounded like a Glock. His stolen gun. Regardless, it resulted in exactly what Jason had dreaded.

The crowd swirled and stampeded in terror. What was once a storm became an F-5 tornado. People screamed and cursed, trying to get out of the area as quickly as possible.

Jason curled up in a ball on the ground and covered his neck with his good hand. Shoes kicked and trampled him for what could have been hours. His nerves shut down so he wouldn't have to feel more pain. That would come later.

A foot gently prodded his shoulder, but he didn't react. He didn't want to come out of the shell he'd rolled himself into. But then a voice said, "Flynn." It was *Cabrón*.

Jason peeked out. *Cabrón* hovered next to him, forcing the crazed crowd to split around the two men, as if *Cabrón* were a stone in the middle of a river. The Japanese man turned and offered his cuffed hands. Jason reached out, grabbed the fingers, and pulled himself to his feet.

Cabrón must have lost Marco in the chaos, then circled back. He gestured with his head to a side-street. "Tobin," he said.

Jason perked up slightly. "He's that way?"

Cabrón gestured again.

"Thank you…" The words tasted foreign to Jason. He walked in the direction *Cabrón* had indicated, but he only made it a few steps before his spinning head forced him to stop and brace himself. He wanted to lean against the other man, use him as a crutch, but they hadn't developed *that* much trust yet. "Thank you," he repeated and kept walking.

"Akio."

Jason looked at *Cabrón*, confused.

The Japanese man nodded to Jason and said, "Flynn." Then he puffed out his chest. "Akio."

Jason got it. "That's your name?"

The man—Akio—said more in his native language. Jason didn't know what, but he responded, "Nice to meet you too, Akio."

The two men navigated the crowd and slipped down the side-street, avoiding the cartel's attention for the time being. Jason hoped they wouldn't encounter those men again. But he'd never put much stock in hopes, and he wasn't about to start tonight.

20

The roar of the crowd faded as Jason and Akio walked away from the shell of an electronics store, deeper into the neighborhood. Well, Akio walked— granted, with the pace of a man who had just finished a marathon after staying awake the previous night—but he walked upright all the same. Jason stumbled and limped, barely able to stay on his feet.

Jason's battered right hand hung lifelessly at his side. Thanks to gravity, every heartbeat felt like barbed wire being pulled through the veins and tendons, but he was too exhausted to hold his arm up.

His throat, lips, and entire body cried out for water. He was simultaneously dripping with sweat and dying for moisture. Part of him wanted to flop back down onto the pavement and slip into the abyss. In his mind, at least, he could be chugging a soda with two good hands, far away from this hellscape. There would be no guns, no cartel, no riots, no earthquakes…No fear, no uncertainty, no emotions, nothing.

All he had to do was lie down and stop trying. Sweet surrender. Release himself into dark oblivion.

But no. He staggered onward.

He looked around at Royal Heights. The damage from the earthquake was everywhere: burst fire hydrants, cracked sidewalks, capsized cars, downed electrical poles…But the real disaster came in the aftermath: violence, paranoia, confusion. Jason could feel it in the air. Smell it. Taste it.

A rustling sound caught his attention. A few dozen yards away, he saw a person moving haphazardly in the shadows. In the daylight or under streetlamps, he would easily be able to see who it was, but in the evening, aided only by the occasional small fire, he couldn't make it out.

He listened closer. It sounded like shifting rocks, and every now and then, he heard a small grunt. A boy's grunt.

With every shaky step he took, the scene took further shape.

Suddenly, he stopped and gasped.

An entire building had been reduced to rubble. Not a single brick was left on top of another. Throughout Royal Heights, he'd seen fallen walls and cracked foundations, shattered windows and leaning structures. But this was total destruction.

He turned his head away, not wanting to look too closely. Not wanting to see the stray shoes, the bent dinnerware sets, the hundreds of toys scattered in the wreckage.

And, undoubtedly, there would be bodies. Somewhere under all the metal and mortar, there would be bodies.

It would take emergency services days to reach this part of L.A., if not weeks.

The boy grunted, and the rustling sound continued. Jason looked and saw lanky Tobin Vivek in the middle of the debris, on his hands and knees. The kid dug through the dirt, shoving bricks out of the way. Every few seconds, he huffed and grimaced with the effort. Or maybe it was his grief trying to break free.

This is his apartment. Jason sighed. *Was.*

He slowly entered the debris and, with great effort, knelt down beside Tobin. He used his left hand to sift through the bricks. He didn't know what he was looking for, but Tobin sure did, and Jason tried to mirror the kid's urgency.

Jason remembered that, earlier in the mechanic's garage, Tobin had said they should head to his apartment and hide out. *"We'd be safe,"* Tobin had insisted.

Seems it was more than just a suggestion. He really wanted to get back here.

Akio stood back, in the middle of the street, watching them pick through the rubble. Occasionally, the noise of the distant riot flared up, and he turned to make sure the coast was clear.

Minutes passed. Or maybe hours, or seconds. Jason's left hand was scraped raw by the bricks, and his right throbbed in pain. He opened his mouth to say something, but only a dry croak escaped. He tried again: "Tobin…"

Suddenly, the kid stood and wiped his hands on his pants. "They're not here." He spoke with hollow defeat—heartbroken but not surprised.

Jason stood too. "I'm sure your family got out. People helped them, for sure. Or they got somewhere safe, surely…" He tried to mask the doubt in his voice with words of confidence. It didn't work.

Tobin looked up at him, confused for a moment. It was only a moment, but Jason caught it. "Oh yeah," Tobin nodded, "yeah, I hope. I hope…"

His family isn't on his mind at all. Jason swallowed as a bead of cold sweat sliced down his spine. He wasn't sure why Tobin's attitude gave him such pause, but then a question prodded his mind:

Are people worried about me? Wondering where I am? Looking for me? Looking for my body?

He shook his head to banish the thoughts.

Tobin examined the detective's blanched face. "You good?"

"Yeah…" Jason rubbed his forehead. "It's just…It's just my hand." He held up his wounded right hand. Even in the low light, it looked bad.

Tobin recoiled. "Whoa! That thing looks like a squashed bug!"

Jason groaned. "Thanks, doc." He regretted showing Tobin at all and started shuffling out of the debris, back to the street.

"No, seriously." Tobin followed, not dropping the subject. "That looks like what they'd serve at a one-star roadkill restaurant. It looks like a prop in a horror movie. If a buzzard was starving in the desert, and all it could find to eat was your hand, it'd call its mom to say good-bye."

A hurricane of a headache brewed in Jason's skull. "What did I say before about being a smart aleck?"

"You said that people with guns and driver's licenses make the rules. But a driver's license'll do you jack-squat out here, and it looks like you lost your gun."

Jason wanted to retort, but he didn't have the energy...or a good comeback. So as he passed Akio, he gestured forward. "You walk ahead of us," he said to the Japanese man.

Akio must have understood the motion, because he started moving down the road, not fast enough to outpace Jason and Tobin, but slow enough to accommodate their slower gaits.

Seems like he's sticking with us. For now. Jason was glad he didn't have to worry about Akio bolting every few seconds, but he was also cautious. Akio was clearly pretty smart. Or, at least, not an idiot. Jason would keep an eye out and try to expect the unexpected.

But then again, the day had already been filled to the brim with the unexpected. A historic earthquake, cartel gunmen, a random kid swiping a car that happened to have a hostage in the trunk...

Jason didn't know if he could take anymore.

"...and I'd say, 'Throw that thing in the trash, it's past its expiration date.'" Tobin was still insulting Jason's hand.

"Can you please go bother Akio for a minute?"

Tobin's mouth kept running as his brain took in the new information, then he said, "Who's Akio?"

Jason realized Tobin wasn't there for a few key details. He bobbed his head at the man walking ahead of them. "That's our handcuffed friend's name. It seems that he's really pissed off a cartel, and they're gunning for him. Him and the morons who helped him escape...That's us."

Tobin took a breath, swallowing the horrible news whole and pushing it deep down, where it couldn't scare him. Then, "Cartels are drug people, right?"

Jason jostled his shoulders. "In a nutshell."

"Huh..." Tobin kept walking, quietly thinking. In the still streets, far away from the riots and gunfire, he appeared unfazed by their situation.

But Jason knew Tobin had to be terrified. He was a thirteen-year-old kid. He'd started the day normally, probably excited for summer vacation, and now he was running for his life.

A memory flashed in Jason's mind. He quickly punched it into submission, trying not to let it linger and take hold, but it was too late—a mere flicker of a memory was more than enough.

In the early part of his son Ted's life, the boy was abysmal at hiding his emotions. Up until the age of seven or eight, what he was feeling was as plain on his face as a flashing neon sign. When he was happy, he laughed. When he was sad, he teared up. When he was ashamed, his cheeks flushed. Emotional deceit was impossible for young Ted.

But as he grew, he began to take after his father in certain ways. Anger became a prevalent state of being. Instead of simply expressing it, though, he tried to wear a mask. He would clench his jaw, twitch his eyes, and stew in unsaid words.

It pained Jason to know that his son would rather bottle up his anger than share it with his dad—a man extremely familiar with the emotion. Over time, however, Jason got very good at reading Ted's concealed moods.

Jason tried to resurrect these skills and use them on Tobin. It was hard to see the kid's face in the blurry darkness, but it looked like he was chewing on the inside of his lower lip. He also fidgeted with his fingers a lot.

He's terrified, tired, and desperately trying to hide it.

Tobin lowered his voice and tilted toward Jason as they walked. "So, uh…Why don't we get rid of him now?"

"Get rid of him?"

"Yeah…" Tobin sucked on his teeth like he didn't quite want to finish his sentence. But then he did anyway. "Kill him."

Jason flinched. "Where'd you get that idea?"

Tobin gestured at the world around them. "Desperate times, man. And besides, you're a cop. Cops kill people all the time."

"I'm a detective," Jason said. "And I don't kill people all the time."

I know this man's name now, and he saved me from Marco. How can I kill him? He didn't say that, though. Instead, he said it in a way he figured a thirteen-year-old would understand: "We need to be the opposite of bad guys."

"Good girls?" Tobin flashed a toothy, over-the-top grin.

Jason wasn't in the mood for banter. "You've always wanted to be a hero, right?"

Every kid wants to be a superhero in their own story. Save the day, do what's right, all that crap.

Tobin shrugged and nodded.

"Well, the cartel is the villain. If the cartel wants him dead, we need to do the opposite and keep him alive."

Tobin mulled that over. "Fine. As long as you're the sidekick."

Jason didn't respond, much to Tobin's chagrin. The kid had clearly thought his response was worth either a chuckle or a snarky comeback. Or both.

As they walked, Jason continued thinking: *In order to be a hero, do the opposite of what villains do. The cartel is bad, and they want to kill this man. So if we want to be good, we should not kill him. Logical.*

Abel killed people, and Roger Shore killed people.

And I tried to kill Roger Shore. I only didn't because Danielle Zahn stopped me.

I'm not the opposite of a villain. For all intents and purposes, I'm a killer too.

Tobin spoke again: "Where are we going?"

Jason scratched his head, trying to forcibly evict the pestering thoughts. He answered, "There's an old, crumbly church with a stained glass window in this direction. If it's still standing, that's where we're headed."

"Oh yeah, I know that place." Tobin searched his mental files. "It's called Rebirth. Or Restoration. One of those. Nice people. Why are we going there?"

"To hide."

Tobin snickered and shook his head. "Hiding. And whose bright idea was that?"

Jason gave the kid a win. "Yours."

"And *when* did I have that idea? Before or after you got squished in that crowd?"

"Don't press your luck," Jason sighed.

They walked quietly for another minute. Every few seconds, Tobin's eyes twitched toward Jason's wounded hand. Eventually, he unwrapped the necktie from around his forehead. His mangy hair flopped over his eyes as he handed the cloth to Jason. "Here. To wrap up your fingers."

Jason's heart fluttered, but a dark cloud in his chest swallowed his words of gratitude. He nodded awkwardly and took his necktie back.

He took several short, quick breaths, bracing himself. Wrapping the cloth around his fingers was going to hurt like nobody's business.

21

What a day. What a hellish, chaotic, whirlwind of a day.

Akio kept a steady, even pace, a few meters in front of the policeman and the boy. He kept his hands — which were bound behind his back — open and splayed, so that the Flynn man knew he wasn't up to anything suspicious.

Just a nice, helpful, docile hostage. Nothing to see here.

Akio had been planning on ditching the Americans as soon as possible. He knew very little about Los Angeles, and he definitely wasn't an urban survivalist, but navigating the earthquake by himself had seemed like a better prospect than being hitched to a policeman and his shaggy-haired pet. He might as well have traded one kidnapper for another.

But then he saw the riot in the street. The roiling cauldron of human fear and anger, spewing in every direction. And on top of that, Marco and his partners were on the hunt. If it were a lower-level cartel operative, Akio might have chanced it on his own. But the sight of Marco, combined with the scope of the disaster, convinced Akio to stay with the policeman.

Flynn could brawl, for sure. He had dispatched a few other fighters quite handily, all while exhausted and dehydrated. True, he had lost against Marco, but Marco was a behemoth. Even Dwayne Johnson would take one look at Marco and run the other way.

Yes, Akio would stay with Flynn for as long as necessary.

The metal cuffs dug into his wrists. They'd been agony at first, then they were sore, but now, his hands were numb. That was worse than any pain.

Much like the thought of Madoka, his friend, the man with whom he'd been kidnapped.

When Akio woke up in the trunk of a car, alone and handcuffed, he'd assumed the worst: Madoka had undoubtedly been killed. For a moment, he was devastated. Then he had pushed the sadness from his mind, focused on the issues at hand.

Now, after hours of adrenaline and confusion, the thought of Madoka barely stirred his heart. And that was the worst of all.

Akio flexed his ears to listen to what Flynn and the boy Tobin were talking about behind him. "Behind his back," he believed was the American idiom. It didn't make much sense, though—if something was "behind his back," that was make it within his sight, right in front of him. But never mind the colloquialism. He'd resigned long ago to the fact that English was hard to learn and even harder to understand.

To this day, he understood a handful of English words. About a hundred, if he had to estimate, but he'd played dumb when talking with Flynn. Best to let the two Americans think he was totally lost.

The two spoke in a conversational volume, their words skipping down the empty neighborhood street. Fires crackled in small patches here and there, and Akio could still pick up sounds of yelling rioters. Other than that, it was quiet.

"*Gun*," he heard.

Then "*hand*."

His own name, "*Akio*," came up in conversation.

"*Kill*."

Akio's blood turned to ice, but he tried to keep his posture the same. He couldn't let them know he'd understood any of their conversation.

But then, after "*Kill*," Flynn kept talking in an even, disarming tone, as if explaining something very complicated to a child. Which, Akio supposed, he was likely doing. The boy Tobin was quite young— between ten and twelve, if he had to guess.

Besides, Flynn didn't have a gun. Akio could kick and run, if he had to.

A minute later, the conversation between Flynn and Tobin drifted to an end, and they didn't attack Akio. It seemed they wouldn't try to slit his throat just yet.

Then, Akio heard a sharp wince and a yelp, similar to the sound his pet dog had made when its tail got caught under his car's tire. Akio instinctively spun around and saw Detective Flynn huddled over his wounded right hand. The necktie that had been around the boy's head now bandaged the policeman's fingers together. Tears stained Flynn's cheeks.

Akio sympathized with the man. He wouldn't go so far as to call the policeman a friend — not by a mile — but they were certainly allies in this situation.

He faced forward and continued walking down the street. The pair of footsteps followed.

In spite of everything, Akio smiled. He hadn't thought of his dog in years...Toshi. His best friend in childhood. Such a good boy.

Back then, everything had seemed simple. Cause and effect were a straight line — when he got good grades, he got a dog, and so on.

His parents were fairly typical: nice enough, drank a bit too much. They never beat or chastised him when he did something they disapproved of...but they only did good things for him when they were pleased. Treats like candy, vacations, and his dog Toshi were withheld from him if his chores were sloppy or his grades fell. If he was caught lying or he disobeyed them, meals and baths were on the chopping block.

Cause and effect. Do well, get good things. Simple.

Then, when he was fifteen, his parents died in a car accident. In one fell swoop, he was alone, and the philosophy of his entire life had been upended. He hadn't done anything wrong, so why had his family been taken away? He didn't understand, and if he was really honest with himself, the question still haunted him well into adulthood.

Orphaned and disenchanted, young Akio buried himself in his studies. Schoolwork had always reaped reward in the past, right? In the following years, he became a human calculator, looking to expand his mathematical knowledge more and more. Eventually, his skill with numbers peaked...and instead of being a fifteen-year-old orphan, he was a twenty-year-old one. His intellectual success hadn't changed the fact that he had nothing in the world.

So he turned to drink. Then drugs. Then gambling. All in fairly quick succession. Those were fun years, but he realized something was missing. Every high and buzz he attained was too easy — they were "effects" without "causes." He needed to earn the fun things in his life, just as he'd earned his candy and baths and Toshi.

His genius-level skill with numbers led him to become an accountant for a high-rise company. Then he worked for a few clients off the books. Then, one thing led to another, and the Yakuza got a hold of his number.

He handled the finances of one of the mid-tier sects — very basic and frankly menial tasks. But it gave him the "cause" his life needed. Anytime he bought an expensive bottle or sat at a poker table, he knew he'd earned the money he spent.

Never before had Akio imagined he would work in organized crime. He was just an orphan with an affinity for numbers. He wasn't a gangster or a gunman.

For a while, he actually believed he could go through life divorced from his employers. He thought he could cash his paycheck without having to deal with the reality of the waters he swam in.

Then, his bosses sent him and his friend Madoka to Los Angeles to scope out the territory. Madoka was a fellow accountant, genial and always quick with a joke. As they stepped off the plane, Madoka had whispered, "Think we'll get discovered?"

Akio's blood ran cold. Had the local cartels already caught their scent? "Discovered?"

"Yeah, by a movie producer?" Madoka laughed. "Hollywood! Woohoo!"

Within an hour, the two were beaten, blindfolded, and stuffed into the trunk of a sedan. The cartel hulk named Marco had smiled as he slammed the lid shut.

As Akio lay there in the stiflingly hot darkness, legs cramping, head pounding, heart throbbing, he thought about how every decision in his life had led to that moment.

Cause.

And effect.

He wondered if anyone was looking for him and Madoka. They were low on the ladder of the Yakuza operation, but he liked to think that he was at least a little important. He definitely knew things about the organization. Account numbers, schedules, addresses — all sorts of things that made him valuable.

Maybe his bosses and handlers were on their way at that very moment. Akio allowed himself a moment of fantasy:

A helicopter swoops down, carrying a battalion of armed gangsters. They smile at him and cut off his handcuffs. The Yakuza lieutenant gives Flynn a stern glare, but doesn't harm him.

Then, Akio sees that Marco is on the helicopter. The cartel hulk is beaten and bound, en route to Tokyo for a bit of Yakuza justice. Akio and his colleagues get on the chopper and fly out of this ravaged sewer of a city.

But in reality, Akio was by himself. Handcuffed, fatigued, and in an unknown neighborhood.

Yes. He nodded to himself as he walked with a slow, steady pace down the deserted neighborhood street. Yes, he'd stick with the policeman Flynn. He stood a far better chance of surviving the night with him as an ally.

And he couldn't let anyone know that he was a mere accountant. He could yell and pose and pretend all he wanted, but the truth of the matter was that he'd never held a gun or been in a fight in his life.

But perception was reality. As long as people *thought* he was a dangerous Yakuza gangster, he *was* a dangerous Yakuza gangster.

He straightened up and puffed out his chest a little.

Dangerous.

22

Except for their footsteps against the pavement, it was quiet. Then Tobin said, "Man, I'm thirsty."

Jason wanted to pant like a dog and agree, but he had to appear strong and stoic, large and in charge.

He was thirsty too. Dehydration had dug its claws into him hours ago, and he knew he was in trouble. Even walking at a steady pace was difficult, as if he were marching while wearing full uniform. His head was full of wool, and his mouth couldn't remember what drool felt like.

If he didn't get a drink soon, he'd collapse and not be able to stand back up.

A gas station stood on a street corner at the end of the block up ahead. The signage displaying the gas prices had the structural integrity of the Leaning Tower of Pisa. Jason nodded toward it. "Let's try there."

Tobin perked up. "Ooh, some jerky and Flamin' Hot Cheetos sound good." Before Jason could shoot him a glare, the kid held up his hands in surrender. "I'm kidding, I'm kidding, geez."

A clattering sound came from a side-alley. Jason's heart slammed into overdrive. He grabbed Tobin's wrist and hissed, "C'mon!" He got Akio's attention and dragged them behind an overturned dumpster. They all huddled on the ground, hopefully out of sight.

A second later, a large dog bounded down the street. Jason couldn't be sure, but it looked like the same dog he'd seen right before the earthquake struck. It was mangy and wild, with a matted tail and claws that clicked as it ran. Its nose pointed straight ahead, as if running from a predator.

Sure enough, a group of men followed the dog.

No, wait. Jason risked peeking farther over the dumpster to get a better look. *Not men. Boys.*

Five or six kids ran after the street dog. They were ten years old, max—not even teenagers. But they yelled and cursed and stomped with the unfiltered anger of adults. They threw stones and cans at the dog. One waved a crow bar around, another wielded a splintered plank.

The dog didn't look aggressive or malicious in any way. Only scared. Fleeing for its life. But the kids chased it as if it were Frankenstein's monster, the source of all their fears. If they could just kill it, everything would be okay.

But the dog was too fast. It disappeared into the night. The kids followed. Their bellows faded.

All was quiet again.

It took a few tries before Jason could lunge to a standing position. Under his clothes, he bet his body looked like a cheetah's—getting kicked and trampled by the riot had undoubtedly given him tons of bruises. He tried to say something to Akio and Tobin, but all that came out was a groan. He blamed his lack of eloquence on dehydration and exhaustion...not the sense of defeat that was slowly growing in the back of his mind.

They trudged across the remaining No-Man's-Land toward the gas station. The neon and fluorescent lights were out, and most of the windows were either spider-webbed with cracks or missing entirely.

In fact, the glass door was gone. Not broken or damaged—gone. Jason didn't have the energy to imagine the Great Gas-Station-Door Heist, as much as his sarcasm wanted him to. He entered the dark building.

The shelves were empty, except for the occasional crumpled box or smashed snack cake. Wrappers and bottles covered the vinyl floor, announcing their every step with plasticky crunches. The ATM and cash registers were busted open.

And the refrigerators on the back wall were cleaned out. Even the milk, which would have been warm by now anyway, was gone.

Tobin deflated. He'd been able to joke around earlier when the prospect of water was on the horizon. Now that the possibility had been taken away, however, he looked dejected, like a boxer after a round with the heavyweight champ.

Akio too looked about to crumble to dust. Although he gave off a gruff demeanor, sweat poured down his face. His knees trembled.

Jason wiped his own forehead, and then dabbed Akio's. The Japanese man nodded his thanks.

Nothing here. Jason was about to leave the store when he heard Tobin gasp. The kid's posture straightened up as if he'd remembered something, and he sped off, deeper into the gas station.

"Hey, Tobin..." Jason's voice came out gravelly and painful. He forced his words through his Sahara of a throat. "Tobin, slow down! We don't know what's in here."

Or who.

Tobin yelled over his shoulder, "The bathroom!"

Despite himself, Jason felt a smile tug at his lips. Finally, sweating and cooking under the sun all day, he might be able to get a drink from a faucet.

But then his rational mind fought back to the forefront, and his gut clenched. "Tobin, don't!" He raced after the boy to the back of the store, weaving between empty shelves. He saw a door with a male silhouette, swinging a little on its hinges. He held up his hands to burst into the bathroom...and he lowered his wounded right hand at the last second.

He slammed into the door. The gas station bathroom looked slightly worse than usual, with grimy smudges on the floor, mirrors hanging askew, and toilet paper strewn all over. He heard water sputtering from a spout and plinking into a sink.

"Tobin..." he wheezed. An invisible iron band wrapped around his chest. He badly needed water — but he couldn't get it here. "Tobin, don't..."

But the boy stood a few feet away from the sink, not drinking the runoff, not even touching it.

Brown, murky water streamed out of the faucet. When it splashed against the sink, particles and hunks of grime were left behind.

The three of them stared at the dirty water, silently begging it to get clearer. If they waited just another minute, maybe the contaminants would move out of the pipes, and the liquid would run crystal clear. Then they could drink and bathe and gargle to their hearts' content.

A full minute later, the water was still brown. Jason had a feeling it would be for months.

Finally, he muttered, "Let's go."

They staggered back to the street, thirstier than ever. Each step was a challenge, every breath a miracle.

Jason tilted his head back as he walked. The sky looked so far away. So deep and enormous. Pitch black—not a single star.

Is this all a dream? A Matrix simulation? A test from some scheming, omniscient god, trying to put us through hell on earth?

He sent his thoughts out into the universe. Into the void, hoping to receive an answer. Any answer. He'd take anything at this point. His questions shot through the air...

...and they ricocheted back to him. No one—neither on the earth nor in the blackness of heaven—had a response.

He kept trudging along, answerless.

23

"Where could they be...?" Marco massaged his neck as he and Ajax wandered down the street.

A hijacked police cruiser shot past them, sirens blaring. Ajax could tell it was hijacked because half of the red and blue lights were shot out, the back door had been ripped off, and the driver was a shirtless man holding his middle finger out the window.

Idiot. Ajax hated idiots.

"We need to be smarter about this," Ajax said. The other four gunmen were scattered around, kicking in doors and sifting through apartments. It was a needle-in-a-haystack search. A huge waste of time, but they didn't have any better ideas yet.

"Okay." Marco nodded. "You're right."

Part of Ajax wanted to scoff "*I know.*" But that wouldn't help, so he held it in.

Marco slicked back his hair—he was so sweaty, it stayed. "Safety. They'll want to go someplace safe."

"Nowhere is safe. Not here."

"I doubt the cop is from around here." Marco's interaction with the cop during the riot had been brief, but it was more than nothing. "He's a city man. This neighborhood doesn't suit him."

"They'll need a car to get somewhere he knows."

"And we'd be able to hear a car engine from a mile away."

Ajax pulled on his Hawaiian shirt again and again, trying to fan himself. "So they have to walk. And they'll need..."

Marco clapped and finished his sentence: "Food!"

"And water." Ajax wasn't as excited as Marco. He didn't like the fact that he needed to talk it through with someone else in order to reach such an obvious conclusion.

About a half-mile ahead was a gas station, nearly toppled by the quake. Its innards were no doubt picked clean by urban buzzards, but it was worth a look. Ajax nudged Marco, and the big man nodded to confirm he was thinking the same thing.

As they walked, they approached a body laying across the sidewalk. It was an old man, one of his legs bent at a nauseating angle. He wasn't moving. Marco held his breath and moved around the body. Ajax stepped right over it.

They reached the station. The air smelled of spilled gasoline, and Ajax instinctively looked at the pumps, making sure none of the mechanisms were sparking.

"I'll look around inside," Marco said. "Hang back, make sure no one comes out." He drew his pistol and entered through the empty space where the front door used to be.

Ajax loitered in the middle of the street, sweating in the darkness. To be honest, he hadn't realized how hungry and ravenously thirsty he was. The back of his throat felt like sandpaper, and his stomach growled.

He frowned and forced his body to submit. "You're fine, Heck. You don't need water. You don't need food." His quiet admonitions quelled the growling…for now.

Mind over matter. Maybe he should make a motivational tape series of his own. He almost laughed.

Someone approached. Ajax strained his eyes to see in the dark. He set his hand on his hip, inches away from his gun.

The figure took shape as it sauntered closer. It was a tall, slim man. Athletically built. Wearing all black. Heavy boots made his footsteps thud against the pavement. With both hands, he carried a tactical machine gun.

Ajax's heart thudded a little bit faster.

The man raised his hand to get Ajax's attention, then stopped about twenty yards away. Far enough to be courteous, but close enough to make his intentions clear.

At this distance, Ajax could see the man was Japanese. His face was sharp and very serious, as if he had walked right off a battlefield. He said something in his native language, and each word had the power of a bullet.

Ajax didn't understand anything the man said, but even if he did, he wouldn't have responded. He straightened his posture and tried to mirror the stranger's confidence.

The man said something else, this time in Korean. Then in Spanish, and Ajax finally understood: "I'm looking for two men. Have you come across anyone who answers to the names Akio or Madoka?"

Gooseflesh raced down Ajax's arms. The Yakuza were in the city, looking for their lost men.

One of them was dead in a warehouse.

The other was nearby. On the run.

Ajax took his hand off his hip, moving it far away from his pistol. As much as he wanted to appear tough and intimidating, he knew that this situation called for him to act his age. He slumped his shoulders a bit and mustered every ounce of seventeen-year-old angst he had. "No, I haven't," he moped. "Why would I?"

The Yakuza operative rolled his eyes and kept walking.

"If I do see him," Ajax said on a whim, before he could stop himself, "how can I let you know?"

As the man strolled past the gas station, he answered, "We'll be around. We're not hard to find." His boots thumped down the street, until he turned a corner and disappeared.

Ajax ran to the gas station's entrance and called to Marco. "We need to go. There's another party at play."

Marco's muscular frame jogged out of the shadows. "The faucet in the bathroom was on. Dirty water."

"We need to round up the others and get moving," Ajax said. The encounter with the Yakuza gunman had lit a fire in his chest.

"They aren't here." Marco sighed. "What now?"

"Like you said before. If they didn't find food or water, they'll look for safety." Ajax took off, almost running. Suddenly, the night had become a race. "I saw a church close by. Find the others and meet me there."

24

As they rounded the corner, Jason couldn't believe his eyes.

For the previous few blocks, he had heard the murmuring of a large crowd up ahead. He'd braced himself for more chaos and violence. He briefly considered avoiding the crowd and hiding, but the prospect of getting to the church won out in the end.

So when Jason saw hundreds of people surrounding the church, chatting with each other, helping the injured, carrying boxes of supplies, and distributing food, he was astonished.

Earlier that day, it had looked like the church was setting up for a picnic. Now, tables and chairs covered the lawn. Every seat was filled, and most squeezed in two or three extra. Others sat on the grass or sidewalks, or they stood around in clumps. They ate from sack-lunches or drank from water bottles and juice boxes.

Light bathed the grounds, thanks to dozens of electric lanterns that were scattered on the grass. There were even a few gas ones that looked like they'd been dug out of a dusty closet.

Voices filled the air, but none were shouting. They spoke comfort to one another. An elderly couple near the church building was even leading a few songs. Not many joined in, but the faint melody carried throughout the crowd, as if keeping everyone in the same mellow rhythm.

It was remarkable.

Tobin held out his arms. "Now this is more like it."

Akio didn't say anything, but his eyes scanned the scene, then scanned again, then again. Finally, after not finding any threats or sources of danger, the tension in his shoulders relaxed.

The rustle of paper bags and crinkle of plastic water bottles almost made Jason salivate. The only thing stopping him was the complete lack of moisture in his mouth. "Whaddya guys say we have some dinner, huh?"

"What's on the menu?" Tobin asked.

"Food."

Tobin smiled. "My favorite!"

The three of them stepped onto the church lawn and approached the building. The gathered people looked like they'd been through a war. Some smiled and waved, some merely nodded, most didn't acknowledge them and remained focused on their own group.

Despite all the grime and blood on their clothes, a sense of relief shrouded the lawn. Maybe even the entire block.

Iron letters fixed to the side of the church building stated its name: "Rebirth." *So that's what it's called. Tobin was right.*

The letter-board sign on the lawn was damaged and askew. What used to be a Bible verse had been reduced to a jumble of letters with gaps in-between. The building itself also bore a few vertical cracks, and it looked like a strong wind would take it down. The earthquake had taken its toll.

As they approached the building, Jason caught sight of the stained glass window on its side. Only a few lights shone from within, but the colors were vibrant. It depicted a haloed Jesus seated on a rock, preaching to the masses. Somehow, it had survived both the earthquake and the ensuing turmoil. Amazingly, Mother Nature hadn't destroyed it, nor had a brick thrown by a rioter.

I'd almost call it miraculous.

He heard a small chain rattle, and he saw Akio adjusting his wrists within the metal handcuffs. Jason felt for the man. It must be painful and tiring to have his arms bound behind his back all day. He could see deep red marks where the metal has dug into Akio's skin. Once Jason found whoever was in charge here, he would ask if the church had a pair of bolt cutters they could use.

The front door of the building popped open and a man stepped out, balancing a stack of boxes between his hands and knees. Jason's memory prickled a bit…but he didn't get a good look at the guy's face.

No way. Is that…?

The man set down the boxes and wiped his forehead. His boyish eyes twinkled in the orange light of the gas lanterns.

Red!

Raul Rojas, nicknamed "Red" by his friends at the L.A.P.D. He spoke Spanish, English, and Tagalog fluently, so he'd had a knack as an undercover operative in countless cases. Jason had last seen him at the arrest of a drug dealer named Shane Drake last year.

After the Abel fiasco, Red had quietly retired. Jason didn't know the exact reason, but he could imagine. There was no going-away party. Red didn't make a scene. One day, he simply didn't show up, and his small desk was cleared.

As Jason looked at the man now, and he felt a smile forming, he realized…He barely knew anything about Raul Rojas, other than his name.

Does he have a family? Kids? Wife? Where did he learn to speak so many languages — in school or in his everyday life? Where did he grow up? What drives him to wake up every morning?

Jason craned his neck to look around the crowd of people, hoping to get a better look at his old friend. Red wore a short-sleeved collared shirt with a logo on one breast — probably the church's. People greeted him warmly.

He raised his hand to wave, but Akio said, "Flynn." His voice was taut.

Jason looked at Akio, who gestured with his head down the street where they had come from.

In the distance, barely visible in the dark, was a man in a suit. A cartel soldier, eyeing the crowded church exterior.

Surely he can't see us from so far away. We haven't been spotted. Jason clenched his jaw. *Yet.*

"Tobin, stay low." He put his hand on the kid's shoulder and shoved him down so that he was hidden among the crowd of people.

"Hey, hey, what're you —"

Akio squatted too. "Cartel."

Tobin snarled. "Are you kidding? Here?!" He paused, then stared at Akio with wide eyes. "Wait, you can talk? In *English*?"

Akio smiled and said, "*No hablo inglés.*" He laughed heartily, enjoying his own inside joke.

"They're coming," Jason said as he zipped between bodies, headed for Red. Tobin and Akio stayed close behind.

With every step, Jason could feel the cartel men closing in, and his heart thudded harder. It felt as though an unseen sniper rifle was aimed at the back of his head.

"Red!" Jason couldn't take it anymore. He broke into a sprint and grabbed the ex-cop's shoulders. More words tumbled out of his mouth before Red could even react. "Red, we need to hide. Now."

Raul Rojas stammered for a moment, jarred by the panicky stranger. But then a flicker of recognition passed over his face, then a wave of memories, then a dump truck of grief. Jason felt a pang of guilt—Red had left the L.A.P.D. for a reason, and now Jason was dredging up those dark thoughts again.

"Jason...?" Red's brows stitched themselves together, wondering why this figure from his past had shown up so frantically.

But then, the adrenaline, the wild look in Jason's eye...It all passed directly to Red. Jason could see it all—the dormant instincts in Red's chest started to flare up. He looked out at the darkened street, and he could see the shapes of the encroaching cartel men. His intuition whispered to him, "*Danger.*"

In an instant, Red's questions disappeared, and he nodded once. "Come with me."

He led the three travelers to the church's front door and shoved it open. The old wooden door resisted at first, but a moment later, they were inside.

A couple of electric lights barely illuminated the sanctuary. Long shadows cloaked most of the room. From what Jason could see, it was clear this church had been built nearly fifty years ago—the carpet was an ugly sea-green, the light fixtures were full of dead bugs, and the pews looked horrendously uncomfortable. But an air of security permeated the whole place, as if they had entered a bunker rather than a church.

Sanctuary, Jason thought. *The word makes sense.*

The Rebirth Church consisted of one large room in which the congregation worshipped, and very little else. A few small offices and closets were connected to the sanctuary, but ninety percent of the building belonged to the room Jason was now running through.

The rows of pews faced a pulpit that was probably bought at a garage sale. A stubby altar ran along the front wall, and a heavy, two-foot-tall iron crucifix sat atop it, in case anyone forgot to whom they were supposed to be praying.

The beautiful stained glass window loomed over the altar and pulpit. From the inside looking out, the colors were much darker — Jesus preached at night rather than in daylight.

"There," Red huffed, "hide behind the altar at the front. Duck down and don't make a goddamn noise. I'll try to cover your tracks outside."

Tobin chuckled dryly, disguising his terror. "You can cuss in church? Well, shi —"

"Hey!" Red pointed a well-worn finger in Tobin's face. "Only I can." A twitchy smile played across his face. His humor put Tobin at ease, but Jason could tell that the impending threat was pushing Red to the edge.

Jason gripped Red's shoulder his with good left hand. "Raul, thank you."

"Don't thank me yet." He grabbed a handful of his shirt and wiped his sweaty face. "Now get behind that altar."

As the three of them trotted down the aisle between the pews, Akio's handcuffs jingled, and the noise caught Red's attention, just as it had caught Jason's. He eyed the cuffs briefly, but then turned to leave.

"Red," Jason called out, "these guys are bad news."

As he exited the church, Red replied, "My specialty." He smirked and closed the door.

Thud. The old carpet absorbed much of the door's volume, but enough of it bounced off the hard pews and walls...and even the metal crucifix seemed to ring a bit, like a struck bell.

Jason, Tobin, and Akio reached the front of the room and vaulted the altar. They clustered behind it, their backs against the wood, staring at the stained glass window.

Jesus's eyes were flat. Lifeless. It was odd, because the rest of the window was so vibrant, full of movement and energy. But it seemed like the artist had fallen ill before designing Jesus's eyes, and his less-talented cousin had taken over.

Typically, Christ's eyes are sparkling, full of joy and love. Not here.

Jason tilted his head to stare at the carpet instead. His heartbeat ricocheted throughout his body, but in his injured right hand, it *throbbed*. The makeshift bandage felt like plaster, squeezing his fingers and constricting blood flow.

"Oh, thank you, Jesus," Tobin sighed as he stuck his hands under the altar. He pulled out the most beautiful thing Jason had ever seen: an unopened two-gallon jug of drinking water.

Jason could barely speak. "Open it, open it, open it." He tried to keep his voice down, in case the walls were thin and the cartel soldiers were outside, but his excitement couldn't be contained.

Tobin ripped off the plastic lid and tipped the jug over his mouth. Clean, clear water *glug-glug-glugged* down his throat for what seemed like an hour. Then he lowered it with an "*Ahhhh*" and handed it to Jason.

It felt like a bar of gold in his grasp. Heavy, unwieldy, and once he finally had it, for a split second, he didn't know what to do with it.

He snapped out of his stupor and held the jug's opening to Akio. The Japanese man looked taken aback. Jason muttered, "Drink. Quick. We don't have long."

Akio nodded his thanks and gulped his fill. He came up for air, heaved a few breaths, and then drank even more.

Between Tobin and Akio, the jug was half-empty. Jason lifted it to his mouth with one shaky hand and sipped. Then drank. Then guzzled. The water was tepid and tasted a little plasticky...but at the moment, it was heavenly. He felt the liquid run down his dry throat, all the way to his stomach. It seemed to flow through his veins, fill the empty cracks throughout his body.

Outside, a voice: "*Hola, predicador.*"

The water ran down the wrong pipe, and Jason nearly choked. He dropped the jug and clamped his hand over his mouth, holding in the cough. Holding in for dear life.

It sounded like a teenager. The cartel kid in the floral shirt. The guy who'd stood in front of a speeding car and a hail of bullets without flinching. *Magnum*, as Jason had dubbed him.

They're here.

Jason squished himself behind the altar, hugging the floor. "Get down, and don't breathe."

Tobin and Akio had heard the voice too. Tobin looked scared, and he followed Jason's orders...but Akio looked terrified. His lips trembled, and tears formed at the corners of his eyelids.

Christ...If a tough guy like Akio is this scared of these cartel soldiers...

Jason leaned against the back of the altar and breathed a prayer to Red. "Please, Raul, please."

The chatter outside had gone quiet. No one wanted to speak in the presence of the men with guns.

Then, Red's voice: "*Puedo ayudarlos a todos? Comida y agua—*"

Magnum cut him off: "*Dónde están ellos, predicador?*" He sounded young and confident, which meant he probably didn't react well when people didn't give him exactly what he wanted.

"*No soy un predicador,*" was Red's only reply.

Jason wasn't fluent, but he got the gist: Magnum wanted to know where they were, and Red wasn't obliging.

The teenaged voice barked something angrily, and then, Jason heard an unmistakable sound, like a baseball landing in a mitt.

Thwack! Red cried out in response to being punched—likely in the cheek, judging by the sound.

Jason winced, helplessly huddled inside the church. Tobin sat with his face on the floor, knees pulled underneath his torso, hands over his ears. He shook uncontrollably.

Akio locked watery eyes with Jason. His trembling mouth formed a noiseless word: "Sorry..."

Red's voice trembled, "*No sé a quién estás buscando!*" His plea was muffled slightly by the old walls, but not much. They were thin, with only a layer of peeling wallpaper separating Jason from Red's pain.

Jason barely stayed behind the altar. *Why is no one helping him?!*

But he knew the answer. The hundreds of people on the church lawn weren't coming to Red's defense for the same reason Jason had asked for Red's help in the first place: They were scared, and they knew that if they opposed the cartel men, they would lose.

"Ugh," Magnum scoffed, then suddenly switched to English. "This is stupid." His English was heavily accented but quite good. He spoke with great confidence and no hesitation. "Marco, Manny, watch the streets. Make sure no one with guns bigger than ours shows up."

Why did he say that in English? Jason wondered for a moment, but then he heard the church door creak open, and Magnum's footsteps padded inside.

So that we could understand it and know we're surrounded.

Jason clenched his left hand to keep it from shaking. His right one, though, shook like a dead leaf. He thought it should be hurting, what with all the movement, but he felt nothing. His whole body was numb.

"Hey!" Red shouted as he stormed into the church, right behind Magnum. "You can't come in —"

From his hiding spot, Jason couldn't see exactly what happened next. But when he heard a shout and a scuffle, he couldn't help but risk a quick peek.

He immediately wished he hadn't.

By the church's entrance, the teenager in the floral shirt loomed over Red, who was doubled over on the floor. Magnum held a pistol in one hand, and the other was balled in a fist. Red's cheek was darkened from the punch he'd taken outside, and his right shoulder was severely popped out of place.

Magnum placed a foot on Red's back and shoved him out the open door. "Marco! Hold him out there."

Slowly, Magnum turned away from the door and faced the shadowy sanctuary, and Jason retreated back behind the altar, hoping he hadn't been spotted.

Footsteps plodded across the crunchy carpet, inching toward the front of the room. Toward the pulpit, the crucifix, and the altar.

Tobin was still wrapped up like a turtle in hiding, face on the floor. Except for his trembling, he didn't budge.

Akio's eyes were clamped shut, and frightened tears dripped down his cheeks. He struggled against his handcuffs, trying in one last effort to break free of them. Jason reached out a hand to gently stop him — the rustling of the chains might give them away.

The young, forceful voice spoke: "You're in here...I know you are."

It didn't sound like he was smiling or enjoying himself. That was unusual, in Jason's experience. No, Magnum sounded strong and dominating, but on the verge of desperation — slightly scared, as if finding them was the only way to prove his strength and domination.

"I can do this all night," he said, then kicked over a pew. The *clunk* of wood-on-wood echoed throughout the sanctuary as a line of pews knocked each other over, like dominos. "How long do you think you can outrun me?"

A huge shadow appeared on a wall. Jason knew this meant Magnum was passing one of the electric lights that battled the darkness inside the sanctuary. He was getting closer and closer to the front of the room.

Glass shattered, and the room got even darker — Magnum must have kicked the lantern too. "Scared of the dark, kid? I bet you are. It's a dark night all over this city."

He's talking to Tobin. Jason put a reassuring hand on Tobin's shaking back. He hoped the boy wasn't listening or didn't understand that the gunman was speaking directly to him, but no such luck. Tobin's breathing thickened and he trembled even more.

Sweat beaded Jason's forehead like dew. His heart pounded so hard, he almost choked on it. He stared at the empty holster on his belt, willing his Glock to magically reappear. Again, no such luck.

Step by step. Second by second. Magnum got closer with every silent breath Jason took. He'd be on top of them in less than a minute.

Jason looked around his immediate surroundings. What could he do? There was the half-empty jug of water. Old gum stuck under the altar. The crunchy carpet. And...the iron crucifix, sitting on the altar right above Jason's head.

It looked heavy. It could do some serious damage, if thrown hard enough at just the right skull.

No, that won't do anything. If I attack Magnum — even if I knock him unconscious in one blow — there are five other cartel men out on that lawn. Injuring him won't do us much good.

Jason's eyes continued to scan his hiding spot. Naturally, they landed on the most eye-catching aspect of the whole church, which happened to be right in front of him.

The colorful window. Jesus addressing the crowd. Jason could throw the crucifix through the glass, and they could hop through and escape…hopefully before Magnum shot them down.

The footsteps were close. Twenty seconds.

Crash. The gunman knocked over another pew. "Come out, *pendejos.*"

It'd be risky. The crucifix wasn't that big — only about two feet tall. It wouldn't make a very large hole in the glass, so they'd have to use their bodies to make it all the way through. Plus, they'd have to stand up. Expose themselves to Magnum's bullets.

But the sanctuary was pretty dark. Maybe his aim would be off.

All these points raced through Jason's mind. He strained to hear how close Magnum was…

And then, the church door flew open.

Magnum spun around to yell at whoever was interrupting him.

Red's voice boomed through the air: "Catch, asswipe!"

This is it. Red's distracting him so we can run.

Jason hopped to his feet — or, he tried to. His legs had locked up and gone to sleep while he was huddled on the floor. He staggered and knelt at the altar, regaining his bearings.

He quickly sized up the situation in the dark sanctuary. Magnum had his back to Jason, facing the church's entrance. Red bounded in, holding one of the gas lanterns from the lawn. He cocked his good arm back — the other hung limply at his side, seriously dislocated — and threw the lantern like it was a major-league fastball.

Jason wanted to cheer Red on, but he knew he couldn't waste the moments Red had given them. As the lantern soared through the sanctuary, Jason grabbed the iron crucifix, turned, and chucked it at the stained glass Jesus.

The heavy cross blasted through the window and opened a jagged hole...about the size of a car tire.

And then...*Crash.*

A scream pierced the air.

The gas lantern hit Magnum's torso, exploding in a burst of glass, wire, and flame. The teenager flailed his arms as he screamed, all professionalism and confidence gone in a flash. He waved his hands, trying to put out the flames, but it was too late. His floral shirt had caught on fire.

Jason grabbed Tobin's arm and yanked the boy to his feet. He hissed right into his ear: "Go through the window and run. *Run.* We'll find each other!"

Tobin sputtered, frozen in confusion and fear. "But—"

"No!" Jason yelled. "Run!" He shoved both of his hands under Tobin's armpits and hoisted him up. His wounded right hand screamed at him, but he bared his teeth and tossed the boy through the broken window.

Tobin's lanky body widened the hole the crucifix had made. He landed with a painful *thud* on the church's back lawn.

"Akio, go!" Jason said, still trying to keep his voice down. He doubted it was a problem, though—Magnum was too busy rolling on the carpet to notice them escaping.

The next thing Jason knew, he was alone behind the altar. Akio had leapt through the window. Jason peeked through the jagged hole—Tobin's long frame sprinted into the dark neighborhood, and Akio stood right outside, waiting for Jason to follow.

"Come!" Akio beckoned feverishly.

Jason braced himself and dove through the window. A hanging piece of broken glass nicked his arm, but he didn't have time to feel the pain. He landed on the lawn in a heap, his hand erupting in agony. He ignored it and stood. "C'mon."

Before heeding his own advice and running, he turned to look through the shattered window.

Magnum had put out the fire that engulfed his shirt. His bare chest was bright red, burnt, smoking. The skin would be scarred forever. He stood in the sanctuary, stunned, like a shell-shocked soldier in the middle of a battlefield.

Red heaved a breath as he supported his dislocated arm. His eyes flitted to Jason, and he nodded once.

Then, Magnum raised his gun and fired. The shot tore through the air and buried itself in Raul Rojas's forehead.

Jason opened his mouth to scream, but no sound broke free. He felt frozen in time, unable to move, to speak, to think.

From the front lawn, a cartel man yelled, *"Que fue ese ruido?"*

Then...

BANG. BANG. BANG.

Gunshots. People screaming in terror. Feet running on grass.

Bodies hitting the ground.

Magnum's gunshot inside the church must have spooked the rest of the cartel men. And they were opening fire on the people gathered outside.

Jason couldn't take it. Tears of fury sprang from his eyes. Or maybe they were beads of sweat. Or drops of blood. He didn't know anymore.

He began to charge back through the window, ready to tear the kid in the burnt Hawaiian shirt limb from limb. "Hey, bastard —!"

Akio bounded in front of Jason and shoved his body against Jason's. "No!"

Jason snarled, his sights set on Magnum. "Get out of —"

"Run!" Akio dug his heels into the grass like a linebacker, and pushed Jason away from the church. "Gone. Run!"

Jason stopped fighting.

I'm sorry.

Inside the sanctuary, Magnum turned away from Red's corpse and glared through the broken stained glass window. He locked eyes with Jason.

I'm so sorry.

Jason and Akio sprinted into the night, leaving the massacre behind. The howls and cries of the survivors who had witnessed the bloodshed followed them. With every step, Jason's raw shame grew. For the rest of his life, he would remember the sounds of those gunshots and screams…and his shoes on the concrete as he ran away, abandoning the dead bodies he'd helped put in their graves.

25

"There!" Magnum's shout chased them down the street. "That way! Go, get them! They're right there!" His fury was tinged with pain, no doubt from the burns on his torso.

Jason tried to leave the teenaged killer far, far behind him, but he couldn't escape the fact that their sanctuary had become a slaughterhouse, and the cartel soldiers were still hot on their tail.

He strained his eyes to look ahead, to see where he was going. The road was filled with burning cars and hovering smoke, which provided some brightness, but made everything look faint, dirty, and orange.

Over the course of the night, the streets had gone from chaotic to apocalyptic.

Footsteps echoed behind him. Jason risked a look back—a lone gunman in a suit ran after them. He was still in the dark distance, but catching up. The man was athletic, professional, and likely hydrated. He'd be on top of Akio and Jason in a matter of minutes.

Jason urged his body to run faster, but his legs didn't cooperate. They felt sluggish, like he was running in a swamp rather than on a paved road. Those few gulps of water in the church had done little to rejuvenate him.

Guilt stabbed his heart at the fleeting thought of the church he was running away from.

Click.

Amid the running and panting, Jason's ears caught a quiet but unmistakable sound a couple dozen yards behind him: a handgun's slide being pulled back. The pursuing cartel man was ready to shoot.

He needed to take cover, to lose the gunman.

There. Up ahead. A short, wide building with a bent flagpole in front. It looked like a small middle school.

Hallways, lots of rooms, desks to hide under.

He set his course for the school's entrance, and Akio followed right behind him.

The door hung ajar on limp hinges, and Jason shouldered it aside. The flooring was sticky linoleum, designed to look like a black-and-white checkerboard. Or maybe they were maroon-and-tan. It was hard to see—the only light came from the smudged windows.

As soon as they stepped inside, Akio took off down a hallway. His footfalls dissolved into nothingness, leaving Jason alone by the open door.

Splitting up is probably a good idea, he tried to convince himself.

Jason took a breath and felt a lump in his chest. He grumbled, forcing the phlegm out of his lungs, and spat. A lump of black saliva splattered on the floor. "Beauty."

The cartel man was just a few seconds behind. Jason turned a corner and jogged deeper into the school, trying to keep his steps light and quiet.

He heard someone run in. The cartel gunman had arrived.

Then, a new voice echoed against the walls. "Hey!" It sounded like a large man, confronting the cartel soldier. Likely, he'd taken shelter inside the school too. "This place is taken. Who're—?"

BANG. A gunshot ripped the air into a thousand pieces. Jason heard a body hit the ground, and, throughout the school, shoes squeaked as people fled. There must be dozens of refugees hiding in here, and the sudden explosion of violence prompted them to find new hiding spots.

There's another corpse I'm responsible for—

Jason shook his head to clear it as he turned down a hall. A bulletin board featuring a cartoon owl informed him that the English classrooms were housed here. Child-sized lockers were mounted to the walls—not nearly big enough to hide in. Several doors lined each side of the hall, all of them open. He chose one and peeked inside.

Twenty desks. Bookshelves. Abandoned backpacks and supplies. A dry-erase board covered in notes—it looked like the class had been discussing Toni Morrison's *Recitatif* on the last day of school.

A crack bisected the classroom, as if the linoleum was trying to swallow itself. A few ceiling tiles had fallen out, and a snow globe of New York City had fallen off the teacher's desk. The Statue of Liberty sat on the floor, surrounded by glass shards, fake snowflakes, and dirty water.

Good enough.

Jason eased the door shut, not latching it entirely, and tiptoed to the back of the room. He picked a desk and slid under it. The desk was designed for a middle-school-aged kid, so it was small, scratched, and pretty flimsy. But it would have to do.

He curled up on the floor and forced his breathing to slow down. In his nose, out his mouth. In and out. His hammering heart reluctantly braked.

And then.

Silence.

Not a sound. It was so quiet, he could hear his eyes blink.

Clomp. Clomp. Footsteps in the hallway. Slow and steady.

Jason stopped breathing altogether.

And then.

Creeeaaak. The classroom door swung open.

Jason clamped his eyes shut. *Crap crap crap.* He wanted to punch himself. *I shut the door when all the others were open. Stupid, Jason, stupid.*

Too late. The cartel man stepped into the classroom. From under the desk, Jason could only see his legs, but judging by his stance, the man held a gun and knew how to use it effectively.

The classroom was cramped and shadowy, but it was only a matter of time before the gunman found Jason. Only a matter of seconds, really. The man walked quickly between the rows of desks.

Jason shifted into a crouched position under the desk, and he waited. *One Mississippi, two Mississippi...*

Right when the gunman stepped in front of Jason's desk, Jason sprang upward. He launched the small desk into the man, shoving the gun out of the way.

"Gah!" the cartel man cried out. The faux-wood desktop smashed against his face. Jason wouldn't be surprised if his two front teeth were knocked out, but he didn't stick around to find out. He sprinted out of the classroom and down the hall, putting as much distance between himself and the gunman as he possibly could in the few seconds he'd bought.

As Jason rounded a corner—a construction-paper Earth with a face told him he was in the social studies hall now—he heard a grunt behind him, then a bellow: "*Vuelve aqui!*" Then rapid footsteps. The cartel man was hot on his trail.

Surrounded by classrooms and lockers and colorful bulletin boards, yet chased by a killer with a gun, Jason felt a chill race down his spine.

The chill stopped right above his waist. It was a cold spot on his back, about the size of a grape. The spot where, every second, he anticipated a bullet would land.

In the middle of the stretch of hallway, he saw a large, clunky air conditioning unit smashed on the floor. Ceiling tiles and fluorescent light tubes were scattered around it. Jason weighed his options: *Keep running, or take cover and try to get the best of him?*

If I wear myself out, he'll gun me down in no time.

But if I think I can take him in close quarters and I'm wrong... That'd be game over too.

The gunman's shoes squealed as he rounded the corner, a dozen or so yards behind Jason.

Snap decision.

BANG.

Jason slid and crouched behind the metal unit as a bullet tore over him. He'd been a millisecond from having his head blown off.

The cold spot on his back didn't go away. A bullet had his name on it—he just knew it.

He wiped sweat from his eyes and focused.

The gunman kept firing rounds into the air conditioning unit. The bullets pinged against the metal like deadly hail, and the deafening noise almost made Jason's ears bleed.

He sure isn't worried about wasting bullets. Bad sign.

Suddenly, a bullet punctured the unit. It exploded past Jason's body and buried itself into a locker.

He cowered on the floor, nestling his head between his arms, as if that would protect him. A desperate plea erupted from his chest: "Help! Someone, help!" He cried over the gunshots, hoping one of the people hiding in the school would come to his aid. Maybe someone would distract the gunman, or toss Jason a weapon, or…do something. Anything. Jason wasn't picky at the moment. "Anyone! Help!"

No footsteps. No voices. No one was coming.

"Akio! Help! Akio!" He called out for his ally.

They weren't friends. Jason barely knew his name. Within moments of meeting, they'd beaten the snot out of each other. But Akio had saved him from Marco during the riot. They were in this hellhole together, for better or worse.

"Akio!"

Nothing but gunshots slamming against metal.

Still, no one was coming.

Crap crap crap.

Pause. An empty magazine clattered to the floor. The gunman rapidly approached the AC unit as he reloaded.

Fine. Jason readied his good left hand. *Come and get me.*

The cartel soldier was a few paces from Jason's cover when he finished reloading. Jason rolled into view and hopped to his feet.

They glared at each other for a split second. The gunman raised his weapon to shoot, but Jason was too close to get a good shot, so he swung his gun at Jason's jaw instead.

Duck and strike.

Jason swerved under the attempted pistol-whip and, as he rose, brought his fist up into the gunman's ribs.

It was a solid hit, but not nearly strong enough to debilitate the guy. He winced but brought his arm around again to try to hit Jason.

The cartel man's gun was loaded, which was good news and bad news.

On the bad front, obviously, was the fact that the moment he got an opening, he could shoot Jason point blank.

But on the other hand, once Jason got the gun, it would be locked and cocked, ready to be used against its owner.

The cartel man swung and swung, again and again, trying to smash his solid metal pistol against Jason's head. Each time, Jason barely managed to twist out of the way.

Duck. Duck. Duck.

"Akio!" He tried again to call for back-up. "Akio! Now would be a good time—" But he had to dedicate every ounce of brain power to dodging the gunman's strikes. If he lost focus for one second, it'd be the end of the road.

Duck. Duck. Duck. Duck.

He was getting tired. And dizzy. The gunman's plan seemed to be one of attrition—keep swinging either until one of his strikes connected, or Jason collapsed from exhaustion.

And it was working. Jason's vision blurred as he veered and weaved away from the cartel man's pendulum-like arm.

One last effort: "Akio! Help, goddammit!"

Nothing. The cartel man cackled, and his swing slowed ever so slightly.

Just what Jason was waiting for.

Duck. Duck. Duck.

As he dipped under a swing, Jason snatched one of the fallen fluorescent light tubes.

Goose.

He stood and cracked the tube across the gunman's head, and the glass shattered. The gunman staggered a bit, but didn't fall. Then, Jason brought the jagged tube back and slashed it across the man's hand—the hand holding the gun.

He yelped and dropped his weapon.

Jason held the saber-toothed glass against the man's throat, and they both froze. Panting. Drained. One defeated, the other victorious.

"You're done," Jason snarled and kicked the gun to the side of the hall, far out of the man's reach. He cocked his head toward an open door and pressed the shattered tube into the man's fleshy neck. "Go."

The cartel man held up his hands and inched toward the door, glaring at Jason every step of the way. Jason allowed a few feet of distance to open up between him and the disarmed man, so that they couldn't get into another close-quarters scuffle. As they moved into the classroom, Jason's eyes flicked to the gun sitting on the floor, partially under a ceiling tile.

Should I go for it? Instantly, Jason decided against it. He only had one good hand, and it was currently holding the sharp glass. *I'll get it later.*

The two men edged into the classroom, and Jason elbowed the door closed. "Coat," he said. "*Saco. Apagado.*"

The cartel soldier glowered but obeyed. He removed his suit coat and dropped it, revealing the empty shoulder-holster that had carried his handgun. The man's white shirt was drenched with sweat, practically see-through. Unarmed, exhausted, and with a bloody hand, he looked utterly dejected.

In his own white shirt and black slacks, and with a bandaged right hand, Jason imagined he was in a similar state. But he hadn't looked in a mirror all day.

And he didn't care.

With his makeshift knife, Jason gestured to the front row of desks. "Sit."

Again, the man obeyed, plopping himself into a chair that was made for someone twenty years his junior. His knees scrunched up under the desk's surface, and he clamped a hand over his bleeding wound.

Jason quickly glanced around the room. Maps on the walls, hand-drawn copies of famous paintings, stacks and stacks of *National Geographics*—he recalled that this was the social studies hall. He grabbed the teacher's chair and dragged it in front of the room's only occupied desk. He sat on the edge of the seat, still keeping plenty of space between himself and the cartel man.

He took a deep breath, trying to fill the cracks of his tired body and mind with oxygen. *Things are looking up,* he told himself. *I'm not dead yet.* He stared at the equally-tired cartel man sitting behind an undersized desk, and he couldn't help but feel a sense of mild victory.

For the first time all night, Jason had the upper-hand.

"Listen…" He spoke in a low, even tone, as if he were a teacher giving a lecture. "I'm going to ask you some questions, to try to find out what's going on, okay? If I hear a hint of '*No hablo inglés*,' I'll stab this dirty glass into your knee, and then work my way up. I heard the guy in the flowery shirt talking to you goons in English, so I know you understand. Now…your name."

The man's jaw trembled as he stared back at Jason. His eyes narrowed. A mixture of emotions crossed his face—emotions that were difficult for Jason to decipher. The man looked simultaneously angry and terrified.

But Jason felt no sympathy. Not after the day he'd had. He tightened his grip on the broken fluorescent tube. "Test me."

The room was quiet. The cartel man saw something in Jason's eyes that tipped his internal scale toward the "terrified" side. He cleared his throat, stammered, and finally answered. "Manny."

"Alright, making progress. We're doing well." Jason leaned back in his chair. "The guy in the flowery shirt. The kid you work for. Who is he?"

Manny bristled. "I don't work for Ajax!" Immediately, his face looked regretful, but then he smirked aggressively, as if he had intended to give Jason the kid's name.

Jason pressed for more. "And Ajax is?"

The cartel soldier didn't respond.

"If you don't work for Ajax, who do you work for?"

Akio is pretty positive these guys are cartel. But it's better to hear it from the source.

Manny's smirk turned genuine. "Gore Rodriguez," he said with relish.

The name made Jason's stomach clench, and, despite his best efforts, his hand shook. When Manny saw the glass tube quiver, he laughed.

"You've heard of him?" Manny also leaned back in his chair and unfastened the top button of his shirt. He even tried to cross his legs, but the desk was way too low.

Yeah. Jason swallowed. *Yeah. Dang it.*

The cartel led by Gabriel Rodriguez was infamous around the world, but dreaded and reviled in L.A. The ocean of drugs that flooded into the city was largely thanks to him. The body count of those who overdosed on his meth and heroin ticked upward each year.

But drugs were a commonplace problem—people could get them from gangs, dealers, and chemists on every street, if they sought them out. What made Rodriguez's cartel so notorious was its militant brutality.

Jason couldn't remember the exact name of the cartel, but every law enforcement officer in California could tell you about Gabriel "Gore" Rodriguez.

Violence wafted off Rodriguez like a foul smell. Executions. Explosive packages. Shoot-outs. More disappearances than the U.S. and Mexico could keep track of.

Rumors said that Rodriguez lived in an opulent compound called "Xanadu," and, if he so chose, he could launch a full-scale war. The estate housed a small army, along with enough artillery and vehicles to make any government nervous.

Rodriguez's private troops outgunned the police of any American city, even Los Angeles. Not only did they have thousands of rifles and grenades, and they were trained to use them, but their body armor was superior, their cars were faster, and the soldiers were ruthless. Very few institutions could stand against his cartel and survive, much less win.

It was hard for Jason to believe, but he, Tobin, and Akio were actually lucky that only a handful of gunmen were after them, considering the resources Rodriguez wielded. If Rodriguez had unleashed the full might of his cartel, all three of them would be dead by now, their bodies dangling from a clothesline outside City Hall.

That thought must have been plain on Jason's face, because Manny let out a big, booming laugh that bounced off the walls of the classroom. "We'll kill you very soon, little man—"

Jason sprang to his feet and lunged at Manny, jagged glass outstretched. Manny dropped his smirk and shrieked, shielding his face with his forearms.

But Jason stopped a foot away from Manny, panting, glaring, wanting nothing more than to drive the glass into the cartel man's thigh.

No. Then I'd lose my only weapon.

Oh, and he might bleed out. That too.

Jason returned to the teacher's chair. He eyed the cowering Manny and exhaled. "Little man?"

Manny lowered his arms and sneered. "Mock me. Kill me. Doesn't change that you'll be dead within an hour."

Jason tried not to think about the fact that Manny was probably right. He struggled to come up with a retort.

Then, Manny stiffened in anger. His gaze shot past Jason. "Oh. You."

Cautiously, keeping Manny in his sights, Jason turned to see what the cartel man was looking at. Standing outside the classroom door, visible through a smudged, rectangular window, was Akio.

Anger and annoyance flared up in Jason's chest. *Oh, now he shows up?*

When the bullets were flying and Jason had been pinned down, begging for help, Akio had stayed hidden.

Jason glared at Akio, and the image he had held of the handcuffed man all night—that of a gruff, dangerous gangster—evaporated. Instead, Jason saw a small, helpless weakling.

Coward.

Akio's shoulders slumped as he met Jason's glare, then his eyes dropped in shame. He didn't try to open the classroom door and come in...and it took Jason a moment to realize he couldn't, due to his handcuffs. Jason didn't move to open the door for him.

Turning back to Manny, Jason asked, "What do you want with him?"

The cartel man looked at Jason as if he'd asked the dumbest question possible. "To kill him."

Get in line.

"And the kid," Manny continued. "And you."

"Alright, alright," Jason said as he stood, "I get the idea." He put one foot on Manny's coat, which was crumpled on the floor, and dragged it to himself, several paces away from the seated cartel man. He knelt down next to it and shifted his makeshift weapon to his injured hand. He shot Manny a sharp glance, reiterating his earlier warning: *Test me.*

It was agony to hold the glass tube with his smashed right hand. But Manny didn't know that. Jason buried his grunts of pain and used his good hand to rummage through Manny's suit coat. He emptied the pockets onto the floor:

A Zippo lighter. No cigarettes.

A half-empty pack of spearmint gum.

Three spare magazines of ammo for the gun, which was abandoned in the hallway under a ceiling tile. *Score. I'll grab that as we leave.*

A receipt for groceries, dated last Sunday.

A small ring holding a few stubby keys.

Jason almost laughed in disbelief. Another stroke of luck in their favor. He considered buying a lottery ticket, but then remembered the L.A. lotto probably wouldn't be up and running again for several months.

He stood and strode to the door, jingling the keyring in his left hand. He opened the door, startling Akio, and spun his finger like a tornado. "Turn around." The Japanese man put his back to Jason, and Jason stuck one of the keys into the cuff's circular keyhole. On the third attempt, the unforgiving steel manacles popped open.

Akio let out a groan of relief, as if he were sliding into a warm bath.

"Yeah," Jason chuckled, in spite of his annoyance with Akio. "I bet." He took away the cuffs and, in the school's low light, saw the damage they'd done to Akio's wrists over the course of the day. The man's skin was both red and purple, sliced and bruised. It looked excruciating.

Akio didn't act like he was in pain, though. He smiled and held his arms close to himself, blissful, as if he'd been carrying a heavy trunk for hours and was finally able to throw it down.

Jason turned his attention back to Manny. The cartel man had been creeping forward in his chair, preparing to charge Jason while his back was turned. But Jason switched the glass tube back to his good hand

and held it out. "Nope. Down." Manny grimaced and settled back into the seat.

What do I do with him now?

To Jason's horror and grim satisfaction, he instinctively looked at the weapon in his fist. He sighed and shook his head.

Don't kill him. Don't kill him.

But it'd be so easy. Stab him once and leave. I definitely can't take him with us, and if I leave him unrestrained, he'll go back to Ajax. Or he'll kill us himself.

"Actually…" Jason got an idea. "Stand up."

Manny got his legs out from under the middle-school-sized desk and stood. A few drops of fresh blood escaped from his wounded hand and dotted the floor.

Then, Jason said to Akio, "Catch," as he tossed the cuffs. Akio instinctively caught them, eyes wide, as if the cuffs were from a long-ago nightmare he'd hoped to forget. Jason cocked his head toward Manny. "Cuffs."

Akio nodded briskly.

Manny was none too happy. He sniffed and took a few aggressive steps forward. "If you think I'm gonna just let you—"

Jason matched Manny's pace, which caught the cartel man off guard. Jason flew into Manny's face and pressed the jagged glass against his gut. "Cuffs or death. You pick."

I don't make threats. Jason nudged his weapon until it poked through Manny's shirt and skin. A small, bloody flower blossomed from the soldier's stomach. *I make promises.*

Again, Manny backed down from Jason's hateful, murderous gaze. Through gritted teeth, he rumbled, "Fine."

With Jason holding the glass tube like an orchestra conductor's baton, Akio cuffed Manny's hands behind his back, surrounding a leg of the teacher's desk. It wasn't the perfect solution, but the desk was the heaviest thing in the room, and it would at least slow Manny down.

Akio snatched Manny's fallen suit coat from the floor. He slapped some of the dust off the shoulders, then folded it over his arm.

Standing there in his jeans and penny loafers, holding a coat several sizes too big, he looked more than a little ridiculous.

But Akio seemed set on taking the suit coat, for some reason. *Maybe to steal a piece of his former-captor's wardrobe? Or am I overthinking it?*

Jason caught a glance of Manny's scowl. The cartel man glowered at the sight of Akio holding his suit coat.

Ah, so he wants to tick off Manny. A worthy goal.

Jason looped the jagged glass tube through his belt. He gave Manny one final look, then left the classroom, Akio scuttling behind.

"You better run!" Manny bellowed. "Rodriguez will have your heads! You'll never —"

Jason slammed the door shut and wedged a fallen ceiling tile under it. *Should be a pain to get this open without using your hands, eh, little man?*

But even though the gunman was beaten and in handcuffs, even though Jason had survived, even though the danger had passed for the moment...he still felt the cold spot on his lower back where he'd been certain a bullet was going to rip through his body.

He shuddered and tried to ignore it.

It was almost pitch-black in the hall. The weak light from the outside world had waned to almost nothing, and Jason had to squint to see where he was walking. He slid his good hand along the wall of lockers, his feet scouring the ground for the fallen handgun.

Eventually, his toe nudged the fallen ceiling tile the gun had slid under. He squatted and patted the ground. He searched and searched and searched, but all he felt was grime and tufts of insulation.

Crouched on the floor, he hung his head in defeat. Someone else hiding in the school must have snatched it. He'd been counting on having that weapon when he emerged into the outside world.

He resisted the urge to punch a locker — partly to assert dominance over his emotions, but mostly because he couldn't afford to have two injured hands. He straightened up and began marching down the hall, toward the exit.

Akio's footfalls were close behind. He cleared his throat to break the ice, clearly sensing the tension between himself and Jason. He asked, "Tobin?"

Manny's sneering voice filled Jason's mind: *"We'll kill you very soon."*

"Yeah," Jason answered. "Gotta find Tobin."

Before Ajax and the others do.

26

Ajax writhed in agony. Anguish. Affliction.

All the words he knew didn't cover the level of pain he felt. The burns on his chest stretched their serrated fingers into every corner of his body. His toes curled, his teeth ached, each hair felt like it was on fire. And all the while, his burned torso pulsated and simmered.

There was no ice to put on his chest. No medicine. Not even clean bandages. As they had fled the church, Marco had grabbed a handful of donated clothes, which he had cut into strips and offered to Ajax. But the pain was too raw to wrap cloth around the wound yet.

So Ajax laid on the ground, shirtless, sprawled under a stretch of highway, writhing in agony, anguish, and affliction. Screaming curses to the empty air.

After they had opened fire at the church, everyone had panicked — the civilians and gunmen alike. Everyone except Ajax. The pain of the burns hadn't made it from his chest to his brain yet, so he calmly stepped over the preacher's corpse, walked out of the church to the lawn, and saw the carnage. At least twenty bodies laid on the grass, blood leaking from the new holes in their flesh. His men all looked like frightened deer, unsure what to do or where to go.

Ajax had barked, "That way! Go, get them!" He wanted to get his hands on the three targets, but moreover, he wanted to leave the church. All the parishioners had been screaming and scrambling, but soon enough, some of them would try to be heroes and tackle the gunmen. It was best to get out of there.

As he searched for the targets, the pain started. He could barely move without antagonizing the wound, so he had to stop.

And to add insult to injury, his Hawaiian shirt had been burnt beyond recognition. The front disintegrated into ash, and the rest fell off as he ran.

The bright colors that made him stand out among the hardened adults of the cartel…gone. Turned to dust.

About a mile from the church, he'd seen a large concrete overpass that had been damaged in the earthquake. The elevated road had cracked in half and fallen to the ground, one end still attached to the rest of the road, forming a sort of lean-to.

Without a word, he had broken off from his men and huddled under the highway. No one followed him. They must have known he needed space and time to breathe. Either that, or they were scared he would shoot them too, as he had the preacher. Both possibilities were fine with him.

Now, finally, the pain started to ebb. At least, it had receded enough for Ajax to wrap the strips of cloth around his torso. He sat up, which almost made him flop right back down, and laid the first piece across his skin.

He'd underestimated how much it would hurt to press the cloth against his burns. But he couldn't stop halfway, so he braced himself and kept wrapping.

"*GAH!*" His howls echoed under the fallen highway, seemingly dulling his pain. The louder he yelled, the less he thought about the burns.

What else could he think about?

His men were so unprofessional. One gunshot and *pow*, they start blasting everyone in sight.

Anger. Resentment. He ground his teeth together, which helped with the pain.

The Yakuza prick, the cop, and the kid had gotten away. Again. And they had been right in front of him too! Meters away. Dumb luck had been on their side. If it weren't for the preacher lighting him on fire, those three nuisances would be dead, and he could get out of this wrecked city.

Frustration. Fatigue.

He felt a tightness around his ribs, and he realized he was done bandaging his burns. He hadn't even noticed, he was so lost in his thoughts. The phrase "Time flies when you're having fun" popped into his head. He let out a dry chuckle, which he immediately regretted.

He leaned against a fallen chunk of concrete and let out a long, deep sigh.

It'd been a tough day.

In the darkness of the night, sheltered by the overpass, he closed his eyes. What had led him here?

The shiny black BMW idling by the curb.

Rodriguez's stocky form, standing silently in the middle of the warehouse.

Crumbling. Cracking. Shaking. Shattering. The world rocking back and forth.

The stench of sweat and fear.

Kicking over pews. Searching the church.

BANG.

Screams. Blood. Murder.

His first kill. That annoying, meddling man in the church was the very first life he had ever taken.

For years, he'd been curious. He had wanted to know what it would feel like to snuff out someone's soul. To steal their very breath.

Ever since he'd seen Gore Rodriguez kill that bodyguard named Salva in broad daylight, he'd been itching to try it himself.

And now, he'd done it. He had pointed the barrel of his gun at a man's head, pulled the trigger, and ended his life forever.

It was so...so...mundane.

Easy.

Ajax was surprised to find out he felt this way. Surely not. Surely killing a man was at least a little thrilling. A little satisfying. He searched his feelings and interrogated his memory, hoping to find a spark of excitement somewhere in there.

But no. He'd felt nothing killing that man. No fear, no thrill, no fulfillment.

That made Ajax's heart sag. If killing held no pleasure, what was he doing? He had no adventure to look forward to, no peak yet to summit.

He staggered to his feet, gradually and carefully. Then he paced back and forth under the fallen overpass, trying to get used to the soreness of his torso. He breathed and stretched a bit. The wounds were getting better, he thought.

Killing someone wasn't too difficult, really. It had been hyped up as some strenuous, life-altering action. In reality, all it took was good aim.

Ajax scoffed. Gangsters, assassins, soldiers, and hitmen weren't all they were cracked up to be, after all. If he—a seventeen-year-old guy with no real experience or training—could do it, anyone could. Not very impressive.

Footsteps approached. Marco stepped between the sea of wrecked and abandoned cars, making his way to Ajax. Glass crunched under the big man's shoes, disturbing Ajax's alone time.

"What is it?" Ajax called out.

Marco didn't respond until he had fully arrived under the cracked highway, which irked Ajax to no end. He could've spoken as he walked, but he instead made Ajax wait. Finally, Marco said, "We can't find Manny."

Ajax inwardly rolled his eyes. "Fine." He still had four cartel men who could hunt down the escapees—five, counting himself.

"Here." Marco threw something light and airy to Ajax.

But in the dark shadows, Ajax couldn't see clearly and cried out. He flinched and hid behind his arms.

A shirt landed on Ajax's shoulders, clean and unburnt. It didn't have any colorful designs—in fact, it looked plain and gray—but it was in one piece.

Marco laughed. "You okay? Did it cut you?"

Ajax didn't dignify the quip with a response. He gingerly put on the shirt, taking care not to strain his bandages too much.

To Ajax's delight, Marco's laughter turned to pained grunts. The dark bruise on his jaw gave him trouble when he opened his mouth too wide.

Excited shouts emanated from the street. It sounded like the other cartel gunmen. Marco's head whipped toward the sound, and he and Ajax hustled to see what was happening.

"I got him, I got him!" One of the suited cartel men approached the crumbled overpass — Ajax hadn't bothered to learn his name, but he had a lazy eye, so Ajax thought of him as "Walleye." The remaining two gunmen huddled around him as he walked, so Ajax couldn't see what all the commotion was about.

But then one of the men drew his pistol and pointed it at Walleye's waist.

No, the gun wasn't pointed at Walleye. It was pointed at the person Walleye was escorting.

The kid. The shaggy little snot who was running around with the cop and Yakuza hostage.

Walleye must have found the kid while searching for Manny, and he was bringing him to Ajax to show off, like a hunting dog presenting a wounded pheasant to its master.

But another of the gunmen had decided to take matters into his own hands and was seconds away from splattering the kid's brain all over the road.

Ajax pulled his gun from his waistband and fired a round into the air. "Hey!" he shouted. The three cartel men froze and looked at him. "No one kills the kid."

The deafening report of the gunshot echoed in the night. It mixed in the air with the sounds of distant police sirens and helicopter blades. But those were miles away, toward the center of town. Here, in the neighborhood, Ajax was king.

The man who had been about to shoot snarled. "Why not? I thought that's what we were doing out here — finding and killing 'em."

Ajax shook his head. It was exhausting being the smartest person in a group. "We are. But we need the others too. If they see the kid's dead, they'll take off, and we'll start this stupid chase all over again." He turned to Marco. "Take him under the highway and watch him. But keep him just exposed enough so the cop can see him from the street."

It was enjoyable to see Walleye's face turn from pride to dejection as Marco took the kid—his prize—away from him.

"Fan out," Ajax said to his three soldiers. "When the cop and the Yakuza show up, be ready. We need to kill all of them at the same time, so none of them can slip away."

The men nodded and moseyed around, checking the ammo in their guns, wiping sweat from their faces, and looking generally sluggish. Lethargic. Ill-prepared. Ajax groaned. He would have thought that Manny disappearing would put the fear of God into them.

He felt the heft of his gun in his hand, then tucked it back into his waistband. Maybe he'd have to take over for God.

"*Hola!*" The kid hollered at Ajax from a seated position under the damaged overpass. He had a moronic smile on his face, typical for a thirteen-year-old puke challenging authority. He continued in English, "Hey, hey, my Spanish teacher at school taught us this little thing to help us remember the vowels. It goes like this..." He dramatically cleared his throat. "*A, E, I, O, U...El burro sabe más que tú!*" He cackled to himself, rocking back and forth, clearly very proud of his recitation.

Ajax slowly waltzed back under the highway, until he towered over the kid...but the kid didn't stop. He just kept giggling and giggling. The sound of the young, high-pitched laugh also mixed with the distant sirens.

Now that Ajax was closer, he could see the tension in the kid's shoulders, the small tears in the corners of his eyes, the forced nature of his laughter. The kid was giggling only because if he wasn't, he'd be weeping.

The kid looked up at Ajax. "Hey, hey, I've got a secret. C'mere."

Ajax kept a stony expression on his face as he knelt.

"It's a big one," the kid whispered loudly, still putting on a show to cover up his fear. He dramatically cleared his throat again. "Y'know the car? The black one with the guy in the trunk?" He paused to let the night lean in and listen. "I'm the one who took it. I stole it from you. And it was by accident." He crossed his arms. "Can't even drive yet."

Marco, who was standing guard nearby, grumbled and tilted his head back. "Great. A child unwittingly took a hostage from us. I hope Rodriguez never finds out."

Ajax let a small smirk tug at his mouth. He found it funny that they were both younger than their country's legal age to drive, yet this whole situation had started with a car.

He patted the kid's knee. "I'm excited to kill you."

The stupid smile vanished from the kid's young face, and he looked close to vomiting.

Ajax stood, feeling slightly hopeful. He realized it was true—he *was* excited to kill the kid. Maybe it would be more thrilling and satisfying than shooting a man.

Not yet, though. Soon.

As he walked away, he snapped at Marco, "And by the way…A child unwittingly took a hostage from *you*. Not *us*." He went to find a dark perch where he could hide and wait for the kid's rescue party.

27

"Crap." Jason had been peeking around the side of a dumpster, watching the group of cartel men shout and argue as Tobin stood there, terrified but trying desperately not to show it. Then Marco took Tobin under a damaged chunk of highway, and the gunmen began to spread out…and now, one of them was headed right for him and Akio. "Go, go, go," he hissed to Akio, and they scurried into a dark alley.

The ground seemed to rankle and shift as they hid themselves in the shadows. Unseen animals hissed and clawed at their ankles. The alley smelled like old piss and turds that had been in the hot sun for weeks.

But it was better than being out in the open, where the gunmen had clear shots.

And it was *definitely* better than where Tobin was at the moment: under the watchful supervision of Ajax and Marco, and beneath fifteen precarious tons of concrete that were a strong sneeze away from collapsing entirely.

"Okay…" He slumped against the grimy alley wall and set his face in his palm. "Okay, okay." He hoped that by adopting the posture of a man deep in thought, he could trick himself into coming up with a grand plan for rescuing Tobin.

So far, it wasn't working.

He was hamstrung by his injured right hand—his dominant hand—so he couldn't brawl his way through. Besides, the heat and exhaustion of the day had weakened his body and slowed his mind.

And Akio, his only ally, had revealed himself to be a coward, useless in a fight.

But he successfully distracted Marco during the riot in front of the electronics store. He's good at getting someone's attention, then disappearing.

Akio looked like he wanted to lie down, drape Manny's huge suit coat over himself, and hide like a hermit crab in its shell. Any semblance of the dangerous Yakuza gangster had dissipated. Now, he was terrified and confused. He clearly wanted to run away and leave Jason, but he also knew he had no place to go.

Then Jason stopped. He looked down at himself—more specifically, his clothes. Black shoes, scuffed from a day of running and crouching. Black pants, dirty and torn at the knees, with spots of unseen blood. A white button-up shirt, stained brown and gray, soaked with sweat.

The cartel men were dressed the same way…except he was missing a suit coat. And they all had darker hair than he did.

In the darkness of the alley, he dropped to the ground and ran his left hand along the corners of the alley. There had to be something he could use…

His fingers slid into a pile of something soft and mushy. He suddenly remembered that a horde of animals had been here before they arrived, and he slowly, fearfully lifted his hand to his nose.

Aw hell.

He recoiled, and the foul stench almost made him black out. He wiped his hand on the concrete and decided he needed a new tactic.

Jason yanked the suit coat out of Akio's grip, then shoved his bandaged hand into Akio's face. "Stay," he said as if commanding a dog.

Anger flared in Akio's eyes, but he leaned against the wall and obeyed.

Jason pulled the shattered glass tube out of his belt loop and gave it to Akio. "Here. If anything you don't like comes close, poke it." Akio took the weapon, and Jason slunk out the other end of the alleyway, emerging in a quiet street. He eyed the lines of abandoned cars—some parked long ago, some crashed and askew. As he tramped on the sidewalk, looking for a prime target for his plan, he slid into the suit coat.

The heat almost killed him right then and there.

Good grief, is this wool? How have these guys been wearing this all day?

Even in the dark of night, the L.A. heat was stifling. The city had been tossed into an oven and forgotten about.

He wiped sweat from his eyes with the sleeve of the coat, and he tried and failed to ignore the material's strange odor—some ungodly mix of Fritos, body spray, and armpit. He also unhooked his L.A.P.D badge from his belt and tucked it into a pocket.

Then, footsteps. Frenzied, sporadic, coming in hot.

Jason ducked behind an old clunker and peeked around the tire.

An old man shuffled down the street. His facial hair and tattered clothes suggested he had lived under the sun and stars for a few years. His eyes were wide, hands in pockets, jaw clenched. He grumbled to the air, "You kick me off my corner? Police and armymen on your side, so you think you can kick me off my corner? I'll show you…Someday I'll show you…" He lumbered past Jason and turned a corner.

The entire city has become homeless, pushing the original vagabonds even further to the margins. We've taken to the streets, and thus, we've become invaders.

Jason shook his head to refocus.

The car he was crouching behind looked to be from the '70s or '80s. *As good as any.*

Knowledge of automobiles was a major blind spot for him. In most other subjects, he was functional, but if someone asked him where the drain plug was or what to do when a light on the dashboard started blinking, he could only shrug.

He wriggled midway under the car and wiped his good hand across its dirty, grimy belly. His fingers came away black. Good. He gathered up as much grease and oil and muck as he could, then got back on his feet. He raked his fingers through his hair, scraping his scalp and ruffling intensely, as if doing the most vigorous shampooing of his life.

He lowered his hand and hoped that his black pants, the stolen coat, and his darkened hair were enough for him to slip past the cartel men's attention, in only for a few precious seconds.

Okay, okay, okay. He hyped himself up in his mind. It would take every ounce of nerve he had left in the tank to walk past them without trembling.

What do I do? Traipse right past the gunmen and Marco and Ajax, and just grab Tobin and run? That's ridiculous.

He didn't have an exact plan. But time wasn't on his side. Eventually, the roaming cartel men would find him and Akio, or Ajax would tire of waiting and shoot Tobin, or more of Rodriguez's guns would show up, or an aftershock would hit and send L.A. spiraling into the sea.

Given enough time, something horrible would happen—Jason was sure of it. That was true for the present moment, as well as life as a whole. So he had to act quickly and get away before inevitable tragedy struck.

He turned to make his way to the fallen overpass, where Ajax and Tobin were, but something caught his eye. A flash of white, toward the top of his vision.

Wait. I recognize that.

An ivory spire peeked over the neighborhood of Royal Heights. Jason exhaled. "No way..." He had thought he'd never see that building again. A subconscious part of him had believed the earthquake had surely leveled it.

City Hall.

The words he had once told Ted rippled through his mind: "*If you're ever lost, just make your way to that skyscraper, or to the precinct right next to it. You'll find friends there.*"

City Hall was just a few blocks from the precinct. The Chateau. Jason would give anything to see its boring, beige architecture at that moment.

Friends.

Jason knew what he had to do.

He had tried to hide in plain sight in the riot at the electronics store, thinking the cartel men wouldn't attack them in public. He'd been wrong.

He had fled to the Rebirth Church, thinking the cartel men wouldn't attack them there either. He'd been wrong again. Dead wrong.

Now, he could only see one option: get back to his precinct. Go to the one place he knew for sure he had allies.

And he was staring at a tall, concrete landmark that could lead him there.

Maybe Garth would be there. Hopefully Cheyenne.

Oh, Cheyenne.

That was the first time all day she'd slipped into his thoughts, and he couldn't stop a flood of worry from overtaking him. She was brave and strong, but she had only been the acting captain of the precinct for four months. The new boss was scheduled to arrive soon. They had started the morning going through piles of paperwork, and everyone—Cheyenne most of all—had anticipated a monotonous workday.

How is she dealing with this? Did she even survive the—?

He didn't let himself entertain that notion.

She's still alive. She has to be. Both she and Garth are at the precinct, establishing order, whipping things into shape.

He started walking.

Please.

The rumble of a large engine emitted from a few blocks over. It almost sounded like a tank. *What in the world...?* His curiosity took over, and he sneaked around a few buildings and took a peek.

It was a huge SUV. Dark. Probably armored. Heavy-duty. All the windows were rolled down, which seemed to invite attention. Jason twisted his neck to see inside.

The vehicle was full of armed men. Japanese men, by the looks of it. Each of them held an assault rifle, un-holstered, ready for action. Their expressions were hardened, piercing. And they scanned the streets. Looking for something.

Or someone.

Akio.

Are these Yakuza men, searching for him?

Jason slunk away, headed back for the overpass. If the Yakuza was willing to sift through a broken city to find Akio, they were likely willing to use any means necessary to get him back.

I'm already in a scrape with a cartel. I don't need to add the Yakuza to the list. What's next? The mafia? Triads? The Galactic Empire?

Jason's destination became clearer than ever. He needed to make it to the precinct, to safety. *It's getting crazy out here.*

He was close to the fallen highway. As he walked briskly down the road, he refocused on the task at hand.

The streets were empty, as far as he could see. And hear. In the far distance, toward the middle of the city, the sounds of chaos echoed: sirens, engines, screams, crackling fires, and still-crumbling infrastructure.

But here in Royal Heights, it was like the bottom of the sea. Dark, motionless, silent. And it felt like, at any moment, a vicious predator could emerge from the shadows.

Footsteps. About a block away. Around the corner. Slow, meandering.

Likely one of the cartel men, patrolling around the highway.

Jason took a deep breath. Then another. *If I keep my distance and act like I belong, no one will notice. No one will look close enough to see I'm an imposter.*

He kept walking toward the footsteps, on the opposite side of the street.

Should I nod at him? Are they friendly to each other? I don't know any of their names, except Ajax and Marco.

The footsteps were seconds away from revealing their owner.

This is insane.

At the last moment, Jason dashed between two buildings. A cartel man strolled into view, his gun held slightly aloft. He must've heard Jason's footsteps on this street.

Jason leaned against the wall, heart hammering, close to hyperventilating. His every instinct told him to take cover from men with guns. It felt like suicide to stroll past one of them, out in the open.

He looked around at his entire situation and nearly laughed at the lunacy of it all.

This is more than insane.

Detectives are supposed to conduct interviews, make phone calls, fill out reports, follow clues, build actual cases...not go to war with cartel soldiers after the worst earthquake in L.A. history knocks the city to its knees.

Combined with Abel's reign of terror last summer, his encounter with Roger Shore in December, and this nightmare of a day, it was shaping up to be the worst year of Jason's life.

It was all too much to believe. Hard to stomach.

Not to mention Ted's death. That was the rancid root of his misery. As absurd as it sounded, Jason believed that if his son hadn't died at the hands of a madman, things would better — if not the outside world, at least Jason's psyche.

But with my luck, if Abel hadn't killed Ted last summer, Roger Shore might have killed him in December. Or he could have been crushed in this horrific earthquake.

Jason forced himself to stop speculating. He sidled through the alley, passing another duo of people — a woman and a child, dirty and shell-shocked. They barely acknowledged him as he passed, like they were ghosts...or perhaps he was the ghost.

After a few minutes of sneaking through circuitous routes, he poked his head out from behind a squat laundromat. He had a clear view of the crumbled highway. Tobin sat under it, Marco loomed next to him, and Ajax paced on the street. Two cartel men were also in the vicinity, spread out, guns drawn.

Ajax's floral shirt was gone, replaced with a steel-colored one. He winced as he moved, doing his best to not move his upper-half and, as a result, walking like the Tin Man.

Jason briefly wondered why Ajax had switched his wardrobe, and then he remembered: Red had hit him with a gas lantern. A satisfied smirk played across Jason's lips...but then the full memory came back. Gunshots, bodies, grief.

Despite the hot coat, he shivered.

A voice splintered the air. A male voice, far away. Shouting angrily. In Japanese.

Akio. He sure is good at getting someone's attention, then disappearing.

The voice definitely got Ajax's attention. He bristled at the sound, then started barking at his men. "Go!" he brayed. He staggered — even yelling seemed to agitate the burns on his chest — but he kept giving orders. "Find them and bring them here. Alive. Marco, you go too. Don't let them get away."

Marco and the cartel soldiers sprinted out of sight, toward Akio's voice. Jason hoped Akio had quickly tucked himself away. The gunmen were simultaneously exhausted and restless. They weren't playing around. If they found Akio, mercy would be far from their minds.

And then, Ajax and Tobin were alone. Tobin sat with his knees under his chin, arms around his legs. His shaggy hair covered most of his face, but Jason could see his tapping toes and white knuckles. The boy was scared stiff.

Jason had to act now. The cartel soldiers could come back at any second, and his window of opportunity would slam shut.

Before he could talk himself out of it, Jason stepped out from behind the laundromat. It felt like jumping off a diving-board and into an empty pool.

As soon as he emerged, it struck him how ridiculous his grimy, oily hair must look. His bandaged right hand was a dead giveaway of his identity, so he held it behind his back. And the stolen suit coat was several sizes too big for him. He felt swallowed by material meant for biceps much larger than his.

But it was too late. Ajax had spotted him.

Can't turn back now. Onward.

He walked as quickly as he could without immediately arousing Ajax's suspicion.

Ajax tightened his gaze and yelled something at him. "*Qué estás haciendo?*" He left his gun tucked into his waistband.

From this distance, he thinks I'm one of his. He doesn't recognize me. Yet.

Jason picked up the pace slightly. It was a double-edged sword — the closer he got to Ajax, the more likely Ajax was to recognize him, but the faster he moved, the sooner this would all be over…one way or another.

Tobin, positioned behind Ajax, squinted at Jason, then perked up. He saw through Jason's shoddy disguise, and he was much farther away than Ajax.

The cold spot on Jason's back iced over again. The spot where he'd been sure a bullet was going to land. He ignored it and kept walking.

Ajax moved to meet Jason. His furious face contorted as he shouted. *"Te lo dije—"* His words died in midair, and he snarled. "You!"

Busted.

Without thinking, Jason floored it. He sprinted straight for Ajax. Before Ajax could draw his gun or even say another word, Jason slammed himself into Ajax and tackled him to the pavement.

After all this time, after a full day of running and cowering, it felt good to actually touch Ajax. Moreover, it felt good to hurt him.

Jason landed on top of Ajax's wiry body, and he rammed his knees into his chest—the area the gas lantern had burned most severely.

Ajax howled like an animal caught in barbed wire. He tried to swat Jason off, but the pain almost paralyzed him. His punches were weak, and tears streamed down his face. He screamed curses at the top of his lungs: *"Gah! Te mataré a ti y a tu familia, nunca te librarás de mí!"*

A primal urge overtook Jason's body. His left arm cocked back, seemingly of its own accord, and his fist rocketed against Ajax's jaw. He snarled and roared as he punched again and again.

Ajax thrashed under Jason's weight, screaming from the burns, his face becoming bloodied. He reached out and grabbed the detective's left wrist, halting an incoming strike.

But Jason's instinct would not be so easily stopped. Without a thought, he balled up his injured right hand and pounded it against Ajax's chest.

The agony that rebounded through his body nearly blinded him.

He cradled his bandaged hand close to his body, like it was a baby bird.

Someone grabbed his shoulder from behind. "C'mon!" Tobin dragged him off Ajax.

Jason staggered to his feet and gave Ajax one last look. The cartel teen was sprawled on the ground, taking shallow breaths so as not to agitate his burned chest. Jason wanted to kick his teeth in, but Tobin was right. They had to go while they had a chance.

They sprinted away from the toppled highway, toward the labyrinth of buildings and alleys in which they could hopefully hide. A gunshot sounded, and a window shattered. Jason risked a look over his shoulder and saw that Ajax had drawn his gun. The shot had missed completely—blood was in his eyes, and he was still writhing on the concrete—but it had done its job. The shot told the cartel soldiers that something was wrong, and they'd be on their way back.

The two skidded around the corner of the laundromat and made their way down the street. Jason didn't know where they were headed, just that they had to get away.

As he pumped his lanky legs, Tobin peered up at Jason. He gestured to Jason's hair. "That color doesn't look good on you."

Jason wheezed. "Shut up and run."

Commotion and raised voices came from behind them. The cartel soldiers were on the hunt.

Jason mentally ticked off how many enemies were left. *There's Ajax and Marco, and I think I saw three more suits. Five of them total, armed and trained, coming after us.*

They flew past a group of pedestrians wandering the road. It was a larger group—seven or eight people, seemingly unhurt, but definitely lost and hopeless. One man yelled at them, "Have you seen a little girl?"

It pained Jason not to respond, but he couldn't slow down. By the time it occurred to him that he should've warned them about the pursuing gunmen, he was too far away.

Tobin deviated from their course, headed for a line of parked sedans. "I'm gonna get us a car."

"No," Jason said, out of breath, "too noisy! They'll know exactly where we are, all the time."

Tobin shook his head. "We can be noisy or fast. I choose fast." He selected a red car and clattered to a stop beside it. He tapped on the driver's window and waggled his eyebrows at Jason. "If you please?"

Jason gritted his teeth and reluctantly stopped with Tobin. "If you haven't noticed, we're in a foot chase." He bent his left arm, twisted his hips, and then channeled the full force of his body into his elbow as he smashed the car window.

"Exactly." Tobin unlocked the car, wiped the glass from the seat, slid in, and shut the door. "Let's change that." It might have been Jason's imagination, but it looked like a shadow of a smile crossed

Tobin's face. "Time me," he said, then ducked under the steering wheel.

While Tobin twiddled with wires inside the car, Jason stared at the spot where he was certain the five gunmen were going to appear. About a hundred yards away, at the intersection of two streets. Any second, they were going to catch up and shoot them in the street, while he stood there, waiting for Tobin to—

Vrrooom. The sedan sprung to life.

Jason couldn't lie—he was more than a little impressed.

The broken car window framed Tobin's beaming face. "Time! How'd I do?"

"I have to level with you, I wasn't paying attention."

"What?!" Tobin looked like his pride had taken a hit. "That was world-record stuff, and you were *distracted*?!"

"I'm a little busy." Jason jogged around to the passenger's door. "How'd you do that so fast?"

"I'm good with my hands."

Jason started to respond, but an angry shout cut him off: "There they are!"

The cartel men had arrived. Tempers aflame. Guns blazing. They stampeded down the street, straight for Jason and Tobin.

Jason went for the door handle, but he missed a few times, his spike in adrenaline making everything ten times harder. Finally, he wrapped his fingers around the handle and pulled. But nothing happened. He yelled into the car, "Will you unlock it?!"

"Oh!" Tobin scrambled for the locking controls. "My bad, my bad!"

"Yeah, your bad!" *Click.* The door unlocked, and Jason ripped it open and cannonballed onto the seat. "Go!"

Tobin didn't need more encouragement. He slammed his foot onto the gas pedal. The sedan squealed forward, and Tobin flipped on the headlights. Dirty beams of yellow light shot out of the car's nose.

Jason squinted to see a street sign up ahead. "Hang a right and honk a few times," he said quickly.

Tobin hesitated for a fraction of a second, then nodded. "Aye-aye." He whipped the wheel to the side, and the sedan nearly toppled like a tumbleweed. But they made it, and he bashed his fist on the center of the steering wheel.

The old horn bleated into the neighborhood, and Jason studied the dark streets, silently willing Akio to show up. This was near the alley where they had parted ways.

"Slow down a bit," Jason said.

"Are you crazy?!" Tobin yipped, even as he eased his foot off the gas. His eyes also studied the alleys and shadows.

Then...

Clip clap clip clap.

The unmistakable sound of penny loafers slapping against concrete.

Akio popped out of an alleyway, clutching the broken fluorescent tube like it was a relay-racer's baton. A bit of blood decorated the glass's jagged end, and Jason hoped it belonged to a nosy cartel soldier.

Tobin's face lit up. "Hey," he yelled out the window, "hey, Akia!"

"Akio," Jason corrected.

"Yeah, Akio!" Tobin said without missing a beat. "Here!" He hit the horn again. "Here!"

Akio sprinted toward the car, just as, down the street, a few cartel men rounded the corner. They snarled and shouted and let loose a volley of bullets.

BANG SMASH BANG THUNK.

The sedan's back window shattered, and it sounded like the trunk was being drilled full of holes.

Good thing Akio isn't in that trunk—

Jason cut off his internal gallows-humor. He slapped Tobin's shoulder. "Speed up! We need to get out of here."

"But Akio!"

"He'll make it," Jason huffed as he wriggled his way into the backseat. He hit his bad right hand a few times, which made him want to vomit, but he had no choice but to ignore the pain. "Faster!"

The sedan revved as Tobin pressed the gas as much as he dared. Buildings and dead lampposts whizzed by.

Jason opened the back door and gestured to the sprinting Akio. "C'mon! Get in!"

Akio pumped his arms harder, and his face scrunched up with effort, but he didn't get any closer to the moving car. In fact, the distance started to grow.

"Go, go, go!" Jason stretched out his good hand, trying desperately to close the gap. "You're almost there," he lied.

Akio let out a guttural cry, as if exhaling all of the day's anger and fear at once would somehow propel him to safety.

"I'm slowing down," Tobin said from the front seat.

"You slow down," Jason snapped, "we all die." Then to Akio: "We haven't come this far just to—"

BANG.

Akio stumbled and winced, as if he'd developed a cramp in his side.

BANG BANG BANG.

He dropped the glass tube and toppled to the ground. His momentum caused him to roll for a bit, until he stopped in a bloody heap.

A scream was trapped in Jason's throat, almost strangling him.

Tobin had his eyes fixed on the road ahead, and he obeyed Jason—he sped up. The car zoomed down the street, and Akio's body got smaller and smaller every second.

Jason waited for the Yakuza man to hop up and keep running. Or least move an arm or lift his head.

But no. He didn't budge. Simultaneously limp and frozen.

"C'mon, man!" Tobin shouted his encouragement out the window, oblivious to the fact that Akio was no longer running behind the car. "You can do it!"

Jason settled in the backseat, numb, exhausted, beaten. He slammed the door shut.

Tobin whipped his head around at the noise. His eyes took it all in: Jason's ashen expression, the closed door, the silence.

The silence. The cartel men weren't shooting anymore. They'd accomplished their mission.

The car came to an intersection. They turned a corner and sped onward, leaving the body behind. Out of sight.

28

So hot.

And, at the same time, so cold.

Akio had his face pressed against the pavement. It stung his skin, what with the bits of gravel and residual heat from the day's sun. He tried to wave at the car carrying the policeman and the boy, but he couldn't move. He tried to yell out—"Wait for me! Come back! I'm so scared right now!"—but the words were lodged in his chest.

The straight, unwavering line of cause and effect had led him here.

Turns out, nothing had been able to save him. No matter how good he was with numbers, or how much he drank, or the amount of money he accumulated…Every moment of his life had been a brick in the path that led to this city, this night, and this death.

Footsteps approached him. He couldn't crane his neck to see who they belonged to, but he had a pretty good idea. A foot kicked him over, so he could gape at the hazy sky.

A bloody face stared down at him. A teenaged kid in a gray shirt. Akio could see flecks of stubble sprouting from his chin. The kid couldn't even grow facial hair yet.

Another voice said something in Spanish. A few cartel men gathered around Akio, speaking jubilantly, slapping each other's backs, smiling and celebrating as if they'd just won a casual soccer game.

Not the teenager, though. He stared right at Akio with steely eyes.

It was terrifying.

Marco was there. The cartel hulk who had thrown him into the trunk of a car earlier that day. He man wore a satisfied smile.

Akio would rather deal with the muscular beast than the callous teenager.

The fear, in an odd way, was worse than the actual bullets. He didn't feel his wounds. It was more like he could feel blood leaving his body. Negative-pain. Air seeping out of a hole in a balloon.

But raw fear hammered in his chest with all the force of a battering ram. If he could talk, he'd be blubbering and weeping and begging for his life. Good thing his mouth wasn't cooperating.

The teenager raised his gun, its barrel pointed at the center of Akio's forehead.

Akio wanted to thank him. If this was the way to get rid of the fear, he welcomed it. He just hoped it wouldn't hurt too much when the bullet pierced his skull.

At the last second, he thought of his dog Toshi. He wanted to die clutching a happy memory.

29

The crack of the gunshot vibrated the air, then faded to nothing. A few blocks away, people screamed, but it sounded like they were wise enough to run away from the violence, not toward it.

Ajax wiped blood from his eyes tucked his gun away. His scuffle with the cop had left him with more scrapes than he wanted to admit.

All four of his men stood around, congratulating one another. As if they'd done something important. As if they hadn't spent all day and night chasing a hostage Marco had lost in the first place.

Marco's smile was the biggest. No doubt, he was relieved that the Yakuza man was dead. Thoughts of returning to Gore Rodriguez probably filled his head. Returning to Xanadu and getting some sort of reward. Or, at the very least, not being killed for letting the hostage escape.

It got under Ajax's skin, seeing Marco smile so big. All that muscle and bravado, and he couldn't even catch one man. Ajax had stepped up and taken care of business. He'd even pulled the trigger, when it came down to it.

Marco dug his phone out of his suit coat pocket. He slid to the camera feature, turned on the flash, and took a clear photo of the Yakuza's bloody corpse.

Walleye chuckled. "Think Rodriguez will hang that up in his house?"

Marco laughed in response.

Ajax withdrew his own phone. It was cracked and several years older than Marco's, but it still worked just fine. There was no cell signal, but he didn't need that. He snapped a picture of the body too, then put his phone back in his pocket.

Marco's meaty hand rested on his shoulder. "Good job tonight, Hector."

Under his breath, Ajax hissed, "That's not my name." He kept his temper at a simmer and started walking.

"Where are you going?" Marco called after him.

"To finish things up."

"Huh?" Marco jogged ahead and placed his hulking frame in Ajax's path, forcing him to stop. "The job *is* finished."

Ajax wanted to spit. He said, "Really? You're just gonna let the cop and that kid get away?" He turned and jeered at the other three gunmen. "After you chased them around this neighborhood all night, and they made you look like morons?" His voice rose with his anger, straining the burns on his chest. "They're just gonna go on with their lives!"

"And so are we," Marco said firmly, thinking he'd ended the discussion. He fiddled with a ring on his left hand, which Ajax hadn't noticed until now.

They were all so weak. Ajax wanted to punch Marco in his bruised jaw. Right where it would hurt most.

Ajax skirted around Marco and kept walking in the direction the car had gone. He couldn't stop thinking about pointing his gun in the cop's face. Punching him in the ribs. Plucking out his teeth like berries from a bush.

"The man is dead," Marco pressed. "We're done here."

Ajax didn't slow down, nor did he look back as he spoke. "Then you can be the one to tell Rodriguez that the people who offended him are still breathing. See how he takes it."

They didn't have an answer for that one.

But the truth was, Ajax didn't care about Rodriguez. He didn't care about honor or retribution or his own reputation. He was used to being disliked. He was used to being the smartest person in the room, yet continually disregarded. He was used to being berated and kicked around like an unwelcome dog.

Most of all, he was used to feeling nothing in the face of violence.

From the day he had seen Salva killed outside a greenhouse on the Xanadu grounds, he had felt the itch. He had seen a man murdered in front of him, yet he was entirely unmoved. Not scared. Not repulsed. Not aroused. Nothing.

And today, he had killed two men. Still, nothing. His heartrate barely rose when he pulled the trigger.

He didn't want to kill simply to kill—he wanted to feel something. He wanted to scratch the itch he hadn't been able to reach.

It wasn't bloodlust. It was the *lust for bloodlust.*

And this cop and kid—two people he hated so much—were the best chance he could see. He trembled with anger just thinking about them. Surely snuffing them out would feel incredible.

Or at least...something.

A man followed him. It was the gunman with a lazy eye. Walleye, he called him, since he hadn't learned his name. Nor did he intend to, at this point.

"I'm with ya, Ajax. Let's go kill those cockroaches." He cocked his gun to prove his point.

"Put the safety on," Ajax sighed with venom.

He almost looked back to see if anyone else was coming, but he heard no more footsteps. He didn't care.

He had started the day wanting more than anything to impress Gore Rodriguez—from wearing his colorful shirt, to looking for the missing hostage.

Now, he was walking away from his fellow cartel gunmen and the body of the man they'd been hunting.

"Hey," Walleye said to him, "I don't have any more ammo. Can you spare a magazine or two?"

Ajax growled. "Shut up." This idiot was ruining his moment.

He wondered about the look on Marco's face. Was he sad? Scared? A mix of both?

A quick glance would be worth it, Ajax decided. He bent his neck to see how Marco and the other gunmen were taking this.

But they were already walking away, in the opposite direction. They didn't care either.

"Fine." Ajax decided to pretend that he hadn't looked back. He stamped his feet as he marched in the direction of the people he wanted to kill more than anyone else in the world.

30

Tobin gripped the steering wheel so hard, his fingers started to tingle.

Akio was gone. Tobin hadn't actually seen it happen, but he was certain. The men with guns had been shooting, and then Akio wasn't there anymore.

The scores of dead bodies littered in the street were seared into the backs of his eyelids, and he saw them every time he blinked…and now there was Akio. A man he'd spent the day with and walked beside.

They didn't really know each other all that well. But he had a feeling that Akio's face and voice would show up in his nightmares for years to come.

His feet were going asleep, so he shifted his weight. His legs were pretty long, but in order to reach the gas and brake pedals, he had to perch at the edge of the driver's seat.

He'd talked a big game earlier in the day, telling Detective Flynn that he could hotwire cars. And that was true, but he had very little experience with that. And even less experience driving. His brief escape from Detective Flynn earlier that day was pretty much the extent of his experience.

He knew *how* to drive. But he also knew *how* to play basketball and *how* to make perfect chocolate chip cookies. That didn't keep him from tripping over his shoelaces and burning every cookie he touched.

Still, he was doing pretty well, all things considered. Hands at ten and two, like he'd always heard.

The car's headlights sliced through the night. The streets were choked with crashed or empty cars, and Tobin sometimes had to drive slowly to slink around them. It was hard to navigate, like a maze on the back of a weirdly-themed restaurant's kids' menu. There were a few people walking on the streets too. They would stare at the car as it passed, as if it were part of a sad, lonely parade.

He looked in the rearview mirror, at Detective Flynn. The man had his head in his hand, shoulders slumped. At a glance, with his greasy hair and suit coat, he looked like one of the bad guys. He hadn't said a word since he shut the door…leaving Akio behind.

No. He didn't want to think about Akio. He didn't want to blink either. Any flash of darkness would bring up the dead faces.

Detective Flynn looked about as low as Tobin had ever seen a person, as if a gust of wind would disintegrate him. He seemed really sad about losing Akio…which was weird. Tobin didn't think they liked each other very much.

It didn't matter, though. Well, it mattered that Akio was gone. Tobin didn't want anyone to get hurt, but at the same time, they still had to keep going. They weren't safe yet.

Probably.

For some reason, even though the shooters weren't around, Tobin felt anxious. Like a giant boulder was rolling toward him, but he couldn't see it yet.

Yeah, they weren't safe.

He needed Detective Flynn to get it together. There was no way Tobin could make it alone. He didn't even know where to go.

The solemn man in the backseat didn't look like someone who could lead them to safety. He looked exhausted.

All at once, the day caught up to Tobin. He hadn't eaten or slept for a long time. His senses had been cranked up to eleven since the afternoon. His family was missing, best case. Men with guns had been behind him all day.

He was drained. Empty. A blanket of gauze wrapped itself around his head. Maybe if he closed his eyes for just a minute, he could recharge. Like when he plugged his old iPod Touch into an outlet for a second, and the battery jumped back up. A power nap, is what his mom would call it.

The images of all the dead bodies didn't bother him so much. He was too tired. He closed his eyes and drifted off. Just for a second.

And just for a second, he forgot he was driving.

"Tobin!"

Flynn's voice jolted him awake. The car's headlights illuminated a brick wall five feet in front of them. Tobin didn't even have time to take his foot off the gas.

Part 4:
Aftershocks

31

Jason's forehead slammed into the back of the seat in front of him, jostling his brain within his skull. His body instinctively tensed up, which made the impact even more rattling.

Hisssssssss.

Smoke seeped out of the crumpled hood, and the windshield had cracked like a spider's web. The headlights lit up the brick wall they'd rammed into.

Jason tried to get out of the car, but his bones felt brittle, like porcelain. Every inch was a struggle. He moaned as he opened the door and fell out.

"Tobin?"

The kid sat in the front seat, frozen. Stunned. Dazed. Trapped by a musty airbag.

Jason ripped the rumpled door open. The kid had been smart enough to fasten his seatbelt, so Jason undid it and hauled Tobin out.

Jason assessed the damage to the car. He was no automotive expert, but it looked out of commission.

Fortunately, Tobin had been driving pretty slowly as he maneuvered among the debris in the streets. If he'd been going full-speed, they would've both been killed.

Lucky. They were still alive and had to keep trudging through this hell.

He slumped against the metal frame and nearly lost it. Screams and words and emotions he had been repressing chose that moment to ransack his mind. He squeezed the side of his head, as if physically holding in his rage.

He was hungry. Thirsty. Beaten and broken. Defeated. And so tired.

His head felt fuzzy, full of thick, hot cotton. His eyes itched from the inside out.

With a primal yell, he kicked the sedan's front tire. It did nothing but stub his toes, which made him even angrier.

"I didn't ask for this. I didn't ask for any of this!" He felt abandoned. Adrift on a raft in the middle of a tempest.

Tobin's small voice came from behind him. "I'm sorry…"

Jason spun to face him, practically seething. "I know. Everyone's sorry. Me most of all. Wanna know why?" His unstable emotions tumbled out of his mouth, and as much as he wanted to stop them, he couldn't contain the deluge. "Because everything is my fault. Everything. I could've killed Abel, but I *didn't*, and he killed my son. You got in the one car in the world that made us a target, but only because *I* was chasing you. *I* led the gunmen to the church too, and they killed who knows how many innocent people. I dragged Akio around because he was *my* responsibility. I said I needed to protect him because I had to act like 'the opposite of a bad guy,' and guess what? He's dead now. *I* led him to his death and left his body behind — might as well have killed him. If you were smart," he stuck a wavering finger in Tobin's face, "you'd leave me and find your own way, because if you stick around, odds are you'll be dead soon."

With that, he marched away from the wrecked car.

Everything's wrecked. What's the point?

He recalled earlier in the evening, he had considered lying down on the pavement, closing his eyes, and simply slipping away into nothingness. He had been so bruised and trampled, any other option had sounded like sweet relief.

Now, he wanted to do the very same thing, but for nihilistically altruistic reasons. If he crawled under a dumpster and fell asleep — or died, for all he cared — nothing would matter. The city would still be broken, innocent people would still be dead, and life would continue on its chaotic path. Everything was wrecked, and Jason couldn't fix it.

But at the same time, if I disappeared at this very moment, I might be able to do some good. I wouldn't get anyone else killed. I wouldn't lead anyone else to slaughter. Taking myself out of the equation might be the noblest thing possible.

He looked for a place to go. A car to hide under. A dark corner where his body wouldn't get in the way. He didn't want his corpse to add to the clutter in the streets.

I'll also need something sharp. A quick slice across the jugular…

Small footsteps followed closely behind him. He looked, and Tobin stared right back.

Jason's tight muscles loosened. Just a bit.

I can't leave him alone. Even if I know he's better off without me, he doesn't seem to believe that. As long as he thinks I'm his best bet, I can't desert him.

"So what next?" Tobin's voice was artificially light, an attempt at being his old sarcastic self. Over the course of the day, something had changed in the boy. Something had broken that likely would never be fully mended.

Jason tried to moisten his deathly-dry lips, then pointed to the center of the city. "We're going there."

Tobin noticed the white building peering over the skyline. "What's that?"

"City Hall."

"Why're we going to City Hall?"

"Next to it. That's where my friends are."

Tobin looked up at him. "You have friends?"

"Not a ton."

They walked in silence for a few minutes. The thought crossed Jason's mind that they should get another car, but he felt awkward ordering Tobin to hotwire one. He decided he would soon—his feet felt worn to nubs.

He realized he was still wearing Manny's suit coat. He slid out of the material, let it drop to the ground, and kept walking. Even the slight breeze created by his own movement was better than being cooped up in that woolly cocoon.

His right hand throbbed in its necktie-turned-bandage. Despite his better judgment, he lifted the material to peek at it. His fingers had turned a sickening rainbow of colors—like gasoline in a puddle.

Nausea swept over him, and he regretted looking.

City Hall was within sight...but still so far away. That was one of the greatest pains of L.A. living: A person might be able to see their destination, but it'll take them hours to get there.

Royal Heights was roughly four miles from City Hall. Not far at all, on paper. But when you take traffic and detours into account, it might as well be lightyears away.

And in this case, "traffic" and "detours" meant "damage caused by the worst earthquake in the city's history" and "gunmen out to kill them," respectively.

They passed a low wooden fence, which was a fresh sight, compared to the concrete walls and brick alleys they'd been living in all day. Lawns, driveways, chimneys, porches...They were still in Royal Heights, but they'd left the realm of apartments and small businesses and had entered the swamp of overpriced, underdeveloped houses.

Cars lined both sides of the street, many of them with flat tires or massive dents. Mailboxes were knocked over. Windows were shattered, and a few trees laid on the ground, their massive roots trying to keep them connected to the earth. The earthquake had hit this residential wing of the world hard.

Patches of blood were scattered on the sidewalk and street, but there were no stray bodies left to rot out in the open.

Did people drag the dead and injured inside? That was the only logical option Jason could see.

It looked a lot like the street where Jason had chased Anthony Reynaldo earlier that afternoon. Or was it yesterday, technically? Except that had been closer to the center of the city, where money tended to pool. Here, the cars were cheaper, lawns browner, and houses scruffier.

Jason's feet got in each other's way for a few steps. His body was depleted, and he'd reached the point where his steps were off-track and his head was filled with helium.

If he cared the least bit about his own well-being, he would be desperate for food and water.

But he wasn't.

He wasn't sure what he would do after he dropped Tobin off at the precinct. Strangely, he didn't know whether or not he actually wanted to see Cheyenne and Garth. An hour ago, he would've given anything to be in the presence of his friends. Now, everything was shrouded in an apathetic fog.

I don't care if I eat or drink. I don't care if I keel over in this heat. I don't think I care if I die.

The thought should have shocked him, made him stop and gather himself. It didn't.

I just have to get Tobin out of here. Into someone else's hands. That's the one thing I care about.

An image flashed through his mind, as clear as day, like a morbid Renaissance painting:

Ajax, shooting Red.

Then another:

Ajax, shooting Akio.

Lastly, a premonition:

Ajax, shooting Tobin.

Okay, there's one more thing I care about—I want to be the one to kill Ajax.

I've dealt with some serious scum over the years, but I haven't killed anyone. Not for lack of trying, but still.

That's gonna change today. I swear, Ajax is going to be my first kill.

The world would be better without him.

It's up to me to take out the trash.

Jason's instincts tingled. His ears picked up the sound of footsteps behind him. "Are you serious...?"

He leered over his shoulder, and there they were, like creatures from a recurring nightmare. A man in a suit ran toward them, his face twisted into a gleeful snarl. He seemed all-too eager to get to the killing. Looming behind him was Ajax, his gray shirt blending into the night and making him look like a floating, spectral head.

Jason only saw the one suited gunman.

The others must be close by.

Maybe the rest of the gunmen were circling around the houses, waiting to ambush them farther down the street. He felt surrounded. Trapped.

A shout erupted from Jason's chest. "You already killed him! Leave us alone!"

The suited man didn't listen and kept running straight at them. He was close enough for Jason to see he had intense, charcoal eyes, one of them lopsided like a chameleon's.

Jason shot out a hand, grasped Tobin's shoulder, and wrenched the boy behind his own body. "Stay back," he hissed, glaring at the charging cartel man.

Oddly enough, in that moment, he felt like a bull, and the cartel man was a foolhardy matador who had picked the wrong fight.

The lazy-eyed man didn't divert from his path even slightly. When he was mere feet from Jason, he let out a celebratory trill. "Gotchu, kid! I gotchu again!" He opened his arms, ready to tackle Jason to the ground...

...but Jason was ready. Adrenaline flooded his veins, washing out the cobwebs and fatigue. His vision sharpened, and he moved smoothly for the first time in hours. He knew it was temporary, but it was all he needed.

He swerved under the man's arms, slammed a fist into his gut, and put him in an iron headlock. He held the man in front of himself as a shield, and he said to Tobin, "Move, move while we can." Jason shuffled backward, keeping the stunned cartel soldier between himself and Ajax.

Ajax walked toward them, reaching for his waist.

The man tried to squirm out of Jason's grip, but Jason kneed him in the back and crouched down, so that he was shielded as much as possible.

"Get back, Ajax!" Jason's voice shook the quiet street. "I'll crack his neck right now. I swear, if you take one more step—"

BANG.

The man slumped in Jason's arms, and he struggled to keep the dead weight upright. Tobin exhaled a breath of horror.

Oh God.

Ajax strode toward them, gun outstretched, eyes flashing. "Quit hiding."

The corpse in Jason's arms was as heavy and unwieldy as a sack of rocks. But he couldn't drop it. If he did, there'd be nothing but air between them and Ajax's wrath.

The cold spot on his back multiplied and spread all over his body.

"Stay behind me," he said to Tobin, trying to sound confident, but his voice cracked. Tobin nodded...or, at least, Jason thought he nodded. He could've been shaking so violently that his head bobbed.

Ajax twisted his arm side to side, up and down, trying to get a clear shot around the body Jason was propping up. He grimaced and cried out in frustration, "Just drop it and die!"

"*Hey!*" Someone shouted. The voice made both Jason and Ajax freeze. "Back off!"

A porch door swung open, then clattered shut. Brittle footsteps shuffled down the wooden steps, across the lawn, and into the street. An old woman, as fragile as a newspaper, planted herself between Ajax and Jason. She was armed with nothing but a Depression-era scowl...and a double-barrel shotgun. She leveled the terrifying weapon at Ajax's chest. "Get outta here. Now."

Ajax took a step back, but he didn't lower his handgun. "This has nothing to do with you, *abuela*," he said, trying very hard to keep his voice even.

"This is our street, piss-breath," the woman growled, "so this has nothing to do with *you*."

And just like that, dozens of people appeared on their own porches, clutching baseball bats, kitchen knives, and gardening tools. Not a single one of them was under seventy years old, but Jason wouldn't dare challenge any of them to a fight.

Ajax wavered, his finger against the trigger. Just a small flick would result in a bullet. His hateful glare could pierce a tank's hull, but inch by inch, he lowered his gun. He turned and started marching back down the street.

The woman said, "Leave the gun."

Without turning, Ajax scoffed, "No way." He slid the gun in his waistband and eventually disappeared in the darkness.

Jason released a breath and let the dead cartel man flop to the ground. His hands were covered in the man's hot, syrupy blood. He gave Tobin a glance, and the kid quickly wiped his eyes. He brushed his shaggy hair back, trying to look tough, obviously hoping Jason hadn't seen his tears.

The woman lowered the shotgun as if it weighed a hundred pounds. She gave Jason and Tobin a curious but not unkind look.

A few residents came down from their porches, gathered the dead cartel man, and began carrying him away.

"We've been taking pictures of any bodies we find and looking after 'em," the woman explained. "Figure the government or the city or someone will come by eventually and want to know the full damage. A dead census." She shook her head at the morbid idea.

Jason cradled his damaged hand and stared at the spot where Ajax had disappeared. "You should've shot him. Would've been easier for everyone."

She puffed out a laugh. "Nah, I hate guns." She tapped the shotgun in her hands with a spindly finger. "No bullets. Haven't had any since 1992."

The street had come to life. Every porch had someone standing on it, watching the scene. Despite the heat, many wore cardigans or had blankets wrapped around themselves. There were even a few small dogs at some of their feet, keeping watch.

Jason gave the woman a curt nod and introduced himself. "I'm Jason. That's Tobin."

She slung the shotgun across her shoulders, and, even though Jason knew it wasn't loaded, he couldn't help but shy away from the barrels. She stuck out a hand. "Val."

Before Jason could awkwardly shake her hand with his undamaged left one, Tobin swooped in and grabbed on. He yanked her hand up and down like a wanderer in the desert who had found a water pump.

She smiled, revealing teeth like kernels of corn, "Pleasure's mine, Tobin, Jason. Careful, son, or I'll end up gimpy like your buddy." She pulled her hand out of Tobin's grip and playfully shook it, as if he'd injured it.

Jason cleared his throat to inject himself back in as the leader of the conversation. "We have to keep moving. That madman only left because he thought he would lose. He'll be back."

"Where're ya headed?"

"Center of town."

"Well," she rubbed her forehead, "wish we could offer you some help." The deep wrinkles in her face sagged even more, as if the weight of the day was dragging her down.

"You already did," he said. "Thank you."

"Yeah," Tobin added. "We'd be sliced into salsa right now if you hadn't showed up."

Jason felt that he should say more, or maybe offer the residents some sort of reward. Or at least give Val a hug. But, for some reason, he could only say, "So how much? In your dead census?"

Val sighed. "On our street, seventeen. I bet it was way, way worse in areas with tall buildings. All that glass and stuff falling down, smashing on people, hitting their heads…Sounds like a horror movie."

You're not wrong.

She continued. "A few friends on this street had heart attacks, one got trapped under a china cabinet and bled out. A lot of people from other parts of the neighborhood wandered in, and the injuries they got elsewhere took their toll. They just stopped where they stood and…dropped to the ground. Bam." She nodded, her eyes far away. "Yeah. Seventeen. So far."

The last two words made Jason shudder. He liked Val and owed her Tobin's life, but he was overwhelmed with the urge to get moving. "Time to go." He turned to leave, gaze fixed on City Hall standing miles away.

Without a word, Tobin scuttled away from Jason, up a set of stairs to a house's porch. He knelt down and scratched one of the dogs behind the ears. It was short and floppy. Maybe a beagle, but Jason wasn't an expert.

A minute later, Tobin rejoined Jason, and they started walking down the street, past the patrol of houses, their windows like wide-open eyes, never sleeping, always watchful.

Tobin jutted out an arm, thumb up, trying to gauge how far away the white building was. Jason decided it was more merciful to not tell him.

Only three miles. So close, yet so painfully far away.

32

Ajax stalked through Royal Heights, absolutely fuming. Ready to burst. If he opened his mouth, he would spit bullets.

A phrase from one of the motivation tapes he listened to briefly ran through his mind: *"When anger starts to overwhelm you, remember: Anger is always a bad driver. You're in charge of where your car goes."*

Internally, he told the tape to shut up.

For the first time all day, he was outgunned. Outmatched. The kid and the cop had evaded him for so long by being weasely and slipping out of his grasp. Always just barely, if Ajax could say so himself. But this time, he'd been alone, and a weapon bigger than his had been pointed at his heart.

And…

He kicked a metal garbage can, and it made a satisfying *gong* sound.

And it'd been a bunch of mummies who had threatened him. Dinosaurs with dentures, fuzzy slippers, and pants tugged up to their nipples.

It made him want to kill something.

The bullet he had sent into Walleye's chest hadn't affected him in the slightest. Before, Ajax had been a little disconcerted by the fact that violence didn't faze him. Now, he was frustrated. Angry. Rivers of lava coursed through his body, and he needed to let them out. But he couldn't.

It didn't seem to matter whether he killed a preacher, a gang rival, or one of his own men. It was all the same as stepping on a bug. And, without an effective outlet, the pent-up fury consuming his body grew more and more intense.

He'd been down this street before. At least, he thought he had. The whole neighborhood was starting to blend together.

A group of survivors sat on a curb, passing a package of trail mix between them. Ajax drew his gun and pointed it at the lady currently holding the bag. "I've killed three men today," he said, jumping right in. "Drop the bag and leave."

The lady shook, set the bag on the pavement, and started to crawl away, not wanting to make the sudden moves necessary to stand up. She sniveled like a baby, face scrunched up, heaving for breaths. "Please don't...Please, please."

One of the men in the group decided to be a hero. "Whoa, whoa, punk," he snarled as he stood. "How dare—"

Ajax shot him in the knee. The man shrieked as he fell to the ground, and the rest of the group demonstrated their loyalty by scattering. Like a bunch of bugs. Ajax picked up the bag and dumped a mouthful of trail mix into his mouth.

"I'll rip you apart," the man said between his pathetic gasps for air. "You'll be—"

Again, Ajax didn't wait to hear the rest of his threat. He shot the man in the head. The gunshot rippled through the neighborhood, and all was quiet.

Nope. He didn't feel a thing.

He finished the trail mix and tossed the bag aside. With a dark smile, he wondered if littering would give him the buzz he wanted.

After returning the gun to his waistband, he cleared his throat and started yelling. "Akio! I found him! I found Akio!" He walked down the street like a doomsday preacher, letting the world know that he had found the Yakuza's missing man.

Five minutes passed. Then ten. Thirty. His voice was almost gone, scraping against his dry throat.

"I found Akio..." He tried to swallow, but he had no moisture in his mouth. He wished the survivors he'd come across had been sharing a bottle of Gatorade rather than such a salty snack.

Then, he heard an engine. A big one. An armored SUV rolled around a corner and approached him. A man leaned his head out a passenger window, and Ajax recognized him—it was the Yakuza operative he'd met outside the gas station. One of the soldiers looking for the hostage Ajax had killed.

Ajax raised both hands to show he had nothing to hide, and he winced as the burned skin on his torso pulled upward. The pain kindled his anger toward the L.A. cop, and in that way, it felt pretty good.

"Hi," he said to the SUV full of Yakuza soldiers. "I'm Ajax."

The doors popped open, and six tactically trained men filed out. They moved with precision, not an ounce of energy wasted. Nasty machine guns hung from their belts.

"And? We heard you yelling." The man who appeared to be their leader spat his words like spent ammunition cartridges. "Talk."

Ajax slowly—very, very slowly, making it clear he wasn't going for his gun—pulled his cell phone out of his pocket. He unlocked the screen and turned it toward the men.

They gasped. One even staggered back, as if pushed.

"I found the man Akio like this," Ajax said, simmering with anger. "Shot in the street. Brutal. In the head. And I saw who did it, running away. I'm sure he killed your man Madoka too."

The operatives seethed and reached for their guns. Ajax continued, knowing the answer to the question they were about to ask:

"It was a Los Angeles policeman. He's killed people close to me too, and I want to help you find him."

33

As Jason and Tobin trudged toward the heart of the city, they started seeing more and more people adrift on the streets…and the damage became worse and worse. The taller the building, the farther it could fall. There were fires everywhere. Piles of debris acted as makeshift gravestones, because there were undoubtedly bodies buried under each one that would only be discovered later.

More than once, their path was blocked by an entire skyscraper that had come down. The air was thick with dust, grime, and crystallized glass. Survivors staggered every which way like they were zombies — numb, shell-shocked, and desperately hungry. It was nightmarish, and they had to find circular routes around in order to get back on track.

Jason had never seen a tank before, but he saw one rolling through the Los Angeles financial district.

Chic boutiques, high-end restaurants, prime spots for Instagram pics, powerful places of business…They had all been impacted. At best, they were shaken and would never be the same again. And at worst, they'd been wiped from the map.

Lines of survivors wrapped around the city's center. They waited for clothes, water, food, or information. They waited to hear from their families, friends, or the government. They couldn't do anything, so they waited.

At one point, as Jason and Tobin passed a hundred people in line for water, Tobin muttered, "I wonder if my mom made it here."

It was the first time Jason had heard Tobin mention his family in hours. He didn't respond — it wouldn't help to say that his mom was probably under the ton of bricks that used to be Tobin's apartment building in Royal Heights.

U.S. soldiers and L.A.P.D. cops were increasingly present too. Their uniforms were sweaty and stained with soot, but even the sight of them gave Jason comfort. There was no way Ajax would try anything here.

A few police officers recognized him, but they took one look at his dour expression and didn't say anything to him. One officer sporting a volleyball of hair widened her eyes and stepped aside from him, as if he were carrying an infectious disease.

"Detective," Danielle Zahn murmured as he passed.

"Danielle. Good to see you."

"Mmm." She pursed her lips and nodded once, not directly responding to what he'd said. "Rough night?"

He looked at his ravaged clothes and bandaged hand. "A bit. It's…It's laundry day. My nicer shirts are at the cleaners'."

She didn't smile or laugh. Instead, she fixed her gaze on the other people inhabiting the streets, trying to look busy and move on from the conversation. "Be safe."

Jason swallowed and kept walking. *I may have escaped Fury Road out there, but now I have to deal with my other problems again.*

A horrifying slideshow of Abel, Roger Shore, and Anthony Reynaldo flashed through his mind.

"That one of your friends?" Tobin interrupted his gory thoughts.

Jason nodded and weakly said, "I think so."

They kept walking, past the destruction, past the desperation, past the despondency. No matter what he saw, Jason kept walking, and Tobin plodded beside him.

The traffic issue was far worse downtown than it was in Royal Heights. Wrecked, abandoned, and fire-scorched cars clogged the roads. There was even a city bus on the sidewalk, like a beached whale, its tires and engine having been looted.

And then, he saw it. A beige concrete cube, with a massive window on the third floor. The Chateau. Jason's precinct. Blinding floodlights lit up the block, letting everyone know who was in charge.

Dozens of cars were parked in front of the precinct. Police black-and-whites, mainly. This was probably done on purpose to project an image of strong police presence.

If there were dozens of cars, there were just as many actual cops running to and fro, carrying supplies, relaying messages, or simply looking harried and authoritative.

A few blocks away, City Hall stood tall and proud over the shorter, mostly damaged buildings. Even though it was unlit, the white architecture glowed like a lighthouse.

Standing just outside the Chateau's front door, holding a clipboard and giving orders to a mass of paramedics, was acting-captain Cheyenne Childers.

Jason could barely believe it. His feet felt swaddled in cement, but he started galloping toward her.

She had a black eye, and part of her hair was matted to her neck with dried blood. But she looked okay.

She's okay.

He opened his mouth to shout her name, but instead, someone called his.

"Jason? Is that you?!"

Garth Jameson emerged from the crowd. He was filthy and dog-tired, his perfectly trimmed hair was in disarray, and his shoes had lost their shine, but his slim necktie was still cinched all the way up.

Despite everything, Jason stopped, smiled, and held out his arms. The two detectives collided in an aggressive hug—one that resulted from two people literally thinking the other might be dead.

"I thought you were gone," Garth said into Jason's shoulder.

The two separated, and Jason felt himself nearly collapse. "It's been a hell of a night." His voice caught in his throat as he thought about the church, the cold spots all over his body, losing Akio...The people who were now dead, thanks to him.

Garth turned to Tobin and gave a tired smile. "Is this Tobin Vivek? Never thought I'd see you again. Have you grown since I last saw you?"

Tobin pushed back his unruly hair. "You must have me confused with someone else," he mugged. "I'm a law-abiding citizen who never gets chased in the streets by cops."

Garth exhaled a laugh. "Glad to see both of you."

Jason said, "Garth, I…" He had to fight through a barricade of grief to finish. "Red's gone."

"Red?" It took a second for Garth to connect the words to their meaning. "Raul? He's…gone?" His eyes got heavy. "How? Why?"

Once again, a wave of anguish swallowed Jason. He felt like he wanted to lie in front of the tank he'd seen earlier and let it turn him into paste.

He had no explanation to offer Garth. Not one that would absolve Jason from blame.

Then, a scream pierced the night.

Jason's blood froze. *I thought we'd be safe here.*

An SUV careened down the street, ramming aside empty cars, not paying any attention to the pedestrians in its way. It was headed straight for the precinct. Dark. Probably armored. Heavy-duty.

No no no. Jason spun and started yelling, "Take cover! Get down!"

The vehicle rumbled to a halt, and its doors whipped open. Six Japanese men in black tactical gear leaned out and, using the open doors as cover, unleashed hell on the block.

Rapid bursts of gunfire tore through the air, turning the cop cars into Swiss cheese. Despite the projected air of authority and control, as soon as the bullets started flying, the scene exploded into chaos. Civilians screamed and ran—some officers called for order, while others reached for the guns on their hips.

But any cop who took a stand out in the open, not ducking or diving for cover, was mowed down. Their bodies burst open, and they fell to the pavement.

Jason dragged Tobin behind a deserted car, and Garth followed close behind. As they hid from the gunmen, Garth drew his Glock and Tobin covered his ears.

Garth bellowed over the noise, "What's going on?!"

"Yakuza!" Jason yelled back.

Garth's jaw nearly hit his chest. "What? Are you serious?"

"I wish I wasn't." Jason flattened himself against the ground and peeked under the car. The Yakuza soldiers moved swiftly from their SUV, fanning out and taking cover of their own.

Yep, six of them. Armed to the teeth.

One more person hopped out of the armored vehicle. A teenager, wearing a gray shirt, moving like the Tin Man.

Ajax. Why is the Yakuza working with him? He killed Akio —

It hit him.

He must've convinced them we're the ones who killed Akio. And now the Yakuza has declared war on the L.A.P.D.

Tobin knit his eyebrows together, and the hands over his ears turned into fists. "I'm so sick of this!"

"Okay," Jason thought out loud, "we need to take them out quick. I need to get a gun —"

"No!" Tobin interjected. "If we kill one of these guys, they'll get ultra-pissed, and we'll never get rid of them. They'll be coming after us forever."

"He's right," Garth said as a bullet whizzed over them. "If these are Yakuza, we don't want to make them any angrier. We need to de-escalate."

Jason heard the police returning fire. "Might be too late for that."

Something exploded. More screams.

"What we need to do is call in back-up," he continued. "The National Guard, the army, something. Most of our guys were taken out in a matter of seconds. This last stand won't last long, at this rate."

Oh God. Cheyenne. Is she — ?

"I saw a tank back there!" Tobin jumped in. "The army's in the city. They'll hear all this and come and help."

Jason winced. "Can't count on that. We need to call." He looked pointedly at Garth.

"There's an emergency radio in Cheyenne's office," Garth said. "Third floor."

"Alright..." Jason leaned against the car's tire and sized up the distance. The precinct's entrance was about fifty yards right in front of him...but the Yakuza soldiers were right behind him, eager to shoot anything that moved.

"I can hotwire this pup." Tobin patted the car. "Getcha there."

Garth was impressed. "Dang."

"Okay, Tobin," Jason looked the boy in the eye, "get Garth to that ugly beige building, then up to the third floor. I'll draw their fire, and you get a car started. Got it?"

Tobin nodded, his hair whipping over his face, but Garth wasn't having it.

"That's suicide, Jason!"

But Jason was already moving. He thought dying in a blaze of glory sounded pretty good.

And he wanted a shot at Ajax.

Either way, he dashed out from behind the car.

He heard a voice yell something in Spanish, then someone else yelled in Japanese. The gunfire paused for a fraction of a second, which he used to set his sights on a destination.

There. The broken-down bus.

The machine-gunfire directed itself at him, and he channeled every ounce of remaining energy into his legs. He moved laterally across the street, feeling the heat of the bullets mere inches behind him. Any one of them could have taken him down, but as long as he kept moving, he stayed one step ahead.

He aimed for the bus's broken glass door and dove in. Glass cascaded around him, but he was out of the line of fire. For the moment. He got on his belly and army-crawled down the bus's aisle —
Best to remain a moving target.

His nose crinkled. The bus smelled.

Vroooom.

A car engine fired up, and wheels howled against the ground. Several men yelled in Japanese, and Jason assumed that Tobin had gotten a car started.

He hoisted himself to his knees and peeked through a grimy window. The six Yakuza men had their guns aimed at a sedan that was doing donuts between the shredded police cars as it tried to maneuver itself closer to the precinct building.

But Jason was about to have company: A teenager in a gray shirt was running toward the bus. Gun drawn. Teeth bared.

Jason crouched back down. He was unarmed and one-handed. Done for.

He snarled. There was no way he would let Ajax take him out. But how could he even hope to fight back?

A rectangular object caught his eye. Something sat on the floor of the bus, underneath one of the hard plastic seats. Jason waddled over to it, and he gaped. "You've gotta be friggin' kidding me."

It was a toolbox. A full, heavy toolbox.

The one he'd hurled at Anthony Reynaldo's head earlier that day.

This was the bus he had ridden. The bus he'd accidentally left the toolbox on.

He popped open the lid and took out the hammer he'd used to smash Reynaldo's toes.

"Bring it on, you little puke."

34

Ajax had him cornered. Finally, he was mere seconds away from blasting the cop to pieces. Once that was done, all he would have to do is find the kid and rip him apart too.

As Ajax approached the derelict city bus, he realized something: He didn't even know their names. The two people he wanted to smother out of existence were basically total strangers to him. And yet, they dominated his thoughts. Their faces filled his brain. He wanted to kill them more than he'd wanted anything in his life.

Maybe then, with their blood on his hands, he'd feel satisfied. Or thrilled. Or frightened, even. He'd take anything.

He raised his gun and set his foot on the first step that led into the bus. Then the second. With one last heave, he boarded the bus and stood in the middle of the aisle, finger on the trigger. As much as he wanted to take his time and enjoy things, he knew that the cop was wily. If Ajax had an open shot, he needed to take it without hesitating.

Step. He looked side to side, checked the first row of seats.

Step. Checked the next.

Step.

Something moved very suddenly. A heavy object arced toward him and slammed into his chest. He roared and stumbled back, the pain from his burns exploding throughout his body. "Agh!"

The object clattered to the bus's floor. An old, rusted toolbox.

And then, the cop charged at him, having been crouched in the shadows toward the back of the bus. He let out a war cry and swung a hammer at Ajax's head.

Ajax dropped himself to the floor, and the hammer swept right over him. He landed hard on his tailbone, but he could see that if the hammer had connected, he'd be dead. The cop meant to kill him.

Splayed out in the aisle, Ajax used one foot to scoot himself back, and he kicked the cop's ankles with the other. He put some distance between them and lurched to his feet. He held up his gun, but the cop hit it with the hammer. It flew out of his grip, into a dim corner.

Ajax felt a pinprick of panic in his gut. He wasn't any good at hand-to-hand fighting, and the cop was clearly out for blood. He held up his fists, but they trembled. This was bad.

35

Jason went into a frenzy, flinging the hammer against the body that stood in front of him. He barely even recognized the flesh as a person named Ajax—all he really knew was that he was hurting someone. And it felt great.

Ajax held up his arms to protect his face, and Jason drew back his hammer, winding up for a grand slam. He brought the bludgeon down on Ajax's left forearm, and he heard a sickening crack.

The teenager let out a wolfish scream.

Yeah, I hope that hurts.

Ajax flopped to the floor again and began squirming under the bus's seats. Jason swung at him with his hammer, but Ajax was too quick, sliding farther into the shadows.

"Get out here, you rat!" Jason bellowed as he stalked down the aisle. "Stand up and face me!"

BANG BANG.

Looked like Ajax had found his gun. Two bullets burst through one of the plastic seats and pinged into the bus's roof.

"Crap crap crap."

Ajax began emerging from under the seats, sweating and snarling like a mythical beast. He swerved his gun in Jason's direction.

Fight or survive — choose one.

With a shout, Jason hurled his hammer at Ajax's gun, turned, and leapt through one of the passenger windows. He went shoulder-first, breaking the glass and toppling into the outside world. He landed hard on the pavement, and his collarbone screamed at him. He wouldn't be surprised to see something red and white sticking out of his shirt.

But he didn't have time to check. He heard a clipped voice, and he looked up to see one of the Yakuza soldiers pointing an assault rifle at him.

Come on! he shouted internally. *Give me a break!* As gunfire clattered toward him, he rolled under the bus and felt shards of concrete shrapnel bite his exposed skin.

He scurried on his stomach to the other side of the bus and popped out. A pair of headlights revved toward him, and he yelped and braced for impact.

A neon-green sports car skidded to a stop next to him. Tobin leaned out the driver's window and yelled, "Your Uber's here!"

Jason didn't wait for an explanation. He dove into the back seat, and the car squealed away.

"If you fall asleep again," Jason panted as he caught his breath, "I'm giving you two stars."

Tobin kept his eyes forward and whooped. "Oh, ha-freakin'-ha, the copper's got jokes now."

Jason realized only he and Tobin were in the car. "Where's Garth?"

"My first car got shot up and stopped running. We had to get out and find a new one, and we got separated." Tobin veered back and forth, threading the powerful car through the clogged streets. Its engine sounded like a caged dragon, ready to flex its wings. "I found this bad boy and saw you needed a lift."

Spotlights whizzed past the windows like they were inside a kaleidoscope. Tobin's driving was breakneck, but Jason had to admit, they hadn't crashed, and the Yakuza's bullets weren't hitting them. The kid might have a future in the racing arena.

"You're being pretty cocky," Jason leaned toward the driver's seat, "going this fast with so many cops around."

Tobin shook his head. "Too many jokes. Read the room."

"Swing by the precinct's front door. Slow down just a hair, but don't stop. Then floor it and get outta here."

Screeeeeeech vroooom.

"Aye-aye." Tobin whipped the sports car around and threaded his way past the Yakuza's SUV and the parked black-and-whites.

The Chateau grew larger and larger in the windshield, until Tobin yanked the wheel to position the car so that Jason's door was right next to the building's entrance.

"Five stars," Jason said as he leapt out of the car and sprinted inside.

The car's engine gargled as it sped away. "Too quippy!" Tobin's voice was cut off by the front door swinging shut.

And just like that, Jason was alone. For the first time in hours, he was truly by himself. The small reception area still smelled like lemons. It was a comforting detail—not everything had changed. He passed Lois's desk, where the homely, bespectacled woman usually sat.

Did she make it through this okay?

He patted her nameplate on the desk, then felt time breathing down his neck. He bounded up the stairs, sucking in dusty air as he went. When this was all over, he wanted a long, cold shower.

Into the bullpen he went. The desks were strewn chaotically, thanks to the earthquake. Papers everywhere, framed photos cracked on the floor, useless computers lying around.

The last time he had seen it this empty was the previous summer, when he'd staggered in after being rammed by a taxi in the middle of a rainstorm—

Focus.

He headed for the captain's private office. The wall-sized window had a thick crack running vertically through it. What once had seemed impenetrable and larger than life was now broken and fragile. The glass allowed the spotlights to shine inside, bathing the whole room in ghostly white illumination. It looked like a set on a stage, waiting for its performers to show up and bring it to life.

He surged through the office's door and was shocked by how barren it was. He remembered Cheyenne moving her things back to her desk this morning, but the entire room was spotless. Walls, the floors, the desk…It smelled like she'd even disinfected every surface. He almost smiled thinking about how "classic Cheyenne" that was.

Focus, ya idiot!

He rummaged through the drawers and filing cabinets. He wasn't sure exactly what he was looking for, just that Garth had said —

Aha!

In the bottom drawer, there was a zippered case, containing a bulky yellow hand-radio that would break the floor if he dropped it. He switched it on, pressed the button on the side, and started talking frantically, as if his life depended on it:

"This is Detective Jason Flynn. I'm at the L.A.P.D. precinct next to City Hall. We're under attack. We are *under attack!* Request immediate back-up. Immediate back—"

"Drop it!" A voice boomed through the empty bullpen, and one of the Yakuza soldiers marched across the linoleum floor. His assault rifle was ready to fire, grinning wickedly in the white light, but the man's face was all business. Dispassionate.

Jason held up his hands, but kept a thumb on the radio's button.

"I said *drop*!"

With the gun barrel sneering at him, Jason let the radio clatter onto the desk.

"Out." The soldier indicated that he wanted Jason to exit the office and stand in the middle of the bullpen. "Here."

Jason slowly crept out of the captain's office and placed himself among the desks, a good distance between himself and the Yakuza man. The wide window provided plenty of light, and for the first time in a while, Jason could actually see clearly. He leaned sideways to see past the floodlights and check the sky's color. If he had guess, he'd say it was about three or four in the morning.

He swallowed the bile in his throat and said, "Sir, I'm Detective Jason Flynn of the L.A.P.D."

"Nice to meet you," the man said, his voice cold and smooth. "You will come with me, and you'll answer for your crime."

"I didn't kill Akio. I swear."

The Yakuza soldier stiffened at the name. "I have no reason to believe you."

"Do you have any reason to believe Ajax? Did he tell you he's a member of Gore Rodriguez's cartel?"

Judging by the soldier's creased forehead, Ajax had omitted that detail.

Jason pressed on. "Ajax and his men have been hunting us. Akio and I teamed up, relied on one another. We had to in order to make it through the night."

The man didn't respond. But he shifted a little in his combat boots.

As long as he was alive, Jason kept talking. "Akio was shot, correct? Look—my dominant hand is smashed to hell. I can't even hold a gun, much less make a clean shot. I'd be more than happy to sign my name with my left hand right now to prove it's not my dominant one."

The gunfire and shouts outside were a terrifying soundtrack. The noises made Jason's heart thud in his chest—he could only imagine what the death toll had amounted to.

How many other lives have I cost just in the last few minutes?

"Sir," he continued, "you don't have to believe me. But don't kill me yet. Put me and Ajax together, and we'll compare stories. You'll see through his lies in an instant, I promise."

The assault rifle's barrel began to tilt toward the floor. The man's tight jaw softened the slightest bit.

Footsteps skidded on the linoleum floor. Ajax appeared out of nowhere, pale as a phantom in the floodlights. His breath hitched in his chest, and one arm dangled at an unnatural angle, but his eyes were determined. And one arm was functioning just fine. He lifted that arm and shot the Yakuza soldier through the head.

Jason wanted to cry out, but Ajax quickly turned the gun on him, and the shout shriveled up and died in his throat.

Ajax stood beside the soldier's body, Jason in his sights, scowling like the devil. "I've got you." His quiet words floated in the air, as if they were meant for himself, not Jason.

Jason's hands were still in the air. He had nowhere to go. Nothing to say. "Ajax…"

"So you actually know my name." Ajax snorted once. "Weird. We've been at each other's throats all day, all night, and I don't think I know yours."

"Care to learn the name of the man you're about to shoot?"

The teenager took a breath and seemed to repress a smile. "Nope."

Jason gulped. He saw Ajax's finger tightening around the trigger.

This is it.

He clenched his muscles and wondered what it will feel like to die.

I wish I could wipe that smile off your face, you rat.

"Hey!"

Another voice. More footsteps.

Tobin sprinted through the bullpen and slammed his gangly frame into Ajax's. The cartel teenager was bigger than Tobin, but he was off-guard enough to stumble in the direction of Tobin's momentum. And once he was knocked off balance, Tobin's raw adrenaline kept them moving.

Toward the wall-sized window.

The two bodies slammed into the glass, but Tobin didn't stop.

CRASH.

For one nauseating moment, Ajax and Tobin were suspended in mid-air.

Then, they plummeted from the third floor.

Jason almost retched. "No!"

The next minute was a blur of running, stairs, and sheer panic. The next thing Jason knew, he was outside the precinct, kneeling on the still-hot concrete, next to two bodies.

Ajax had landed flat on his back, and Tobin was on top of Ajax. He hadn't taken the full impact.

Jason set a quivering hand on Tobin's shoulder and slowly peeled him off of Ajax. "Tobin...? Tobin, talk to me."

The only response Jason got was a shriek of pain. Tobin clutched his right arm. A bone had shattered and was sticking through his skin. He wasn't even crying, just screaming and convulsing.

But he was alive. He'd saved Jason's life.

"It's okay, Tobin. It's okay." His words did nothing. They were a Band-Aid on Tobin's broken arm and traumatized psyche.

"We got him, Jason." It was Garth. He and a few medics approached.

Jason suddenly realized...There were no more gunshots. No more sounds of war. The Yakuza had fled. Army vehicles and more police cars were parked as far as the eye could see. Reinforcements were here. U.S. soldiers marked a perimeter, and medical personnel were dealing with the many—far too many—casualties.

The medics and Garth moved Tobin onto a stretcher, and they took him away.

Leaving Jason alone with Ajax.

Jason leaned over and glared at Ajax. The teen's eyes were half-open, his mouth ajar, a trickle of blood rolling down his jaw.

"Come on, get up." Jason shoved Ajax's shoulder.

Nothing. No reaction.

"I know you're alive. Get up!" He prodded Ajax's forearm, where he had hit him with the hammer. That was sure to rile up the little punk. Still, nothing. He pressed down on Ajax's burned chest.

And he didn't feel a heartbeat.

"Wake up!" He clutched the lapels of Ajax's gray shirt and started shaking him with all his might. "Wake up, you rat, so I can send you to hell myself!"

He looked down and saw that he was holding Ajax's shirt with both of his hands. The damaged right hand didn't hurt anymore. It had gone completely numb. Dead.

It was no use. Ajax didn't move. Didn't open his eyes all the way. Didn't breathe.

Jason slumped back, head hung low.

Earlier, he had given himself two reasons to live: to shuttle Tobin to safety, and to kill Ajax.

With the danger passed and Ajax dead, he had nothing.

He felt like he was falling. Tumbling through space, bracing for an impact that would never come.

Ajax's blank face stared at him, and all the anger Jason had repressed for years finally reached a boiling point.

Instead of a wrathful scream or flying fists, all that came were tears. Hot, painful tears.

He needed the release.

He needed the violence.

But there was none to be had. And so…he had nothing.

Jason got to his feet. It was a monumental task.

Garth jogged back toward him. "Tobin will be okay. It's a miracle, but he's…" He stopped a few feet away from Jason, as if he felt the cloud over him. "Jason? What is it?"

Jason looked out at the sea of gurneys, bullet-riddled cars, and spent ammo casings. He whispered, "I deserve death."

"What?" Garth leaned in to his friend, thinking he'd misheard.

"I didn't kill Abel," Jason said. "I didn't kill Ajax. And look what happened. Red's dead. Akio. The Riley boys! All the victims of Jordan Northwood and Anthony Reynaldo! God knows how many people at the church. All these officers, gunned down right in front of me. And it's my fault. I didn't stop it. I led the wolves right here!" His face turned red as it contorted in anguish. "I killed these people! If I…If I could have gotten to Ajax sooner. Wrung his little neck and smothered him before he had a chance to…Before he could've…"

He couldn't finish his thoughts, but that didn't stop him from thinking them.

If I desire violence so much, maybe I should just direct all my anger at myself. Every punch I leveled at Abel, I deserve twofold. Every bullet that I wanted to pump in Ajax should go in me.

"I'm a monster," he said. The words hissed out of him, like air from a punctured tire. "Just kill me."

"Jason," Garth implored, "this isn't on you."

"I let this happen. I'm just as hideous as—"

"Shut up!" Garth shouted, like a volcanic eruption. "Snap out of it!" He paused, seeming to debate something in his head. Then the dam burst. "My heart is broken that Ted is gone, and I know you're hurting. But how arrogant do you have to be to think you're all that stands between order and chaos? Not every bad thing that happens in the world is your responsibility. You're not that important!"

Jason was stunned. Paralyzed on his feet.

The world continued moving around him. But he couldn't imagine ever moving again.

Until.

Two men materialized from the darkness. They wore dark suits, despite the heat, and their faces seemed designed by scientists to be as nondescript as possible. They planted themselves between Jason and Garth.

"Detective Flynn," one said. "Will you come with us." It wasn't a question.

"Who are you?" Garth tried to interject, but they flashed some fancy badges at him and started dragging Jason away.

Jason wasn't paying too much attention. He was so tired. By the time the two men stuffed him in their black sedan, he was asleep.

36

The room was small. Fluorescent lights blinded him from above, and the metal chair he sat in killed his back. But there was AC and coffee.

Jason's third cup sat on the table in front of him, getting cold. He had no idea what time it was—the room had no clock—but it had to be well into the day. He'd been here for a long time. As long as he could remember.

The two men in suits had taken him from the Chateau, driven him out of town, and escorted him into the room. He'd sat down, they'd given him some caffeine, and he'd told them everything.

Tobin. The black BMW. Akio. The riot. Ajax's stupid floral shirt. The church. Manny. The Yakuza. How it all ended.

Every little detail.

They'd taken notes, stood up, and left. That had been a while ago.

Jason was still in his stained, tattered, grimy clothes. He scratched his scalp, and when his hand came away greasy, he remembered that he had colored it with car grunge. Not his finest hour.

He just wanted to lie down. Sleep. And not wake up.

He wanted nothing more than to not wake up.

Then the door opened. A woman entered holding a pretty thick file. She placed it on the table and sat across from him.

She sized him up for a minute. She looked tired too, as if she'd been staring at computer screens for three days straight.

Her question surprised him: "How are you?"

I don't know how to answer that.

"Alive," he said. Even his voice was heavy.

She nodded and adjusted her watch. Jason tried to spy what time it was, but his vision was too blurry.

The woman continued, donning a tone that screamed *federal agent*: "I listened to your story. You've had extensive, life-threatening encounters with both Gore Rodriguez's cartel *and* an unknown branch of the Japanese Yakuza." She swallowed and took a breath, like a surgeon about to deliver bad news. "I just don't see any way around this, Mr. Graff."

His head swam. It seemed the suicidal thoughts and lack of sleep had finally caught up to him, and he was starting to hear things. He slurred, "M-Mr. Graff? That's not my name. That's not me."

She looked at him with sad eyes and slid the file across the table. "It is now."

Jason's hands fumbled with the pages.

Miles Graff.

Social security number. Past records. Family history.

A new identity.

"You'll be on a flight out of the state in twenty minutes, Mr. Graff."

Still, Jason didn't react to the name.

Garth. Tobin. Cheyenne.

I'll likely never see them again.

He set down the file and spoke past the sooty lump in his throat. "Why?"

She sighed. Not in an exasperated way, but in a manner that suggested she truly hated saying this. "If Jason Flynn stays here, he'll be dead in a week. Either at the hands of the Yakuza or Gore Rodriguez."

What if that's exactly what I want?

But he didn't say that.

Instead, he tried to recall the last words he'd said to Garth.

To Tobin.

To Cheyenne.

He couldn't remember.

About the Author

Photo by Casey Swanson

Luke was raised on a steady diet of stories. You can find him with a book constantly in his hand. He is the author of full-length fiction as well as a handful of published short stories. He lives with his wife in Oklahoma City.

Note from the Author

Word-of-mouth is crucial for any author to succeed. If you enjoyed *Epicenter*, please leave a review online—anywhere you are able. Even if it's just a sentence or two. It would make all the difference and would be very much appreciated.

Thanks!
Luke Swanson

We hope you enjoyed reading this title from:

BLACK ROSE
writing™

www.blackrosewriting.com

Subscribe to our mailing list – *The Rosevine* – and receive **FREE** books, daily deals, and stay current with news about upcoming releases and our hottest authors.
Scan the QR code below to sign up.

Already a subscriber? Please accept a sincere thank you for being a fan of Black Rose Writing authors.

View other Black Rose Writing titles at www.blackrosewriting.com/books and use promo code **PRINT** to receive a **20% discount** when purchasing.

www.ingramcontent.com/pod-product-compliance
Lightning Source LLC
Chambersburg PA
CBHW010734100726
47899CB00009B/3041